Phantom

Dark Musicals Trilogy, Book 1

Laura DeLuca

To: Freda
Come join the production!

Laura
De Luca

Library of Congress Catalog Number: 2012936131

ISBN: 9781980785507

Edited by Rosa Sophia
Cover by Elke Weiss
Typeset by Angelique Mroczka

Printed in the United States of America

For the real Lord Justyn Christofel.
May we someday meet outside of cyber space.

AND

In loving memory of Jarad Patko

Contents

Chapter One

"Why are you so nervous, Becca?" Carmen Webber asked. "You've got to be the only person in the school who's had the entire script memorized since kindergarten. Besides, you have an amazing voice. You're going to be fine. Really!"

Her best friend's compliments did little to placate Rebecca Hope's nerves as she waited in the high school auditorium for auditions to begin. Her gnawed fingernails were a testament to those nerves. They were practically chewed down to the stubs. From her shaking hands to her churning stomach, the rest of her body wasn't fairing much better.

It was completely out of character for her to be doing something so outgoing. The first three years of high school, Rebecca had strived to go unnoticed. She was involved in activities, but mostly the kind that no one paid attention to, like the Ecology Club and the orchestra. Places where she could blend in with a hundred other non-descript faces. But when she heard that the drama club was going to be performing *Phantom*, she had done something completely against her shy and quiet nature. She had signed up to try out for a part.

Phantom was her all-time favorite play, her all-time favorite story in general. The sad plight of Erik, the deformed musical genius who lived in the tunnels under a Paris opera house, and the inner struggle of Christine, the beautiful opera diva he took under his wing, was a love story that gave her goose bumps no matter how many times she watched it. She forced her parents to make the three-hour drive from their hometown in Egg Harbor, New Jersey, to New York City every year so she could see it live on stage. She had twelve different movie versions on DVD, including the slasher version. And she owned every soundtrack that was ever put out. Those soundtracks played in her car every morning as she drove to school. For Rebecca, *Phantom* was more than just one of the greatest musical scores ever composed. It was her personal obsession. This was why she *had* to try out for a part. Still, as the butterflies in her stomach threatened to morph into giant birds of prey, she had to wonder if she had made the right choice. Maybe she should have stayed safely hidden in the back rows of the orchestra, clutching her violin and bow, and going completely unnoticed by both the audience and her classmates.

Rebecca took a deep, shaky breath, and turned to her friends. "I think I'm going to throw up." She admitted.

Carmen rolled the deep brown eyes she had inherited from her Cuban mother. Exotic and beautiful, the dark-haired Latina never had to worry about what people thought of *her*. She wasn't nervous about auditioning at all. She was a good enough dancer to guarantee her at least a part in the chorus. Not like Rebecca who could barely walk without tripping and whose mousy brown hair and dull hazel eyes made her the poster child for plain and boring. She must have been insane to even consider doing this. She was going to make a total fool of herself.

Her other longtime friend, Debbie O'Neil, was more sympathetic. Overly tall for a girl and somewhat stocky, Debbie understood what it was like to be less than perfect in a teenage world that required nothing less than perfection to fit in. She patted Rebecca's hand soothingly.

"You're going to be fine, Becca." Debbie consoled. "Just relax. If *I* can do this, you certainly can. Anyway, we still have to get through the guys' auditions before you'll have to get on stage."

Rebecca nodded and settled back into her seat to wait. One way or the other, it would all be over soon. She just had to make it through the next hour without fainting.

"Oh my God, *look*," Carmen suddenly exclaimed. She squeezed Rebecca's wrist so hard it almost hurt. "It's Tom Rittenhouse. Isn't he hot?"

Hot hardly seemed an adequate description. Dreamy. Gorgeous. The epitome of male perfection. Even those words fell short. Multi-talented, rich and handsome—Thomas Rittenhouse was the school's most sought after heartthrob. He was the basketball star, the surfer extraordinaire, and the male lead of all the plays since his freshman year. He was first in *everything*, so it was no surprise that he would be the first to audition. Rebecca had always secretly had a crush on him, but of course, he didn't even know that she existed.

Tom took his spot on the stage, and the orchestra erupted into a sudden, full-bodied ballad that echoed melodically off the high ceilings of the auditorium. Rebecca felt herself melting into the cushions of the seat as Tom took his place behind the microphone. If *Phantom* was her obsession then Tom was her fantasy. And it *was* pure fantasy and nothing more. There was no way that the blue-eyed, blond-haired, would-be supermodel was ever going to notice Rebecca Hope. She had a better chance of being hit by lighting and winning the lottery on the same day.

"He's definitely going to get the lead," Carmen gushed when Tom began his overture. "He's the only logical choice."

"Shhh!" Their English teacher, Miss King, who doubled as the head of the drama club and director of the play, hissed at Carmen and put a manicured finger to her lips. "Quiet!"

Rebecca thought the teacher's thick, plastered on foundation was going to crack from the effort, but she was glad when her friend was chastised to silence. It allowed her to concentrate on the beauty of the music. The male solo was one of her favorite pieces. But Rebecca was more interested in the performer than the performance. Tom's voice was a little rough around the edges, but it was adequate. Their high school, Mainland Regional, had a limited supply of willing male participants in the drama club. Tom was hardly Andre Bocelli, but he always managed to pull off his roles with poise. Besides, it didn't really matter if he gave a less than flawless performance. He had no competition.

Rebecca couldn't help but admire Tom's brown skin as he stepped down from the stage. It was still sun-kissed from the previous summer. She smiled at him as he passed by, but as usual, she was invisible. Tom didn't even notice her as he took his seat a few rows back, accompanied by the other brave boys who had decided to try out for the play. The majority of them were freshman and sophomores who didn't know what they were getting into.

"Jay Kopp!" called Miss. King, as she flipped through her audition list. The answering spitball that landed in her teased hair remained there unnoticed; Jay sauntered up to the stage with the unmistakable air of a class clown who reveled in his title.

Jay cleared his throat in a highly exaggerated fashion as the music started again, and then plunged into the most God-awful singing that Rebecca had ever heard. *Singing?* Squawking was more like it, and even *that* was putting it mildly. As he sang, his arms flailed dramatically and his face twisted into the silliest expressions he could manage. Beside her, Carmen groaned and rolled her eyes.

"Jay is such a goof." She complained. "He's what my dad would call a social hand grenade. He doesn't take anything seriously."

Debbie laughed. "Sure he does. He takes being the comic relief seriously." She covered her ears as Jay hit a particularly sour note. "And I think he's proven his point, so enough is enough already!"

Miss King apparently agreed with Debbie's assessment. "Thank you, Jay," she said, and signaled the orchestra to silence before the second verse had ended. "That's quite enough."

Jay took an exaggerated bow, and Tom and the other guys hooted and whistled as he went back to join them. They all exchanged high fives as Jay took his seat. It was strange to think that Tom and Jay were best friends. They were as different as night and day. Jay was tall and lanky, with a shock of reddish-blond hair and abundant freckles. He could only be classified as a nerd, *if* he could be classified at all. It seemed more appropriate that he would be a flunky than a friend to the popular Tom. Yet the two had been inseparable since junior high. They reminded Rebecca of Zack and Screech from the old nineties' sitcom *Saved by the Bell.*

A few more mediocre performances followed, all of which seemed like masterpieces after Jay's shoddy efforts. While they were tolerable they were hardly *Phantom* material. Rebecca wondered how they would possibly cast both the opera ghost and the hero role of Raoul, the count who was in love with Christine, when they had such limited talent. Not that it really mattered that much. This was high school after all, not Broadway. They could be completely terrible, and the parents and grandparents in the audience would still give them a standing ovation when it was all over.

"Lord . . . Justyn?"

It sounded more like a question than an audition call. Miss King looked slightly baffled as she scanned her paperwork and read the last name on her list of male candidates. Once she was certain she had read the name correctly, she called it out once more with a little more confidence. When she received no immediate response, she seemed ready to dismiss the whole thing as a joke. But then a strange black clad figure seemed to materialize in the corner of the stage, and with practiced grace, he moved towards the center of the platform and the waiting microphone.

"That's Justyn Patko." Carmen informed Rebecca matter-of-factly. Luckily her best friend was the queen of gossip. "He just moved here this year. From Vegas, I think. He's in my Calculus class."

"He's a little creepy if you ask me," Debbie whispered.

Creepy he might have been to some, with his black clothes trimmed with silver chains, black hair, and black fingernails. He was obviously Gothic to the core; a fashion statement Rebecca had always thought was secretly a cry for attention. But for Justyn, there seemed no other possibility. She couldn't imagine the darkly mysterious figure dressed in earth tones or preppy, button-down shirts. They would have clashed with his dark eyes and pale skin. She had seen him in the hallway a few times, but they didn't share any classes, so Rebecca had never really taken the time to study him before. Despite his odd style, there was something strangely appealing about Justyn. In his own way, he was just as handsome as Tom.

The orchestra tuned for its virtuoso, and Justyn stood ready. But no one else was ready for the magical performance he began. Beside her, Carmen was rambling on about something mundane. Rebecca elbowed her to silence so she could listen to the perfectly thrilling tenor. As she listened to the song unfold, the world around her started to slip away. Gone was the high school auditorium. Gone were the rowdy teenagers. The Gothic stranger on the stage had become the embodiment of Erik, and Rebecca watched him in all his dark glory, belting out his tormented love through the words of his song. And she was as breathless with wonder as Christine herself must have been when the masked stranger serenaded her in the candlelit labyrinth of the opera house. In that moment, Justyn wasn't just *portraying* the phantom. Justyn *was* the phantom.

> *"Let the music touch your soul.*
> *Let the darkness make you whole.*
> *Do not fear what is unknown.*
> *Your true path has now been shown.*
> *Listen to the words I sing.*
> *Embrace the peace that night will bring."*

As he continued to sing in his deep but somehow angelic voice, Rebecca found that she couldn't tear her eyes away from him. With every line, her heart began to beat faster. She truly felt the arms of night wrapping her in a warm embrace. She could almost feel the hands of the phantom glide along her body as the words poured forth. The music caressed her. It possessed her—mind, body, and soul. Each word left her longing, yearning for more.

She was gawking so obviously, it was hardly surprising when Justyn felt her eyes on him and steadily met her gaze. She realized her mouth was hanging open in stunned awe, and she quickly snapped it shut. His lips moved into just a small hint of a smile. He never took his eyes off her while he sang the final verse, making her cheeks flush to the point that she felt almost feverish. It wasn't embarrassment but excitement, arousal even, which was sending her mind spinning in so many directions.

When the song was over, and Rebecca had recovered just a hint of her composure, she couldn't help but burst into a healthy round of applause. A few scattered people joined in, including Debbie and Carmen after she nudged them in the ribs. But only Miss King seemed to truly appreciate the brilliance of his talent as much as Rebecca did.

"That was amazing, Justyn!" The teacher gushed.

"*Lord* Justyn." He corrected as he stepped down from the stage.

A few others complimented him as well, but he took it all in stride. In fact, his serious expression never faltered as he stepped down from the stage. He seemed almost bored, like it was all he could do to hold back a yawn, despite the smiles and words of encouragement.

But not everyone in the crowd was pleased as Justyn glided down the aisle, so ethereal in his dark garments that he still resonated the spirit of the Opera Ghost. Miss King might have been excited about the newest male addition to her cast after being limited for many years, but Tom and his group of boisterous companions glared at him as he passed them by. Jay sneered and tossed a balled-up piece of paper in Justyn's direction, but the Goth was quick, and caught it in his hand without missing a beat.

"I think you dropped something," he said.

His speaking voice was no less melodic than his singing voice, but something about his tone made Rebecca shiver. He tossed the paper back at Jay, who was nowhere near as coordinated as Justyn. He practically fell off his seat in his efforts to catch it.

"Hey, vampire," Tom called when Justyn began to walk away. "Are you sure you can handle the competition?"

Justyn smiled, a cool, sarcastic half-smile, and crossed his arms over his chest. "Are *you*?"

Miss King didn't notice the short confrontation, and Justyn vanished from the auditorium as quickly and mysteriously as he had appeared. Only Rebecca had noticed the very real tension between the two boys. She wondered if it was a bad omen for them to start off the production with hard feelings and envy. That could only lead to trouble. The kind of trouble that could end with someone getting hurt. The kind of trouble that Rebecca would do whatever it took to avoid.

Chapter Two

"Settle down, people! We're ready to move on to the girls' auditions!" Lots of hooting followed Miss King's announcement. "Carmen Webber, you're up first."

Carmen bounced onto the stage nonchalantly, no more perturbed than she would be walking up to the lunch line in the cafeteria. She didn't look nervous at all. Rebecca didn't know how she did it. Nothing fazed her. Rebecca wished she had half her confidence.

Carmen gave a fair performance followed by four underclassman of varied inadequacy. But their singing ability wasn't nearly as important as the fact that they had all been going to dance school for as long as they could walk. Their voices would blend well enough for the choreographed dance scenes that they would undoubtedly appear in. Rebecca wondered if she would wind up in the chorus as well. She shuddered at the thought of trying to move in graceful synchronized motions with two-dozen other girls. Her idea of graceful was making it the whole day without walking into any walls.

Even worse, what if she ended up lost behind the scenes as a stagehand, lugging around heavy props and missing half the show in the process? She should have stayed in the orchestra. At least there she would have been guaranteed a part in the music that she loved. There was no telling what was going to happen to her now.

"Wendy Wright!" called Miss King.

"Snob alert," Carmen whispered.

Wendy all but skipped up to the microphone. As far as confidence went, Wendy was brimming over with it. She wasn't so much auditioning as she was warming up for the final encore of her senior year. Her wide smile implied that she had no doubt that she would star alongside Tom, just as she had for the past three years. She *did* have a beautiful voice, and coupled with her stunning mane of thick blonde hair and sparkling green eyes, she was certainly everything that a blooming starlet was made of. She was the obvious choice for the role of Christine. Anyone with eyes could see that.

Wendy made it through almost the entire audition without once faltering, a feat all the other girls had been unable to accomplish. But when she came to the end of the piece, she made a valiant effort but was unable to hit the full range of high soprano notes. Her voice cracked towards the end of the scale. She glared over at the orchestra as though they had penned the score themselves, instead of just following along with the music on the sheets in front of them. But when Miss King seemed unfazed, Wendy regained her momentary loss of composure. The director waved her hand in careless dismissal.

"Don't worry, dear. We can improvise if we must. Those notes are next to impossible for anyone who hasn't been professionally trained."

"She hasn't heard *you* yet," Debbie whispered with a conspiratorial grin.

Rebecca swallowed hard. No, Miss King hadn't heard her yet, and Rebecca wasn't sure she ever would. Maybe it wasn't too late to sneak out a side door. But even as she thought it, she knew her trembling legs would never be able to carry out the command. How was she ever going to go through with this? How could she think she would succeed where the perfect Wendy Wright had failed? She couldn't! She couldn't do it. And she didn't have to. At least not yet.

The next few girls were horrible. Yet, Rebecca found herself wishing their auditions would never end, because as the number of people in the seats dwindled, the closer she came to her own performance and possibly her humiliation.

"Debbie O'Neil!"

Rebecca knew she couldn't leave now. She couldn't fail to offer the same kind of unconditional support to Debbie that her friend had shown to her throughout the last few weeks. She had gone back and forth for weeks, trying to decide whether to stick with the orchestra or actually try out for a role. Carmen had been great too, but it was Debbie who had really boosted her confidence enough to give her the strength to write her name on the tryout list, right below Debbie's.

Oh God—Her name was right below Debbie's. That meant that she was going to be called next! Even if she wanted to escape, she couldn't be rude enough to walk out of the auditorium when Debbie was about to begin her performance. That would be unforgivable.

Rebecca was almost relieved to see that Debbie also looked nervous as she carried her stocky frame up the steps to the stage. She was glad she wasn't the only one who didn't think it was second nature to face down a room full of smirking teenagers. Debbie struggled with her weight and her abnormal height, so she had always been a little shy. But her voice was almost as good as Wendy's. She usually landed at least one of the smaller, secondary roles in the school's productions.

Debbie sang well—better than well, revealing a rich, firm voice. But she had no more luck than Wendy when it came time to reach the highest notes. Her voice faltered and cracked. When the song was over, she returned to her seat with a slight blush to her cheeks.

"Don't worry," Rebecca told her encouragingly. "Even Miss King said she doesn't expect any of us to hit those high notes."

Debbie smiled. "Why don't you get up there and prove her wrong?"

"Rebecca Hope!"

When Miss King called her name, Rebecca felt her stomach do an unmistakable triple somersault. She wondered how she had ever thought a little coward like her would have the nerve to do something like this. She was the bookworm, the nerd, the invisible woman. She wasn't an actress. She wasn't good enough to play Christine. She wasn't even good enough to be a chorus girl.

"Is Rebecca Hope here?"

Miss King called her name for the second time. When she still didn't move, Carmen forcefully pushed her out of her seat and into the aisle. Rebecca wasn't sure her legs were strong enough to carry her to the stage, which suddenly seemed a million miles away. So instead of walking she clung to the armrest of the corner seat.

"You can do this," Carmen insisted. "Have a little faith in yourself."

Rebecca took a deep breath and nodded, forcing her heavy legs to carry her down the walkway, up the three steps and onto the threatening stage front. And that was the easy part. Once she was there, looking down at the dotting of faces spread out along the rows of the auditorium, the real panic started to set in. She thought she might start to hyperventilate. She was gripping the base of the microphone so tightly her fingers had turned white.

"Are you ready, Becca?"

Rebecca didn't answer. She *couldn't* answer. Her tongue suddenly felt thick and heavy and she couldn't quite remember how to make it work anymore. She tried to tell herself this was no different than singing along with her CD in the morning, but she knew that wasn't true. Despite her better judgment her eyes scanned the crowd. She noticed Wendy's smug smile, and Carmen and Debbie's concerned frowns. A little further down, Jay was making obnoxious faces, and even Tom was rolling his eyes. No one seemed to have any faith that she could possibly succeed, including Rebecca herself.

It was then she noticed a dark figure emerge in the very back rows of the auditorium. Justyn Patko watched from the shadows. He watched just as the phantom must have watched Christine at her début performance. Watched through eyes that held her entranced by their intensity, but at the same time filled her with strength and courage. Again, Rebecca had the surreal feeling that she had somehow stepped back into the past. She *was* Christine, and the figure watching her from the shadows was Erik, a dark angel of music, nodding his head in approval. Rebecca felt the stage fright melt away as though it had never been there at all.

"I'm ready."

The orchestra, led by the delicate strokes of the piano, gradually stirred to life. Rebecca continued to focus on Justyn, until the music began to envelope her in its sweet melody. She merged with it, yielded to it, allowed it to possess her until her voice rung out strong and clear, matching the beauty of the instruments. She sang with the passion and the love she felt for the amazing work of art she performed.

> *"When the time comes for us to part,*
> *Carry a piece of me within your heart.*
> *Let our memories carry you far.*
> *Think of me when you wish on a star.*
> *Our love will be a fond memory,*
> *Carried through all eternity."*

Each operatic rhyme rang clearly and fluidly through the wings of the auditorium. Each note resonated in the perfect key and a rich fluid tone. Each word was filled with pure, heartfelt emotion. It almost seemed she was listening to someone else entirely as the song streamed from her lips.

Finally, she approached the final verse of the aria—the part where all other voices had failed. She had managed the difficult scale a thousand times in the safety of her bathroom shower. But would she be able to do it here, in front of an audience of her peers? Not even Justyn's still penetrating stare could help her face *this* challenge. Rebecca closed her eyes and with her voice soaring but unforced, she sang the final lines of the ballad.

> *"Time may pass, the memories grow dim.*
> *But I'll be in your thoughts in a passing whim.*
> *You will never be completely free.*
> *You can never let go of meeeeeeeeeeeee."*

She had delivered the complete aria perfectly, even the dramatic high-ranged notes at the end of the sonnet. With a smile of well-earned accomplishment, she looked into the audience and found a wide variety of stunned faces staring back at her.

At first, she had the horrifying feeling that she had deluded herself. Perhaps she was horribly out of tune, tone deaf to the extreme, and the people who sat speechless simply couldn't begin to express their disgust. Rebecca's heart began to pound with familiar nerve-racking fright as she waited several long seconds for some kind of response. She was rewarded for her patience when she was greeted by a surprisingly loud round of applause considering the small number of people who were present.

"Rebecca Hope!" Miss King exclaimed. "It is absolutely scandalous that for the past three years you've hidden *that* voice behind a mediocre violin ability! That was beautiful . . . *spectacular* . . . really, I'm at a loss for words."

Rebecca blushed as she stepped down from the stage. The magic of the moment had passed, and she was just plain old Rebecca again. The spirit of Christine had possessed her during the performance, but now she wanted only to blend back in with the crowd. The faces hovering over her only made her feel even more overwhelmed. Carmen and Debbie were waiting for her, literally glowing with pride. She tried to weave through the crowd to join them. But before she could reach them, Tom stepped into her path, blue eyes twinkling. Rebecca was pretty certain her already unsteady legs were finally going to betray her.

"You were amazing, Becca!" Tom gushed.

"Umm . . . thanks," Rebecca managed to stutter. She couldn't believe Tom Rittenhouse actually knew her name.

"We'll have to get together and rehearse sometime."

Rebecca was so flustered she almost forgot how to speak. "Yeah . . . sure . . . I mean . . . if I even get a part."

"With a voice like that, you're sure to get the lead."

Again, Rebecca's face grew warm, but this time it had little to do with her singing ability. Carmen was openly gaping at the exchange. As pretty as she was, even she had never succeeded in catching Tom's attention. But Rebecca knew there were no hard feelings when Carmen flashed a thumbs-up.

Before long, others were coming up to her, congratulating her on a great audition, telling her how they were sure she'd get a good role. Rebecca found herself the center of attention for the first time in her life. But not everyone was happy with the day's turn of events. Rebecca noticed that Wendy hadn't budged from her seat. She was glaring at her with an obvious scowl. And from his corner, Justyn looked on at the fanfare with his lips set in a tight frown. Rebecca watched him until he disappeared into the dimly lit corridor, fading into the darkness like the creature of the night that he apparently was.

Chapter Three

"Becca, the cast list's been posted!" Carmen exclaimed. "Aren't you excited? I'm sure you got the role of Christine. You were amazing at auditions yesterday!"

Carmen didn't give her a chance to respond. She grabbed Rebecca's arm and started dragging her across the hallway to the billboard where the announcements were posted before she could even unload her armful of books. Even from the opposite end of the building, she could see a small group of excited students scanning the list for their names. But Rebecca wasn't quite as certain as Carmen was about what the results would be. Yes, tryouts had gone better than she had expected, and Miss King had been happy with her performance, but other girls had done just as well. And girls like Wendy and even Debbie, who had been in the drama club for years, would have seniority over a newcomer like Rebecca. She would be lucky, and grateful, if she got one of the smaller, less important roles. Just being a part of the production at all would be enough for her.

They got a little closer but there were still too many people standing around the billboard to be able to see anything. They stood back a little to wait their turn. Rebecca started biting off what little that was left of her fingernails. This was worse than when she was waiting to get back her SAT scores.

"Woo whoooo!" Jay shouted. He forced a smaller, unwilling freshman to exchange high fives with him. "I got a part! Yeah, man! I'm Buquet!"

Jay pushed his way through the crowd of onlookers. He shoved Carmen and Rebecca roughly as he passed. He knocked into her arm, and Rebecca dropped the stack of books she was carrying. Loose-leaf papers went flying in every direction. Jay looked back only long enough to snicker at her before moving on down the hall, continuing to announce his accomplishment, loudly and obnoxiously.

"Ugh, Jay is such a jerk." Carmen complained as she bent down to help pick up the papers and get them back in some kind of order. "I can't believe Miss King actually gave him a part. Who's Bucket anyway?"

"*Buquet.*" Rebecca corrected with a slight laugh. "He's the stagehand the Phantom kills right before the intermission. He gets hung."

Carmen chuckled. "Do you think Miss King is trying to send a secret message? Anyway, at least we'll only have to deal with him for *half of* the rehearsals. I don't think I could stand spending three full hours a day for the next six weeks with Jay Kopp."

"Jay's not so bad once you get to know him." It was Tom. Suddenly he was kneeling down beside them. "Hey, Becca, I think you dropped this." He handed her a sheet of paper with her calculus assignment on it.

"Th . . . thanks," Becca managed to stutter.

Then she felt like a complete and total moron because she couldn't think of anything else to say. At least not anything that wouldn't make her sound like a babbling idiot. Luckily, Carmen wasn't as easily intimidated by incredibly hot guys.

"Hey, Tom. Have you seen the cast list yet?" she asked as they all climbed to their feet.

Tom shook his head. "Not yet. I was just on my way over there." He turned to Rebecca who was still struck dumb. "Why don't I walk with you? We'll have to get used to each other, you know. We're going to be spending a *lot* of time together."

Tom was confident. But then, why wouldn't he be? He had been the star of all the plays since he was a freshman. But again Rebecca found herself wondering why everyone seemed so sure *she* would get any part at all, let alone the starring role opposite Tom. She hadn't been *that* good. Had she?

"What? Carlotta! Are you *kidding* me?"

Wendy's high-pitched shriek was like a banshee cry as it echoed down the corridor. As Rebecca and the others inched their way forward, she could see Wendy's hands were balled into fists at her side. She kept staring at the cast posting as though whatever she was reading might somehow magically change if she willed it hard enough. Her back was to them when they first approached, but she turned around just as they stepped up behind her. Her face, which was already a blotchy red from anger, turned almost purple when she saw Rebecca.

"*You*!" She spat. "Don't think you've won anything. *Obviously* there's been some kind of misprint. I'm going to talk to Miss King right now. There's no way she would cast *me* in a secondary role my senior year. There's just no way!"

Rebecca was speechless. It was becoming an almost permanent condition for her. She was pretty sure her mouth was hanging open. Beside her, Carmen was wearing a big grin, apparently amused by the whole thing. But Rebecca didn't think it was funny. Wendy wasn't the kind of person she wanted angry with her. Her entire high school life could be over with one word from Wendy Wright.

"Geez, Wendy. I guess the concept of being a graceful loser is foreign to you," Tom said with a smug smile.

Wendy snorted and turned her rage onto Tom. "Oh yeah, Mr. Perfect? Let's see how gracefully *you* take it. I'm not the only one who's been upstaged by some usurping loser from the geek squad." Tom's smile faltered and Wendy was the one who looked smug now. "If you don't believe me, check out the casting list for yourself."

Wendy stalked off with a toss of her blonde hair, and finally they were standing in front of the billboard. Tom tried to act cool, but it was obvious he was a little more nervous now than he had been about reading the results. But he was still nowhere near as nervous as Rebecca. She almost forgot to breathe as she looked for her name on the list. She started at the bottom, still in some way expecting to see her name down there, even after what Wendy had said.

But her name was much higher up. It fact it was the second name listed on the cast.

"Christine – Rebecca Hope"

Her breath caught in her throat. She thought maybe she was imagining things. Or maybe she was dreaming. It couldn't be true. She couldn't have gotten the female lead in the play. She *couldn't* be Christine. It was just too much to hope for. Yet, there it was in black and white. She was the star. For one glorious moment, she reveled in it. She felt all the excitement and pride that the accomplishment deserved. Then reality set in.

What had she been thinking? How was she going to do this? How would she stand in front of an entire auditorium filled with people and sing? Maybe she should follow Wendy into the teacher's lounge and tell Miss King that she agreed with her—that there *had* been some kind of mistake. Maybe Rebecca had been suffering from temporary insanity when she had tried out to begin with.

Luckily, no one noticed that she was having a panic attack. They just went right on talking, not even noticing that Rebecca had long since stopped breathing.

"I got Meg Giry!" Carmen bounced up and down in excitement. "We get to be best friends. Just like in real life."

Meg Giry was Christine's ballerina sidekick. It was a role that called for more dancing than singing, which was perfect for Carmen. Plus, it was the biggest role she had ever landed, so Rebecca understood her excitement. Tom, on the other hand, didn't look quite as happy as he examined *his* placement. His name wasn't above hers as they had all expected. Instead it sat one line below.

"Raoul – Thomas Rittenhouse"

"Congratulations Tom, you get to be the hero!" Carmen was trying to break the sudden strained silence that had fallen around them. But it wasn't working. Tom was still fuming.

"I can't believe they gave that vampire freak *my* role!"

Rebecca wasn't sure what to say to calm him down, especially since she could understand why Miss King had cast Justyn in the role of the Phantom. He really was perfect for the part. Besides his amazing voice, Justyn's presence was ghostlike. He resonated the soul of a tormented artist. He probably didn't even need to act very much. And Tom was really much better suited to play the handsome, lovable Raoul. They both had the same boyish good looks and charismatic charm. At least normally Tom was charming. But at that moment he was too angry to take the casting as a compliment.

"It's not that bad Tom," Debbie said. She had come up behind them just in time to see Tom's reaction. "Raoul's part is just as good as the Phantom's."

Tom was past listening to reason. "And what would you know, you fat cow? You're used to playing the smaller parts. But *I'm* supposed to have the lead!"

Tom didn't wait for any more words of encouragement. He stormed away; following the same path Wendy had taken. Rebecca assumed Miss King would be getting an earful. Hopefully their director had the sense to escape out the side doors before the protestors could lynch her.

"That was completely uncalled for," Carmen muttered. She put her arm around Debbie. "Don't worry about Tom. He's just pissed that the new guy showed him up. Hey, why don't you guys come over to my house for a while so we can run through our lines? After all, Deb, you and I are mother and daughter. We should be spending some quality time together."

Debbie smiled sadly as she ran a hand through her short blonde hair. The fact that she had been cast as Madame Giry, who was the oldest character in the play, probably only made her feel worse. She always got stuck in the frumpy roles, even though her voice was one of the best. It really wasn't fair. Rebecca almost felt guilty that she had gotten the role of Christine. Debbie had just as much seniority as Wendy, and she was a lot nicer.

"That sounds like fun," Debbie told Carmen. Then she turned to Rebecca with a much more sincere smile and reached out to give her a hug. "Congratulations, Becca! I just *knew* you would get Christine. I'm so happy for you!"

"Thanks, Deb." Rebecca returned the hug but it was awkward with her bundle of books still in her hand. "I could never have done this without you. You've put up with all my craziness."

Carmen was rolling her eyes. "Will you two stop being so mushy? We're doing a high school play. It's not like you won an academy award. Now, let's get out of here. I'm starving. We can order a pizza when we get to my house."

"I need to grab my book bag," Rebecca told them. "You guys can wait for me outside. I'll only be a minute."

"Okay, but hurry up." Carmen ordered.

Debbie and Carmen disappeared through the main doors, and Rebecca found herself alone in the eerily quiet hallway. It was a gusty fall morning in South Jersey, and the howling wind sneaking in through the old classroom windows added to the chilling atmosphere. While she had been worrying about casting calls, the rest of the students had cleared out of the building. Rebecca had never realized how creepy the school was when it was empty.

It was getting close to Halloween, and cardboard cut-outs of skeletons and big-nosed witches on broomsticks were taped to the walls. There were smiling cartoon characters that shouldn't have been intimidating, but somehow they were. And even more intimidating was the soft thump of footsteps behind her as she inched her way to her locker.

Rebecca swallowed hard and with more courage than she felt, she swung around to face whoever was behind her.

There was no one there. The hallway was empty, but the door to the gym was swinging on its hinges. Could whoever had been following her have ducked inside? Or was she just imagining the whole thing? Did it really matter? She should just grab her stuff from her locker and get out of there. She was being silly anyway. This was her *school*. She was just as safe there as she was in her bedroom. Yet still, her heart was racing with unexpected fear and excitement. She heard a strong, male voice call out to her in a beautiful and familiar melody.

"Beeeccaaa. Beeeccaaa."

It was the right melody but the wrong name. The song that the phantom used to lure Christine into his hidden underground chamber below the opera house came whispering through the doors. And just as Christine was unable to resist the mesmerizing voice and the gloved hand that pulled her through the secret passage behind the mirror, so Rebecca was unable to stop herself from slipping through the doors of the gym as the phantom voice sang to her.

"Music's dark angel calls you this day.
Come to your angel—come with no delay."

Chapter Four

"Hello?" Rebecca called out timidly as she stepped through the doors of the gymnasium. "Is someone there?"

At first, only silence surrounded her in the empty gym. Rebecca thought maybe the excitement of the day had gone to her head. After all, she wasn't used to excitement. Her life was as boring and humdrum as it could possibly be. But in the past ten minutes she had gotten the role of a lifetime and talked to the man of her dreams. Who could blame her for being a little flustered?

Even though the only light in the gym came through the windows high above her, it was fairly easy to see the whole room. She looked from the bleachers to the side courts. When the only thing she saw was a broom in the corner, she shook her head and turned to leave. Just as she reached out to push the door open, a hand gently touched her shoulder.

Rebecca nearly dropped her armload of books for the second time. She cried out in surprise, swung around, and found herself staring into the dark eyes of Justyn Patko. He observed her jumpiness with a crooked smile. She had no idea where he came from. He had materialized behind her like a ghost.

"Did I scare you?" he asked innocently. His speaking voice was just as beguiling as his singing voice. Deep, but not *too* deep—it was strong and eloquent, and left her feeling just a little giddy.

"N . . . no," Rebecca stammered.

She certainly wasn't beguiling *or* eloquent in any way at all. He probably thought she had some kind of mental handicap. But as far as her not being scared . . . well, it wasn't exactly a lie. While it was true that her heart was racing and her hands were trembling, it wasn't exactly fear that was making her body react so strangely. As Justyn continued to study her with his deep brown eyes, it wasn't fear at all that kept her standing there, staring right back, when she should have turned and stomped back out the door. As much as she wanted to be annoyed with him for trying to frighten her, she couldn't invoke any anger—probably because she was hypnotized by his penetrating gaze, enchanted by his strange, dark appeal.

She had only seen him from a distance before, but now she was able to take in every detail. Although he was pale, with his eyes and lips outlined in black, his face was still chiseled perfection. His nose, his cheeks, and the slight cleft of his chin, all came together to form a walking masterpiece of dark art. Beneath the black t-shirt and black fishnet sleeves, she could see the outline of tight, firm muscles rippling through the fabric. His black hair was long on top and hung dramatically over his eyes, one of which was accented by an eyebrow piercing. Both his ears and his lower lip were also pierced, and the silver studs glittered in the dim light. Carmen had called him creepy, and maybe he was, but he was also eerily beautiful.

"I'm sorry," he said. He apparently didn't believe that he hadn't scared her. And why would he when she was standing as still and speechless as a statue? "I couldn't resist a dramatic introduction when I saw you in the hall."

Rebecca somehow managed to tear her eyes away from his. She blushed because she had been so obviously gawking, and she had to clear her throat before she could speak. "It's okay. You were just getting into character. It's Justyn, right?" She reached out her hand in introduction, and then thought how stupid that must have seemed to him. They weren't at a business meeting.

"*Lord* Justyn," he corrected. He accepted the offered hand, but instead of shaking it as she had intended, he gently lifted it, and brushed her fingers with his lips. "My lady."

Rebecca's heart, which had only just begun to slow down to a regular pace, started to hammer again. The incessant pounding continued as his lips lingered on her hand a little longer then was really necessary, soft as velvet against her skin. An electric charge shot through her hand, up into her arm, and throughout her entire body, until she tingled from head to toe. Even after he lifted his head from her fingers, he still held onto her hand. Rebecca couldn't complain. Speaking had become an insurmountable task. His dark eyes bore into her with an intensity tinged with humor. He knew he had turned her into a tongue-tied mess, and he was enjoying every minute of it.

"I'm glad that you'll be playing the role of Christine. You have an *exquisite* voice."

Exquisite? Who used words like that? Justyn had a way of sounding like he stepped through a time warp, even with his modern Gothic wardrobe. Finally, he let go of her hand. It fell to her side limply, and the trance, if not broken, had lost some of its potency. She at least recovered enough to think of something fairly intelligent to say.

"Thanks. So do you. You were amazing yesterday. Congratulations on getting the role of the phantom. You really deserve it."

"Well, Erik and I have always been kindred spirits."

Rebecca did a double take. Erik was the phantom's real name in Gaston Leroux's novel, *The Phantom of the Opera*. But his name was never mentioned in the musical, which was the script they were working from.

"You've actually read the book?" She couldn't hide her surprise.

Justyn smirked. "Did I give you the impression that I was illiterate?"

Rebecca blushed, feeling stupid again. Could she say anything without putting her foot in her mouth? "No, of course not. It's just that I thought *I* was the only person under forty who had actually read the original *Phantom of the Opera*."

Though she had hardly asked him to prove his case, Justyn did something she never expected. He quoted one of her favorite scenes from the book. A scene, which had touched her heart, and made her cry every single time she had read it.

"I tore off my mask so as not to lose one of her tears. . . and she did not run away! And she did not die! . . . She remained alive, weeping over me, with me. We cried together! I have tasted all the happiness the world can offer!"

For the first time in her life, Rebecca knew what it really meant to swoon. Justyn recited verbatim and completely from memory, part of the dramatic monologue from Gaston Leroux's classic novel. He recited it with passion, his voice filled with such yearning and heartbreak that Rebecca knew her eyes had filled with tears. His voice held all the anguish of the poor, tortured Erik, who was shunned by the world because of his deformity, much like Justyn had been shunned by most of their classmates because of his somewhat eccentric style. The two phantoms really were brothers in darkness.

"Wow." That was all Rebecca could manage to say when he was through. It sounded extremely lame after such a stunning, beautiful narration. "You really have read the book."

"About ten times." He admitted.

Rebecca knew she could top that. "I've read it at least fifteen. And I've gone to see the play in New York every year since I was eight years old."

"I saw it in London."

Rebecca pouted because he had her beat. There was no way she could compete with London.

Justyn was a good sport. "Why don't we call it a draw?" he suggested. "We're both tied for first place in the title of the phantom's number one fan."

Rebecca smiled. "That sounds fair."

He didn't seem quite as mystical anymore, and she started to find it was a little easier to talk to him. But just as she thought she was making headway, his eyes seemed to draw her into their endless depths for the second time.

"I'm looking forward to performing with you, Becca. You really do have the voice of an angel. An angel of music."

He almost sang the last sentence but not quite. Again his voice captured the essence of Erik, and Rebecca wasn't even sure that she remembered how to breathe. Tom and the other boys called Justyn a vampire. For one horrible second, Rebecca thought maybe they were right. Maybe he really was a blood-drinking monster that was going to suck the life from her in the deserted gymnasium. And just like the pathetic, captivated victims of movie vampires, she was just standing there, stupidly waiting for him to sink his fangs into her neck. Waiting because he had bewitched her with his hypnotic eyes.

Even as her mind whirled with all the horrific possibilities, Justyn shifted his weight, and a large silver necklace slipped from behind his shirt into plain view. It made her wonder even more who Justyn really was. The necklace was a five-pointed star locked within the confines of a silver circle. A pentacle. Rebecca had seen enough Hollywood horror films to know that the symbol usually had bad implications. But was it just a statement of rebellion? Or did it really mean something sinister? Rebecca wasn't sure she was ready to find out.

She took a step backwards, and then practically jumped out of her skin when a light thump echoed through the gym. They both turned to see that the broom in the corner had fallen to the ground.

"Looks like company's coming," Justyn stated matter-of-factly.

Rebecca was just about to ask him what he meant by that when the door behind them was yanked roughly open by dirt-caked hands. A grungy, balding, middle-aged man with a cloud of dust around his thin frame stood glaring at them from the doorway with his one good eye. The other was blinded by cataracts, and even behind his thick glasses it was cloudy and lifeless.

"What are you kids doing in here?" he demanded in a gruff voice. "I have to get this floor waxed!"

"Sorry, Mr. Russ," Rebecca told the janitor. "We were just leaving."

"Then get out already!"

The older man continued to grumble to himself under his breath as Rebecca overcame her slight uneasiness about Justyn long enough to grab his hand and hurriedly pull him out the door. She felt herself shiver. If Justyn was creepy, the school janitor, Mr. Russ, was downright unsettling. He was always wandering around the school hallways talking to himself. Most of the kids just blew him off or made fun of him behind his back, but Rebecca felt a strange combination of fear and pity for him. In a way, Mr. Russ had a lot in common with the phantom as well. Except that he had none of the divine musical genius that made Erik so compelling.

"Who was that?" Justyn asked when they were back in the relative safety of the corridor. He didn't seem the slightest bit perturbed by the interruption.

"Just the janitor. He doesn't like it when kids get in his way."

"I kind of sensed that. So." He continued. "Would you want to go grab a cup of coffee or something?"

Rebecca was startled. Too startled to reply for a minute. Was he asking her on a date? That hardly seemed feasible. But even if he were asking her out, was that something she wanted to do? Even though a part of her was strangely drawn to him, another part of her was a little intimated. She was having trouble getting the vampire visions out of her head. Plus, what would Carmen and Debbie think of her if she went out with the Gothic kid they thought was so strange?

Carmen and Debbie! She just remembered that they were still outside waiting for her. They must be wondering where she was by now. It gave her the perfect excuse to get away.

"I . . . I really can't. I already made plans with some of my friends."

She realized she didn't sound very convincing. He must have thought she was just blowing him off. He looked a little hurt when he responded. "Oh, all right. Maybe another time then."

"Maybe." Rebecca felt guilty when his face fell even more. She was being silly and superstitious. Justyn was just the new kid in town. He was reaching out, trying to make a friend, and she was being rude and uncommonly judgmental. It wasn't like her, and she decided she was going to put a stop to it. She gave Justyn a warm, heartfelt smile. "I'll look for you at rehearsal tomorrow. It really is an honor to get to play Christine opposite your phantom."

He seemed appeased. "Until tomorrow then, my lady," he whispered, and actually bowed as she passed by him. It certainly was dramatic, and might have even been silly coming from anyone else, but with Justyn it seemed perfectly natural.

They parted ways, and Rebecca actually made it to her locker without any more interruptions. She didn't notice which direction Justyn had gone and she didn't hear his footsteps in the empty hallway. She was tempted to look over her shoulder to see where he had gone, but the small part of her that was still being irrational was too afraid that he might have vanished into thin air. Or possibly morphed into a bat. So she kept her eyes straight ahead.

Her heart fluttered wildly as she worked the numbers on her combination lock, and she wondered what it was about the Gothic boy that made her feel so . . . so undone. It was like he unraveled her with his eyes. Undressing not her body, but her soul, and seeing things inside of her that she didn't even see herself. Was she attracted to him? She didn't really think so. It was more like she was mystified by him. And maybe a little drawn to his beautiful voice, the same way Christine was drawn to the genius of the phantom. But being enraptured by the music and actually having feelings for the singer were two very different things. Justyn was just a little too strange. She couldn't have a crush on him. Could she?

Rebecca had finally managed to get the numbers right on her combination, and she shook her head to clear all thoughts of Lord Justyn away. She had more important things to worry about. Like how she was going to get through the entire play without having a heart attack.

Thinking again about the auditorium filled with people turned out to be more dangerous than thinking about Justyn. The panic of stage fright was starting to overwhelm her again, and she wasn't even on the stage yet. But when she finally pulled open her locker door, that panic was quickly replaced with fear—a fear that had nothing to do with singing in public.

Rebecca covered her mouth with her hands, and took a few unsteady steps backwards. She was too surprised to scream, and even if she had, there was no one around to hear it. As much as she wanted to, she couldn't tear her eyes away from the grotesque scene that was in her locker.

A doll, dressed in a late nineteenth century gown, dangled limply from her coat hanger, hung by its neck with an elaborate noose. Its eyes were blacked out with markers to make them look closed in death. Above its head there was a note taped to the metal, with a few lines scrawled in large black letters. It was a well-known and eternally foreboding threat from the play they were performing.

"Keep your hands where you can see.
Or the hangman might just come for thee."

Chapter Five

"Keep your hands *where?*" Carmen asked, making a face. "It sounds a little perverted if you ask me."

"The phantom always used a noose to kill his victims. If you keep your hands raised up near your eyes, where you can see them, you would be able to stop the noose from strangling you," Debbie explained.

"Eww, that's gross." Carmen gave a little shudder. "You don't really think someone wants to *hang* you, do you, Becca? That's a little extreme."

It had been twenty-four hours since she had found the note and the doll in her locker, and still, just the thought of it made Rebecca shudder, too. And even though she had thrown the doll in the nearest trashcan, its ghost still haunted her every single time she opened her locker door. And every time she closed her eyes.

"No, of course not," Rebecca said with a sigh. "But I do think they wanted to scare me."

"Don't worry about that stupid note," Tom told her as he tossed his jacket behind the stage. "It's probably just Wendy trying to get you to quit so she can steal your role. That sounds like the kind of stunt she would pull."

"And what about *you*, Tom?" Carmen asked. "Are you still upset that you didn't get the part of the phantom?"

Tom glanced at Debbie and looked chagrined. "Yeah, well, maybe I did overreact a little yesterday. No hard feelings, huh, Deb?"

Debbie smiled. She was way too nice to hold a grudge. "Of course not, Tom. I know you were upset."

"Besides." Tom continued. "Now that I've had a chance to think about it, I'm glad I got the role of Raoul. After all, he's the hero. And in the end, he's the one who gets the girl."

He actually put his arm around Rebecca, and she felt her face flush with pleasure. Tom really seemed to like her. A few of the younger girls were looking at them with envy in their eyes, but Rebecca didn't feel sorry for them. After four years of sitting on the sidelines, she felt she deserved this moment of honor, and she reveled in it.

"It's a shame that life doesn't always imitate art."

Every single person standing on the stage jumped at the sound of Justyn's voice, slightly eerie, somehow almost threatening, yet at the same time as alluring as ever. At least, it was alluring to Rebecca. She was fairly certain that the others didn't see him that way. Especially not Tom, who recovered quickly from the surprise entrance, and glared at the newcomer.

"Can you try to speak modern day English, vampire?"

Justyn stepped onto the stage, darkly clad as usual, and crossed his arms over his chest. "I'm sorry, Tom. I forgot for a moment that you have a limited vocabulary. I'll make an effort to use only one-syllable words when you're around. What I was trying to say was—maybe Becca's not interested in you."

Tom's arm fell away from her shoulders and he took a few steps in Justyn's direction. "And who else *would* she be interested in? *You?*" He gave a small, bitter laugh. "Dream on, vampire! Becca's not interested in satanic freaks."

Justyn frowned, and his face became shadowed. It was as close to angry as she had ever seen him. "If I *am* a satanic freak, don't you think you should be a little more careful what you say to me?"

Both boys were tense, and Rebecca was afraid. She felt like she should be doing something to intervene. Jump in between them, wringing her hands like any heroine worth her salt would do in a similar situation. At the very least, she should be yelling at them to stop. She was so worried one of them would get hurt, she hardly thought about the fact that two gorgeous men were about to fight over her. Over *her*! Rebecca Hope. Three days ago, she couldn't have gotten a guy to look at her if she had flung herself into oncoming traffic. And now, she was watching two men, both of whom she liked, gearing up to bash each other's faces in. She wasn't sure that she liked it very much. In a way, she kind of wished she could go back to being invisible.

The whole room had fallen into silence, watching, waiting. Surfer and Goth were facing off the same way that Raoul and the phantom had faced off for Christine. Rebecca knew she had to move quickly. She pulled away from Carmen's death grip—she hadn't even noticed when her friend had dug her long nails into her arm—and moved to part the two boys. Jay Kopp beat her to it.

"Ha! Back, vampire! Back!" Jay cried as he suddenly leapt from behind the side curtain. In his hands he had two—ball point pens, which he overlapped into the shape of a cross. He jumped between Justyn and Tom, brandishing his makeshift crucifix dramatically. "Back to your crypt, creature of the night! Back before I smite you on the spot!"

Rebecca was never as happy to see Jay as she was at that moment. His tomfoolery had saved the day, though she doubted that was his intention. The other cast members on the stage were laughing, and even Tom was back to his earlier good mood as he exchanged high fives with his best friend. Only Justyn was still annoyed, and it only made sense since the snickers all around them were at his expense. He shook his head in disgust.

"You *both* need to grow up."

Then he stomped to the other side of the stage to wait for Miss King to arrive and for rehearsal to begin. Rebecca felt kind of sorry for him. He was sitting all alone when everyone else was chatting with friends. He *had* been a little rude to Tom, but Tom had started it by always calling Justyn names. The person Rebecca was *really* angry with was Miss King. If their director could just manage to be on time for her own rehearsals, the boys wouldn't have had the opportunity to exchange words at all.

"He is the creepiest guy I have ever met," Carmen said with a small shiver after Justyn had walked away. "Seriously, he really creeps me out."

Speaking of limited vocabularies, Carmen apparently wasn't much better than Tom. How many times and in how many ways could she use the word 'creepy'? And why did it annoy Rebecca so much to hear her best friend putting Justyn down anyway? Why should she care what anyone thought about Justyn Patko, *Lord* Justyn, as he would say? Yet, she felt an undeniable urge to defend him. But before she did, she checked to make sure Tom wasn't listening.

"He's not that bad, you know," Rebecca told Carmen. "I talked to him a little bit yesterday. He's nice. Just a little eccentric."

Debbie wrinkled her nose in distaste. "Eccentric is just a fancy way of saying crazy. I bet that Justyn's the one who put that doll in your locker."

Rebecca thought about it, and found herself realizing that despite the fact that she was so mysteriously drawn to Justyn, it was a definite possibility. He *had* been lurking around in the hallway. He certainly had the means and the opportunity. But why would he want to scare her? What would he have to gain? He seemed to *want* her in the play, unlike Wendy who definitely had the *motive* to try to get rid of her.

"You don't have to worry about that guy or that stupid note," Tom told her. "*I'll* keep you safe."

Rebecca's heart did a somersault as Tom squeezed her hand. She couldn't help but smile, even though she noticed Justyn watching with a frown from the other side of the stage. Before she could respond, Miss King finally walked into the auditorium. The kids in the orchestra starting tuning up their instruments, and the actors were ordered to their positions for the opening scene.

"Okay, places everyone! We're going to take it from the top of the first act. We'll try running through the whole play, minus the dance scenes. Scripts are acceptable this week, but by next week, I expect, no I *demand* that everyone have their lines memorized."

Several students moaned, but Rebecca already knew every word by heart, so the request wasn't intimating. More worrisome for her were the people who would be watching her speak those lines, waiting for her to make a mistake, just so they could laugh at her.

"You're going to be great," Tom told her, and squeezed her hand one last time. "Don't look so worried."

"That's easy for you to say. You're used to this."

Tom smiled and went backstage to wait for his queue. Rebecca took her spot among the chorus girls to wait until she was "discovered". But before she even took one step forward, someone shoved her roughly from behind. The point of their elbow hit her painfully in the lower back, very nearly knocking her to the ground.

"Clumsy much?" Wendy asked with a smirk.

That was only the beginning of a fairly miserable afternoon for Rebecca. She made it through the first half of rehearsal without any major incidents, and aside from Justyn she was the only one that didn't need her script for guidance. But she was still so skittish about even their small audience that her nerves were showing in her performance. She was stiff and unnatural for all that she was able to reach even the highest notes and achieve the most difficult scales. She also kept tripping over her own feet, and even bumped into some of her cast mates a few times, making Wendy's clumsy comment seem only apropos. Rebecca noticed Miss King frowning at her more than once and she wondered if the teacher was regretting her casting decision.

It wasn't until the final scene of the first act that things started to look up. It was the duet between Christine and Raoul, and Rebecca got butterflies just thinking about singing the love song with Tom. It soothed her frazzled nerves when he took her hand and led her to the center of the stage, just like Raoul had soothed the fears of his soon-to-be lover. When he began to sing, even though he had to use his script and was just a little off key, she truly felt that he was singing to *her*. Singing from his heart.

> *"Don't let dark thoughts consume you.*
> *I'm here to sooth your fears.*
> *I'll let nothing and no one harm you.*

I'll protect you all your years.
So take my hand and I'll guide you.
From the darkness of the night.
And when I am beside you,
You'll no longer live in fright."

Rebecca sang her own part flawlessly. Swept away by her feelings, as well as the music, she forgot for a little while that anyone other than Tom was watching her. As they sang, Rebecca truly did feel safe and protected. The note, the doll, Wendy, and even Justyn were all far from her mind as they neared the final verse.

At the end of the song, they were supposed to kiss. And judging from the look on Tom's face, when that time came it would be more than just acting. Rebecca's heart was pounding with excited expectation as the last lines of the song poured forth from them in sweet harmony. Tom's lips moved closer to hers with every word.

"All I ask is that you love me true
Can I ask this simple thing of you?"

Their lips were just about to touch. Rebecca felt her eyes start to close as she waited for the inevitable feel of his lips against hers. But the spell was broken when she heard Carmen's voice cry out in alarm.

"Becca, Tom, look out!"

There were a few more shocked cries, but before Rebecca even had the chance to look up to see what all the shouting was about, she was roughly thrown to the ground and instantly surrounded by darkness.

Chapter Six

Everything was pitch-black. Total darkness surrounded her. Something heavy was smothering her. Claustrophobia set in, and Rebecca felt herself beginning to hyperventilate. She couldn't move. She couldn't breathe. She thought irrationally that maybe she was dead and this was the black abyss that followed. No bright light at the end of the tunnel. No smiling family members there to great her. Just nothing. It was her worst nightmare coming true.

Then something hard jabbed her in the forehead, which was followed by a loud grunt. She realized it was Tom's elbow, and she started to calm down just a little. She *wasn't* dead, at least not yet. But she still wasn't exactly sure what had happened, and it was getting more and more difficult to breathe.

"Becca? Are you all right?" Tom's voice was muffled and even if she had an answer, she was too short of breath to give it.

"Get that *off* of them!"

The new voice was even more strained, even more difficult to hear, because it was coming from the other side of the cloth-like prison. But she was fairly certain it was the frazzled voice of Miss King that was ordering people into action. Above her, something started to shift, but still no light appeared. Rebecca was nearing a complete and total nervous breakdown. She was sure that she could never escape, that she was going to suffocate before they reached her. Even as she thought it, the little air she had seemed to retreat from her lungs, and she heard herself gasping.

"It's okay, Becca." She felt Tom reach out and touch her hand. "We're almost out of this."

Tom's voice was soothing in the mist of the crisis. She felt herself calm down just a little. Before long a crack of light appeared in one corner. A second later, the heavy velvet curtain was completely pulled away with a heave from a few of the stagehands. Rebecca squinted, attempting to adjust to the light after having been plunged into complete darkness.

Carmen rushed to her side. "Becca, are you okay?" She reached out to hug her, and somehow Rebecca found the strength to hug her back, even though her arms were still shaking.

"What happened?"

It was a stupid question. It was plainly obvious what had happened. The main curtain had fallen and covered them. It was still lying on the stage in a huge velvet heap. Around her, half the cast was watching with a mixture of surprise and amusement. Jay was snickering even as he helped Tom to his feet.

"You aren't hurt, are you?" Miss King asked nervously. Tom and Rebecca both shook their heads and the teacher was visibly relieved. "Thank heavens for that! Remember, bad rehearsals mean a great opening night. Besides, I've been trying to get the school to replace this mangy old curtain for years. Now they won't have a choice."

Miss King had the stage crew pull the fallen curtain to the side of the stage. And then had the nerve to expect her to act, literally act, as though nothing had happened. Rebecca wasn't sure how she was going to go back to practice after she had nearly smothered to death. But Tom appeared unfazed by the whole fiasco, and everyone else was falling into line for the next scene, so Rebecca did her best to pull herself together. Her acting was more or less terrible, but they made it through the rest of the play without incident. When it was all over, she joined Debbie and Carmen who were dangling their legs from the corner of the stage.

"You did a great job today, Becca." Debbie gushed.

Rebecca rolled her eyes. "You don't have to be nice. I know I was awful."

"Everyone was awful," Carmen told her. "The first rehearsal is *always* awful. It will get better as we go along and get used to each other."

Rebecca hoped she was right. She also hoped that the next rehearsal would pass without any disasters. She was nervous enough without random things crashing down on her head.

"You kids need to clear out of here so I can clean up this mess!"

Mr. Russ had come in, pushing along his cart of cleaning supplies. He gestured to the auditorium floor. It didn't seem particularly messy, but Rebecca hardly wanted to argue with the odd, old janitor. He stood there, watching them with his one good eye, until they all climbed down off the stage and moved toward the nearest exit. He had blocked most of the aisle so they had to squeeze by him one by one. Rebecca tried to get by without disturbing his cart, but before she could shimmy past him, he roughly grabbed hold of her arm.

"Accidents aren't always accidental." His voice was hoarse and she could smell his stale breath in her face. Rebecca gasped and tried to pull away, but he only tightened his grip on her wrist. "You need to be careful, little girl."

Rebecca wasn't sure what to say. Was that a threat or a warning? Or was Mr. Russ just babbling meaningless nonsense as usual? She had always thought he was harmless. But now she wasn't so sure.

"Leave her alone, you freak!"

It was Debbie who came to her rescue. She grabbed Rebecca's hand firmly, and pulled her free from the janitor's grasp. And since she was significantly larger than him, he could only glare at her for a moment before turning back to his cleaning cart and pushing it down the aisle as though nothing had happened. But he had left Rebecca trembling for the second time that day. As if things hadn't been bad enough. The last thing she needed was to be stalked by the dusty looking janitor.

"What is *his* problem?" Carmen asked as the three of them scampered out into the hallway, trying to put as much distance between them and Mr. Russ as possible. "He is seriously brain damaged or something."

"Don't let him scare you, Becca," Debbie added. "There really *is* something wrong with him. I don't think he knows what he's saying half the time."

Rebecca sighed. "You're right. I really have to stop letting things get to me. At this rate, my hair will turn gray before I graduate."

"Hey, girls!" Tom had just rounded the corner. He spotted them and waved. "I was just going to meet some of the others across the street at Sam's. Why don't you come with us?"

Rebecca's heart started to hammer again, but this time it had nothing to do with fear. It couldn't be considered a date since he had invited all of them. But still, Tom Rittenhouse had asked her to do something with him. It was at the very least worth a diary entry.

"Sure. That sounds like fun." She hoped she didn't sound too anxious.

Carmen's smile couldn't have been any wider as they walked to the pizza shop across the street from the school. It was a small place with only about ten booths, all adorned with red and white gingham table clothes. As soon as they walked in the door, they were greeted by the scent of savory tomato sauce and grilled hamburgers. Rebecca felt her stomach rumble, and realized she was starving. But she lost most of her appetite when she saw that Wendy and Jay were already sitting in the extra-large booth in the corner. Wendy sneered at Rebecca, but with an unexpected and uncharacteristic burst of courage, Rebecca smiled broadly at the blonde girl as she slid into the edge of the booth beside Tom.

"Who invited the Amazon woman?" Jay asked. He blew the cover of his straw in Debbie's direction. She turned red and stared at the tabletop.

Tom reached across the table to punch Jay in the arm. "Dude, don't be a jerk, okay? We're a team now. We have to get along for the next few weeks if want the play to be a success."

"Not much chance of *that* when we're dealing with a bunch of amateurs," Wendy said, and she looked right at Rebecca.

Tom was doing his best to keep the peace. It was a heavy order with the company he was keeping. "Wendy, come on, lighten up!"

Wendy smirked. "If you're such a great team player, Tom, why don't you invite *him* to join us?"

She gestured to the table behind them and Rebecca couldn't resist turning around with everyone else to see who was sitting there. She shouldn't have been surprised to see that it was Justyn. Who else would Wendy use to get under Tom's skin? He was sitting quietly at his booth, with a glass of water in front and him, and a book opened in his hands. It didn't even appear that he knew any of his cast mates were there. Or maybe he just didn't care. Tom, at first, seemed annoyed and even a little disgusted at the possibility of having Justyn join them, but then with a shrug he yelled out across the little restaurant.

"Yo, *Lord* Justyn." Tom called. Justyn lifted one eye from his book. "Want to join us?"

After all the animosity between them, Rebecca didn't really think he would accept the invitation. Tom obviously didn't expect him to either, because his eyes practically bugged out of his head when Justyn closed his book, slipped wordlessly from his seat, and glided down the row of tables. He slid into the end of the booth on the other side of Rebecca, brushing her leg with his own and sending that strange electric current through her in the process. Mouths fell open all around the booth, and only Jay was able to think of something to say, however rude and inappropriate it might have been.

"Hey vampire, does this make you nervous?" He picked up the bottle of garlic salt and waved it near Justyn's face.

Justyn smiled calmly. "Jay, if the smell of garlic could scare me away, I certainly wouldn't be able to tolerate sitting across the table from you. Have you ever heard of breath mints?"

Carmen and Debbie both chuckled, and Rebecca couldn't help but smile. It was the first time in his life that Jay seemed struck speechless. He apparently couldn't think of any retaliation because he put down the garlic salt, and leaned back into the booth with a pout. He could dish it out, but Jay wasn't quite so good at taking it.

"What are you reading, Justyn?" Debbie asked politely. It was the first light topic of conversation anyone had come up with since they walked into the restaurant.

"Tennyson," Justyn replied flatly.

Again the diverse Gothic surprised Rebecca. By now Justyn should have ceased to amaze her with what he did and said. But their common interests still shocked her—by all outward appearances, they should have been as different as night and day.

"I love Tennyson." Rebecca gushed. *"The Lady of Shalott"* is one of my all time favorite poems."

> *"The leaves upon her falling light—*
> *Thro' the noises of the night,*
> *She floated down to Camelot:*
> *And as the boat—head wound along*
> *The willowy hills and fields among,*
> *They heard her singing her last song,*
> *The Lady of Shalott."*

That swooning feeling was back with a vengeance as Justyn's fluid voice recited the verse from the poem. His voice created a magical tapestry in which Rebecca could clearly see the scene come to life before her eyes. Her cheeks burned brighter with each word, and Tom certainly noticed it because she felt him grow stiff beside her.

"Oh please," Wendy said with a roll of her green eyes. "I can't believe you two would actually read that dribble on purpose."

"Just because you're at a third grade reading level, doesn't mean the rest of us are," Carmen snapped, even though she wouldn't have touched a book of poetry with a ten foot pole.

Now Wendy and Carmen were staring daggers at each other across the table. The whole evening was going poorly and Rebecca was relieved when the waitress came to take their orders. It gave her at least a ten-minute reprieve from playing referee. But the peace wasn't destined to last long. Justyn was the last to place his order. Following a string of requests for pizza and hamburgers, his strange choice was bound to start off a whole new round of taunting.

"I'll have the veggie burger, please."

The young waitress smiled at Justyn as he handed her back his menu. He was the only one who said 'please', and his musical tone of voice apparently made other people swoon sometimes too. Rebecca felt just the slightest twinge of jealousy when his fingers brushed against the waitress's hand. But she didn't have time to dwell on it for very long.

"Veggie burger?" Jay snickered. "What are you, a rabbit?"

Justyn raised one pierced eyebrow. "I'm a vegetarian."

"Poetry spouting? Salad munching?" Tom laughed, and it wasn't at all good-natured. "Dude, you really shouldn't try so hard to be manly."

Justyn's voice was not quite hostile, but was openly sarcastic when he responded. "And what makes a man, Tom? A pretty boy face and a string of basketball trophies?"

"It makes me a better man than you, vampire! And who do you think you're calling a pretty boy?"

All pretense of friendliness was gone, and Rebecca was worried she might get caught in the middle of the crossfire if fists were thrown. "Whoa, boys," she said, and laid a hand on each of their shoulders. "No one is questioning anyone's manhood here. Let's all just settle down and try to have a good time."

If settling down translated to sitting in tense silence, then they all complied. Having a good time was a little too much to ask for. Rebecca twisted her napkin under the table nervously while she waited for her pizza to arrive. When it did, she nibbled at it gingerly, hardly hungry anymore.

The tension didn't hinder the appetites of the teenage boys nearly as much. Both Justyn and Tom dug into their dinners heartily and Jay tore into his hamburger with reckless abandon, practically eating the whole thing in three huge bites. But the girls were only picking at their meals. Especially Wendy, who was more interested in shooting Rebecca dirty looks across the table than she was in eating. Even Carmen and Debbie looked like they felt completely out of place, making Rebecca feel even worse for having dragged them into her soap opera existence.

She was relieved when Justyn finished his veggie burger, and picked up his book to leave. He tossed a ten-dollar bill on the table.

"Thank you all for allowing me the pleasure of your company this evening." Only Justyn could sound so overtly polite and yet at the same time have his voice drip with such obvious sarcasm.

"Freak," Wendy mumbled under her breath.

Justyn ignored her. "Becca, I hope I'll see you tomorrow at rehearsal."

"You'll see her all right," Tom told him through clenched teeth. "Standing right next to *me*."

The two boys exchanged one last hostile stare before Justyn turned back to Rebecca. He bent over, picked up her hand, and kissed her fingers with every bit as much grace and poise as any eighteenth century aristocrat. The whole restaurant faded away for a second as their eyes locked. When he finally let go, her hand still tingled.

"Goodnight, Becca," he whispered.

Then he appeared to float out the door. It seemed that there should have been a swirling mist at his feet to complete the exit scene. Rebecca watched him go, and she could hardly breathe. She didn't even realize she hadn't replied. Tom took that lack of response as confirmation that she wasn't interested in Justyn at all, which was probably for the best. Still, Rebecca had to admit to herself that she *was* interested, at least a little. Of the two, Tom seemed the far safer choice, and Rebecca had never been one to take unnecessary risks. And really, once Justyn was gone, she hardly thought about him anymore. Hardly.

When they were done eating, Tom insisted on paying her share of the bill, and insisted even more adamantly that he walk her to her car. She had to drive Debbie and Carmen home, but they lingered knowingly behind to give Tom and Rebecca a chance at some private time. Halfway through the parking lot, he reached out to take her hand. Rebecca hoped her nerves hadn't made it clammy or sweaty.

"So . . . ." Tom said, and leaned back against the side of her little golden Suzuki.

"So?" Rebecca repeated awkwardly when after at least a full minute had passed in which he said nothing else.

"Next week is the Halloween Dance."

"Yeah."

"I was thinking maybe, you know—if you were planning on going, you might want to go with me."

Might want to go with him? This was the moment she had been dreaming of for four years. In those dreams, she had always swept him away with some brilliant, romantic response. Real life wasn't usually quite that interesting.

"Sure, that sounds like fun."

Tom smiled. He was really cute when he smiled, all boyish charm. "Great. Then I guess I'll see you in the morning."

"Yeah, you bet."

Tom leaned down over her, and very gently brushed her lips with his own. There were no electric currents or swooning, but it was definitely nice. It was sweet and gentle, and she thought it was cute that he was actually blushing just as much as she was. Popular surfer or not, Tom was still a little shy.

"Bye, Becca."

"Bye, Tom."

Rebecca had to lean against her car to support her somewhat wobbly knees. Tom waved as he walked away and before he had even turned the corner, Carmen and Debbie were pouncing on her for details.

"I smell love in the air," Debbie said. "Tell us all about it!"

"Tom just asked me to the dance next week."

"He didn't!" Carmen exclaimed. She was actually jumping up and down. "I don't believe it! You *go* girl!"

"Believe it." Debbie smiled. "Our quiet little Becca has become the belle of the ball."

They all smiled as they climbed into her car. Rebecca was still feeling a little dreamy after she dropped her friends off and pulled into her driveway. Before she reached the door, her cell phone started ringing and vibrating simultaneously from somewhere deep inside her handbag. She dropped her keys in her haste to dig it out before the call went into voicemail, even though she knew it was probably just Carmen calling to gush about her and Tom and their possible couple status. Finally, she pulled the phone free, and flipped back the cover without even looking to see who was calling.

"Hello?"

The voice that responded was unfamiliar, and in fact, it didn't even sound human. Distorted and garbled as it was, it was impossible to tell for certain whether it was a man or a woman. But it was threatening and terrifying, and the few lines it spoke made her blood run cold.

The words were meant as a threat in the play when the phantom spoke them to Christine as he yanked the engagement ring Raoul had given her from the chain around her neck. And those same words were certainly just as ominous to Rebecca as she listened to them in the dim light of the autumn moon.

> *"A chain cannot bind you,*
> *Nor take you away.*
> *Your soul I've taken captive.*
> *Beside me you must always stay."*

Chapter Seven

The next day, the weather was every bit as threatening as the strange phone call had been the day before. Thunder crackled and rumbled, and lighting flashed across the skyline. It was so overcast that the morning sky could have passed for night. The wind was whipping at least sixty miles per hour, and the rain was coming down in torrents. It was hurricane season at the Jersey Shore. There was no question about it.

Rebecca's hair was plastered to her head when she finally ran into the school. Her hooded raincoat did as much good as the inside-out umbrella she had discarded in her driveway. She was soaked, and freezing, and miserable. She wasn't really paying attention to where she was going while she tried to shake the water off her clothes, and she collided with Wendy as she turned the corner. She dropped her book bag in the impact, and everything inside tumbled onto the floor.

"Watch where you're going, moron!" Wendy snapped. As she walked away, she made sure to step on as many of Rebecca's papers as possible.

Carmen came up beside her with her hands on her hips. "Someone should really take that pole out of her ass."

Rebecca shrugged as she bent down to pick up her assignments, hoping she might be able to salvage at least half of her soggy homework. "She hates me. I guess I better get used to it."

"She's just jealous," Debbie told her. "She'll get over it eventually."

"I sure hope so." Rebecca shoved the last paper back into her bag, a little more roughly than was necessary. "If she's the one trying to scare me away, she's doing a pretty good job. I don't know how much more of this my nerves can handle."

Carmen narrowed her eyes. "Did something else happen?"

Rebecca told them about the phone call, and shuddered as she remembered the menacing voice. Someone was definitely out to get her. She was starting to feel a little afraid, and it wasn't a good feeling.

"I still think it's Justyn," Debbie said adamantly. "He obviously has a thing for you. And I'm sure he doesn't like it that you chose Tom over him."

Rebecca was a little surprised by the statement. Had she chosen Tom over Justyn? She hadn't really considered that she had a choice. Tom had asked her to the dance and she had said yes. She couldn't even imagine Justyn attending something as commonplace as a high school dance. Besides, Tom was the man she had always wanted.

"Well, *I* think it was Wendy," Carmen argued. "She's still really pissed that she didn't get the lead in the play."

Rebecca shook out her raincoat before hanging it up in her locker. "No matter *who* did it, I guess I shouldn't let it get to me so much. It's just a joke, right? It's not like anyone's really going to hurt me."

"Why would anyone want to hurt you?" Justyn was suddenly behind them, as silent in his movements as Rebecca was squeaky in her soggy sneakers.

"Someone's been leaving Becca nasty notes and calling her and making threats," Debbie said with narrowed eyes. "Do you know anything about it?"

Justyn looked surprised, and then concerned, but Rebecca was aware of his extraordinary acting ability. He could turn emotions off and on at will when he wanted to. The response wasn't enough to eliminate him from the suspect list. He really was the most obvious choice. He was the only one, besides Rebecca herself, who knew the play inside and out. Yet, she just couldn't imagine him wanting to scare her. She knew his black clothes and unusual style made her friends nervous, but she saw something in him that went deeper than his fashion sense. She didn't think he would hurt her. But since when was she the best judge of character? There was a time that she thought Wendy was really nice.

"Do you think it's connected to the curtain falling down?" Justyn asked. "I overheard the stagehands saying the curtain rod had been tampered with."

"Tampered with? How?" Carmen asked.

Justyn shrugged. "I don't know exactly."

Rebecca gasped. Despite the strange warning from Mr. Russ, she had never seriously considered that someone might have sent the curtain crashing down on purpose. Miss King had made it sound like it had been threatening to crumple for years. It made the whole situation seem much more sinister. Was the person doing these things really dangerous? The thought made Rebecca feel a little dizzy. She reached out a hand to steady herself, intending to grab her locker, but found that it was Justyn's arm she caught hold of instead.

"Are you all right, Becca?"

His melodious, almost unnatural voice made things even shakier. Realizing that she was making a complete fool of herself, Rebecca took a deep breath and shook her head.

"I'm fine." She forced a small laugh. "*This* Christine is a lot tougher than she looks. I'm not going to go around fainting whenever something out of the ordinary happens."

She was tough? Boy, was that a blatant lie.

"And *this* phantom isn't really such a bad guy." Justyn smiled and let go of her arm, just as the overhead bells started ringing. "Well, if you ever do decide to faint, Becca, I'd be more than happy to sweep you up and carry you away."

"Don't count on it."

Rebecca tried to sound strong and full of feminist pride, but that smoldering look in his eyes made her wonder if she wouldn't hit the ground at that very moment. And the light-headedness had nothing to do with her mysterious stalker. It was because once again Lord Justyn had her reeling with strange and unaccustomed emotions.

"Come on, Becca, we're going to be late," Debbie told her.

She was still giving Justyn dirty looks, and she didn't even give them a chance to say goodbye before forcefully pulling her into homeroom. But

Rebecca felt his eyes on her until the moment that she disappeared behind the doors, and even then she wondered if he had some kind of x-ray vision because she swore she could still feel his presence all around her. She thought about him all day as she flitted from one class to another in a kind of half daze. If nothing else, it made the dull, rainy day go by a little faster, and before long she found herself back in the auditorium preparing for rehearsal.

The first scenes went well, with no curtains crashing down. There were no accidents of *any* kind. Even the constant rumbles of thunder and the heavy rain pounding against the windows didn't disturb the actors. Rebecca was starting to feel a little more comfortable on the stage, and her movements were a lot less rigid. When it came time for the scene where Christine meets the phantom for the first time, Miss King handed Justyn the signature white mask that was the opera ghost's calling card, and told them they needed to start working on the drama of the unmasking.

Justyn slipped on the mask, and Rebecca had to catch her breath. His standard Gothic wardrobe only enhanced the effect. The black t-shirt with the grinning white skull emblazoned across the front would have been a fashion must for any self-respecting, twenty-first century phantom. And Justyn *was* a modern day phantom, a modern day Erik—a tortured musical genius if ever there was one.

The scene began and Justyn gently led Rebecca across the stage. The orchestra flared to life, with pipe organ blaring, and drums thumping. The constant booming thunder was just another instrument that blended perfectly with the intensity of the organ. She sang the famous, mystical duet with him, *for* him, and she realized that she was every bit as much a modern day Christine, drawn to the mysterious darkness and seduction of an unknown stranger who sang like an angel.

> *"He came to me, an angel in the night.*
> *His voice is like a siren's call.*
> *Now I follow him though I know it's not right.*
> *His commands cannot be denied at all."*

The stage wasn't decorated yet. They had no candles or swirling mists, no underwater stream or flashy gondola. But even if there were, Rebecca wouldn't have seen them. She saw only Justyn's face and heard only the music. His eyes held her transfixed, and with those eyes he weaved a labyrinth every bit as enchanting as the underground fortress of the phantom. And Rebecca wasn't sure that she would ever be able to climb back up to the surface that was reality.

She couldn't deny any longer that she was attracted to him. Her whole body was throbbing with the force of that attraction. Yet, somewhere in the back of her mind, there were still thoughts of Tom waiting for her in the real world. More than ever, she was like Christine. Torn between the handsome blond bearer of light and the dark lord of the night. In her heart, Rebecca had always believed Christine truly loved Erik, but was too weak to overcome her fear of his dark side. Looking at Justyn's masked face, she had to wonder if she was letting fear hold her back from what she really wanted as well.

The duet ended and gracefully transcended into the slower, more passionate love ballad which Justyn sang solo. His voice was like a vocal massage, a gentle resonating whisper. Each word touched her, stroked her, embraced her, until her knees quivered and her breath caught in her throat. She had heard him sing the song before, more than once, but not since that first audition did his voice overwhelm her so completely.

> *"The mysteries of music have been revealed to you.*
> *You will never be free no matter what you may do.*
> *You've journeyed with me to the world of the unknown.*
> *This night I have claimed your soul as my own."*

Now it was not just his words but also his hands that embraced her. Those gentle hands explored her body, sliding along her waist, up her arms, over her neck. He took her hand and lifted it against his cheek. The ceaseless throb in her body turned to an almost unbearable ache, and she longed to feel his touch in less appropriate places.

Rebecca held her breath and closed her eyes. His lips moved so close to the nape of her neck that it made goose bumps appear up and down her arms.

Lips that were so close to her flesh, but never quite touched it. One hand toyed with the ends of her long hair, while the other glided along her waist, squeezing her against him. She waited, yearned for more.

"You're supposed to faint now," he whispered in her ear. His voice was more than a little amused.

Rebecca immediately snapped back to reality. She almost argued with him again that she wasn't the fainting type. But then she remembered that it was part of the scene.

"Oh yeah. Right."

She closed her eyes and allowed her body to go limp and crumple into his waiting arms. She did her best to keep her body relaxed so she wouldn't be too heavy for him. But it was unnecessary because he lifted her effortlessly. She was so close to him that she could smell the scent of his cologne, some mixture of patchouli and sandalwood that was natural but masculine and made her feel even more lightheaded and giddy. He gently placed her down on the dingy, old cot that they were using until the props were complete. She could have been in a bed lined with designer silk sheets, and the moment wouldn't have been any more breathtaking when he leaned over her.

Above them, the thunder crackled so loudly that they could hear it clearly over the stilling music of the orchestra. Justyn stroked her cheek as he sang the last lines of the sonnet.

"It is you alone who inspires me to sing.
Take my hand and watch the symphony take wing."

Once again his heavy breath teased her, tortured her, and left her longing for more. Though her eyes were still closed, she was sure his lips lingered just above hers. She was certain he would kiss her, and was even more certain that she wanted him to. But before she learned for a fact what his intentions might be, the auditorium erupted into terrified screams.

Chapter Eight

Rebecca snapped her eyes open to see what all the shouting was about. At least she thought she did. But even though she swore her eyes were wide open, she still couldn't see anything. The entire auditorium had been plunged into total darkness. Only a few scattered corners were lit by flashing battery powered emergency lights.

Another clap of thunder rattled the sky, and the scared screams settled into startled gasps. As the silence grew heavier in the auditorium, she could hear the rain pounding against the windows and the wind howling through the trees. And even though she couldn't see it, she was sure lighting was flashing dangerously beyond the school walls.

"Everyone stay calm!" Miss King called through the darkness, sounding anything but calm herself. "It's just the storm. I'm sure the electric will only be out for a few minutes. Just stay where you are until the lights come back on. I don't need anyone falling off the stage and breaking their necks."

Rebecca was still lying back on the mangy cot that smelled of stale mothballs. Looming above her, all she could see was the faint outline of the white mask of the phantom, which was still covering Justyn's face. The magic connection they had briefly shared had broken the minute the music ceased to play, and Rebecca had to wonder if it had ever been more than just her imagination. With a sigh of exasperation, she sat up on the cot.

The silence lasted longer than she was comfortable with and Rebecca felt the need to break it. "Spooky, huh?"

She felt the weight shift on the cot as Justyn took a seat beside her. "Not really. I like the dark."

Rebecca laughed lightly. "Why doesn't that surprise me?"

Her eyes were starting to adjust to the dim light, and she was able to see the outline of her companion. Even in the dark room, his silver necklace clearly glittered around his neck. It was the same one he had been wearing in the gym, a star in a circle. It made her curious.

"Can I ask you a question?"

He shrugged. "It's not like I have anything better to do at the moment."

"I don't want to offend you."

She knew he smiled because she saw the white glint of his teeth through the darkness. "I'm not easily offended."

"Your necklace." Rebecca surprised herself with her own courage when she reached out to touch it. "Does it mean something to you? Or is it only for shock value?" He was quiet for a minute and that made her nervous. "I *did* offend you, didn't I?"

He laughed out loud. "Not at all. You just took me by surprise, that's all. I wish more people would ask instead of making presumptions. It's a pentacle. Each corner represents one of the elements." As he explained, he lifted her hand and guided her fingers around the points of the star. "Air, fire, water, and earth. And the center is spirit. I wear it for protection."

Only after he let her hand go was she able to speak. And even then she had to clear her throat. "Protection from what?"

"That's two questions. It's my turn to ask *you* one now."

She nodded, even though he probably couldn't see her. "Okay, that sounds fair. What's your question?"

"Would you give me the pleasure of escorting you to the Halloween dance?"

Rebecca was surprised at first, and even a little excited. But then she remembered she had already promised to go to the dance with Tom. She *wanted* to go to the dance with Tom. She had been waiting all her life to go out with Tom. But she still regretted the answer she had to give Justyn and she found that she was glad for the darkness. He couldn't read the expression on her face, any more than she would have to see the disappointment on his.

"I . . . can't," she told him. "I already told someone else I would go with them."

He sighed, but didn't really sound surprised. "You know, if you continue to turn me down when I ask you out, eventually I might stop asking."

"Really?"

"Yes, but it will take a while. I'm extremely stubborn when there's something I want."

Justyn was staring at her. Rebecca was extremely aware of his presence beside her. She could feel the warmth radiating from his skin, and she could smell his earthy cologne. He was so close, but not quite touching her. Yet, even though they weren't making physical contact, she could still feel an energy seeping from him—that same electric current that shocked her every time he touched her. It was driving her insane. And the most annoying part of it was that he knew he was having this effect on her. She could hear the amusement mingled with the seduction in his voice.

She swallowed hard. "And what is it, exactly, that you want from me, Justyn?"

"I want to know who beat me to the punch. Was it Tom?"

Rebecca wasn't sure that was a safe topic, so she quickly changed the subject. "Oh, no. I answered your question. It's my turn again."

"You're right. You're right."

"So." Rebecca went back to the original line of questioning. "Protection from what?"

"From evil surfers who're trying to steal the girl of my dreams."

Now Rebecca knew her cheeks were scarlet and again she thanked a higher power for the temporary black out. "Be serious!"

"Okay, seriously." He relented. "I'm Wiccan. This pentacle is to me what the cross is to a Christian."

Rebecca felt her mouth fall open. "A Wiccan? Isn't that sort of . . . sort of like a witch?"

"Not sort of. I *am* a witch."

A very appropriate crack of thunder rumbled at that precise moment. In reality, Rebecca wasn't really surprised. It seemed only fitting that the modern day phantom would have some kind of magical ties. Still, Rebecca found herself looking over her shoulder to make sure no one else was listening. Of course she couldn't see anything anyway. But she did hear whispered voices all around her, and wondered who might be eavesdropping on their conversation.

"You're a witch, huh? If I ever do go out with you, will you be picking me up on your broomstick?"

She didn't need to see him to know that he had rolled his eyes. "Ha, ha. I've never heard *that* one before." Sarcasm or not, he still gave an honest chuckle. "If you're really curious, I could give you a book to read, just to explain what it's all about. Wicca isn't what you probably think it is. It's a religion, and a way of life. A good way in my opinion. Our primary rule is, 'If it harms none, do as you will.'"

"It's really important to you, isn't it?"

"It's important to me that you understand who I am. I don't want you to think there's any reason for you to be afraid of me."

"I'm not afraid of you," Rebecca told him, and was surprised that she meant it. Of all the crazy emotions he invoked in her, fear wasn't one of them. "But sure, give me the book. I'm a bookworm. I'll read anything."

"Okay, I will." Then he added. "It's my turn again."

Rebecca forgot that they were playing twenty questions, but she was a good sport. "Shoot."

"What do you see in Tom?"

"He's not *that* bad, you know."

"He has the depth of a puddle."

Rebecca thought about laughing, but it wasn't really a joke. Then she thought about sticking up for Tom, but she couldn't think of any good arguments in his defense. "He hasn't been very nice to you, has he?"

She saw his shoulders shrug. It was getting easier to see in the dark as more and more time passed. "I'm used to being the outcast. It comes with the territory."

"Then why don't you try to . . . I don't know . . . make yourself a little less conspicuous."

"I like who I am, Becca. Why should I change for people who don't take the time to look past outward appearances and preconceptions?"

Rebecca understood his sentiment. But she still wanted to argue that they were in high school after all, and outward appearances counted for ninety percent of their assessment in the eyes of their peers. But before she could open her mouth, the overhead lights flickered, once, then twice, before finally flooding the auditorium with brightness once again. Rebecca was blinded by the sudden radiance.

A few people around her were clapping and hooting. Miss King struggled to regain some order as kids started milling around the stage. They were picking up where they had left off, and Justyn and Rebecca moved to the sidelines because they weren't in the next scene. They watched in silence while the others went back and forth about the mysterious notes they had received from the phantom, leading Rebecca to wonder again who her own personal phantom really was.

"Becca," Justyn whispered suddenly, making her jump. "Do you *really* want to go to the dance with Tom?"

The answer should have been an easy one. But when she turned to meet his steady gaze, her mind was whirling with so many different thoughts, that she wasn't sure anymore that it *was* what she wanted.

She lowered her eyes. "No . . . I mean . . . yes. I mean, of course I want to go with him. I wouldn't have said yes if I didn't."

"You could change your mind . . . if you wanted to."

She shook her head. "No, I couldn't. It wouldn't be fair."

He nodded. "All right then. I won't ask you about the dance again. But that doesn't mean I'm giving up."

"You better give up, vampire. Becca is with me now."

Tom's part in the scene had ended, and he had come to find her. But the lull between scenes wouldn't be much longer, and they all had to prepare for their next curtain call. She tried to use that as an excuse to separate the two boys before they could get into an argument. They glared at each other with such pure hatred that Rebecca had to congratulate herself on her quick thinking as she led Tom to the other end of the stage. Miss King would probably have a stroke if a fight broke out after all the dramatics they had already been through in the last few days.

Rebecca didn't think she had to worry about Justyn anymore as they moved through the next scene. Tom stopped her as she was darting to her spot on the stage with a serious expression on his face.

"You don't really like that vampire freak, do you, Becca?"

She didn't really have time to debate it. She was supposed to be on the stage with Wendy and Carmen. She quickly gave him the answer he wanted to hear, just so he would let it go. It didn't seem to matter whether or not she really meant it.

"No, of course not, Tom."

Tom happily let her go about her business. But what she didn't realize was that Justyn had been standing just behind them, and overheard the brief conversation. When she finally noticed him there, and saw the sad look in his eyes, it almost made her want to cry out that she didn't really mean it. But she didn't have time. They were waiting for her. She decided there would be time to explain later.

The music was already starting. Before she knew it they were already back to the love scene between Christine and Raoul. But before she could step onto the stage for the duet, Justyn caught her arm.

"I'll *never* give up, Becca."

She couldn't have responded even if he had waited long enough for her to find her tongue. Justyn let go of her arm, and took his place hiding behind a gargoyle statue while Rebecca joined Tom. He hadn't really sounded angry, just determined. Yet, Rebecca couldn't help but think that his words had sounded like a threat—a threat worthy of the phantom.

The love scene was a blur, but at least they made it through the whole song without any curtains falling on their heads to ruin the romance of the moment. Tom took advantage of the lack of disasters. His lips touched hers ever so gently as they came to the end of the ballad.

The moment should have been perfect. She waited for the butterflies in her stomach to start fluttering, waited for the lightheaded feeling. There should have been ecstasy after so many years of dreaming of this exact thing happening. But her mind was still on Justyn, worrying that she had hurt his feelings. And even more worried about the fact that he was standing just a few feet away, watching Tom kiss her, just as the phantom had watched Christine.

When Tom finally let her go, the look she saw on Justyn's face was every bit as tormented as the phantom's had been on the cold roof of the opera house when he realized he was losing his love to the gallant Raoul. As she and Tom moved to the sidelines, Justyn took center stage. That torment was echoed and magnified by the desperate, yet beautifully resonating tenor of the phantom.

> *"On my wings your song took flight.*
> *But you betrayed me on this night.*
> *Now as my hopes have been swept away,*
> *So begins our real life play."*

He huddled on the ground, completely in character and beyond. From the sidelines, Tom and Rebecca sang the echoed words of the love song that drove the phantom to unimaginable acts of violence. Justyn captured the essence of that fury as he stood up and stared directly at Rebecca and Tom. The final words of the act seemed as if they weren't just lines from the script, but a serious threat. A threat directed at them.

"This day a curse is on your head.
This opera house will live in dread."

As the menacing words reverberated through the auditorium, Rebecca had to wonder just how much Justyn really had in common with the phantom. What was he really capable of?

Chapter Nine

The weekend was uneventful. Rebecca spent Friday and Saturday with Carmen and Debbie, watching movies, painting nails, and generally immersing themselves in all things feminine. It was a much-needed break from the raging testosterone she had been dealing with for the past week. On Sunday, she gave into self-indulgence and read a historical romance from cover to cover, then soaked for an hour in a warm bubble bath. Best of all, there were no phone calls or notes the entire weekend. When Monday finally arrived, she felt relaxed, revitalized, and ready to take on the world.

The school day went by just as smoothly as the weekend. Tom joined her for lunch, and they actually had their first normal conversation. Rebecca didn't trip over her tongue once, and it only felt natural when they walked into rehearsal together with his arm draped across her shoulders. But the day had gone too well. It couldn't possibly last forever. Especially not when Miss King was running late again, and Wendy and Justyn were both watching her and Tom with open hostility.

Rebecca wasn't ready for the peace to end, even though it was inevitable. But it was the law of averages. All good things came to an end eventually. She did her best to avoid them both altogether, and tried to slip past them to join her friends on the other side of the stage. But Wendy was feeling especially belligerent, and stalked over to Rebecca, waving a piece of paper in her face.

"I suppose you think this is funny?" Wendy spat.

Rebecca had no idea what she was talking about and felt her mouth drop open in shocked surprise. She was glad when Carmen thought of a quick comeback because she certainly wasn't thinking of any.

"If you're talking about the possibility of you actually getting accepted to a four year college, then yeah, it's hilarious."

Wendy's nostrils were flaring, but she ignored Carmen and continued to wave the note in Rebecca's face. "I don't know who you think you are, but you aren't going to get away with threatening me like this."

"What are you talking about, Wendy?" Tom demanded. "Becca didn't do anything to you."

"You think your new girlfriend is so perfect and sweet! Well look at this!" She thrust the wrinkled paper into Tom's hands. "Go ahead, look at it! I found it this morning in my locker."

Tom rolled his eyes but humored her, and tried to smooth out the crinkled paper enough to read it. He cleared his throat dramatically before reading it out loud so everyone could hear.

"'*I tell you, daroga—mirrors can kill.*'" He paused for a minute, looking a little baffled. "Leave Becca alone unless you want to be just as ugly on the outside as you are on the inside."

"You see?" Wendy screamed. "Do you see how she *threatened* me?"

"Wendy, I swear it wasn't me!" Rebecca protested.

"Well, I don't know who or what a 'daroga' is, but I certainly agree with the sentiment," Carmen said as she crossed her arms. "If you'd just leave Becca alone, you'd have nothing to worry about."

"Who *is* daroga?" Tom asked. "It sounds like it should be the name of a car model or something."

"The first line of the note is a quote from the original *Phantom of the Opera* novel," Rebecca explained. "Daroga was the name the phantom called his Persian policeman friend."

"And what other loser but *you* would know any lines from some stupid book that was written like five hundred years ago."

Rebecca could think of at least one other person. A person who dressed all in black and wasn't even trying to hide the fact that he was listening to every word they were saying. But even if she wanted to share the information, Wendy wouldn't have listened to her.

"It wasn't Becca," Debbie told her. "She got notes just like that one. They must be from the same person."

"Of course *you're* going to defend her! She's the only person pathetic enough to actually be friends with an oversized nerd like you!"

Debbie's head snapped back like she'd been slapped. She looked like she was about to burst into tears. As Rebecca watched her friend choke back a sob, she realized that she had finally had enough. It was one thing when Wendy was picking on her, but it was crossing the line when she attacked her friends. That was something even a quiet little mouse like Rebecca wasn't going to stand for.

"Wendy, why don't you just back off . . ." Tom began. Rebecca cut him off in mid-sentence.

"Wait, Tom. I can speak for myself." Rebecca crossed her arms over her chest and took a few steps closer to Wendy, facing her down with more courage than she knew she was capable of. "I've put up with your crap for long enough, Wendy. The jibes. The looks. The nasty comments. Well, I've *had* it. It stops *now*. *I* got the role of Christine. *I* have the better voice. And *you* have been upstaged. Get over it and get on with your life. Being a bitch isn't going to change things."

Wendy looked like she might just have a conniption. Her face turned at least twelve different shades of red, and Rebecca was sure she could actually see the purple veins throbbing in her forehead. For the first time in the four years Rebecca had known her, Wendy Wright was struck speechless. But it was only a temporary condition. Again, Rebecca reminded herself that good things never last long.

Wendy snatched the piece of loose-leaf paper out of Tom's hands, crumpled it up, and tossed it at Rebecca, aiming for her face. She missed, and it bounced harmlessly off her chest before falling onto the floor.

"This isn't over, Becca. If you want a war, you're going to get one."

"Bring it on, honey." Carmen insisted. Rebecca was tempted to slap her.

Wendy huffed, turned on her heel and stomped across the stage. Justyn snickered at her as she passed by him and it was more than she was willing to tolerate.

"What are you looking at, freak?"

"Ugliness incarnate," Justyn replied.

He was suddenly straight-faced and very serious. Wendy gave him one last dirty look before joining a few of her friends from the chorus. She didn't notice that Justyn continued to glare at her as she waited for rehearsal to begin. But Rebecca noticed, and it made her nervous.

"Wow, girl, I can't believe the way you just stood up to Wendy!" Carmen exclaimed. "When did you go and get a backbone?"

"Everyone has a breaking point," Debbie said. "Even Becca."

"That's pretty much it," Rebecca told them. Now that it was over, she was kind of shocked herself. "I guess I went a little crazy for a second there."

"You should go crazy more often." Tom teased. "You're kind of hot when you're mad."

Rebecca knew she was back to her old self when she felt her face flush with embarrassment. But she held her ground once rehearsal started and refused to let the daunting stares and nasty remarks of Wendy and her friends bother her. Miss King had no reason to doubt her casting that day. Rebecca performed flawlessly beside both Justyn and Tom. When it was time for Wendy's main scene, she wondered if she would do half as well, and in uncharacteristically bad sportsmanship, almost hoped that she wouldn't.

Rebecca watched from the sidelines, waiting patiently for the next scene in which she would have to join Wendy on the stage. It wasn't a scene she was particularly looking forward to, but it appeared she would have at least a few moments of reprieve. Scene shifting was taking a little longer now that most of the props had arrived. The transition between the phantom's lair and back to the main opera house was challenging because there were so many pieces involved. Dozens of people were running around behind the curtain, bumping into each other in the dim lighting, knocking things over, and cursing under their breath as they banged their shins and elbows. The whole fiasco was a maze of confusion. Things were finally getting under control and Wendy was ironically waving a phony note in Tom's face as her character, Carlotta, accused Raoul of trying get rid of her so Christine could take her place.

She watched as Tom made his adamant denials and stalked off the stage, leaving Wendy alone to sing her solo with the two freshmen who played the managers of the opera house. She didn't see where Tom went. Carmen and Debbie were also missing in action, and Rebecca found herself standing alone as she waited. Across the stage, she caught a brief glimpse of Justyn's metal-toed boots. Soon, even they had vanished behind the curtain.

Rebecca had the distinct feeling of being utterly alone, even though she was surrounded by dozens of people. The feeling was followed by an eerie sense of premonition that something horrible was about to happen. Her heart started racing for reasons she couldn't explain. And her eyes darted nervously from one end of the auditorium to the other, finally resting disturbingly on Mr. Russ, who was lurking in the doorway just outside the hall. His one cataract plagued eye was oblique and almost glowing, even from the distance. Rebecca found herself stepping further back behind the curtains in the hopes that he wouldn't see her. He had never really bothered her before, but lately there was something about Mr. Russ that she found extremely disturbing. And it was more than just his shady, disheveled appearance.

Back on the stage, the opera house managers were trying to console their star. Wendy was certainly dramatic enough. The role called for a bit of overacting and that was definitely her specialty. She stalked around the stage, flailing her arms like any self-respecting diva, as the managers begged and pleaded with her to perform. But as Wendy was heading toward her newly supplied dressing room table to feign preparations for that night's gala, Rebecca noticed something thin and shiny along the floor of the stage. It was a long, thin line that sparkled under the spotlights. It would have been next to impossible to see almost anywhere else, but from Rebecca's vantage point, it was clearly visible. She strained her eyes in an attempt to figure out what it was, and why it was there.

It all seemed harmless enough; probably just the binding from one of the prop boxes that someone had dropped. That explanation seemed unlikely when Rebecca realized that the line lead all the way back behind the curtains of the stage. And even more unlikely when, just as Wendy walked towards her dressing table, completely immersed in her song, the sparkling thread was jerked up and lifted several inches from the ground.

It all happened so quickly, there wasn't any time for Rebecca to call out a warning. The glittering cord came up in the exact second that Wendy was walking by it. Her ankle caught around it, and she started to fall. There was nothing for her to grab hold of. The two freshmen saw her going down and both of them reached out to catch her, but it was too late. She stumbled forward, her chest slamming hard against the dressing table, knocking the breath out of her.

It seemed like that was going to be the worst of it. Rebecca heaved a sigh of relief, thinking it was all over, that the disaster had passed. She didn't notice the dresser mirror tremble and give way until it was already falling. She didn't notice it come tumbling down until the instant that Wendy lifted her head. The mirror crashed down and shattered into pieces right on top of Wendy.

She wasn't the only one who screamed as shards of glass tore into her beautiful face, and blood starting to drip into a puddle on the floor of the stage.

Chapter Ten

"My face! My face!"

Wendy cried out in horror and tried uselessly to stop the flow of blood with her hands. At first, Rebecca could only watch, still as a statue as the sticky red blood seeped through her fingers. Wendy's desperate calls for help finally spurred Rebecca into action, along with everyone else. The madness of the scene change was nothing compared to the mayhem that ensued. Suddenly, there were dozens of people swarming around on the stage, front and foremost being Miss King who was doing her best to calm the hysterical girl even though she was pretty close to hysterics herself.

"It's going to be all right, honey." Miss King consoled, and patted Wendy's shoulder. "Help will be here soon."

"My face, not my face."

Tears were mixing with the blood that ran from the deep gashes on Wendy's damaged face. So much blood that it was impossible to tell exactly where it was all coming from or how serious the wounds really were. The blood, Wendy's sobbing, Miss King's nervous pacing, it was all too much for Rebecca to take. She had to turn away from the carnage to keep from gagging.

The minutes seemed to tick by like hours as they waited for something, anything to happen. Thankfully, more than one cell phone had flipped open as soon as Wendy hit the ground, so in reality it wasn't long before help arrived. Wendy was put into a neck brace as a precaution before they loaded her onto a stretcher, still crying and wailing. Rebecca was watching the whole calamity with silent horror, wanting to help, yet knowing the best thing she could do was stay out of the way.

"Now *that's* gonna leave a mark."

Only Jay could be that crude and make light of such a serious situation. He had materialized from behind the curtains along with Tom. Debbie and Carmen were coming from the opposite direction. Rebecca had lost track of her friends during the last scene, but was happy for their presence. Even Jay and his off color comments were better than being alone.

"Try to have a little couth, would you, Jay?" Debbie told him.

Jay's response was to stick his tongue out at her, which only annoyed Debbie even more. The rest of them just ignored him.

"What happened?" Carmen asked. "Did you see her fall?"

"She must have tripped over something." Tom reasoned.

They all watched in silence as Wendy was carried out of the auditorium. Everyone from actors to stagehands watched and waited, unsure what they were supposed to do next. Everyone, Rebecca noticed, except Justyn. His was the only face missing from the crowd of concerned onlookers. She looked around for him and finally noticed him lurking behind a curtain near the back of the stage. He wasn't even looking at Wendy. He didn't even seem to care that one of his classmates was seriously hurt.

Rebecca wondered if he really didn't care, or if he was just trying to remain unnoticed. The shiny cord that had tripped Wendy had come from exactly the spot where Justyn had been standing. But when Rebecca looked down for the telltale wire, it was gone. Had she imagined it? Or had someone managed to move it during the frenzy that followed the accident? Whoever it was would have had to move quickly to avoid being seen. Of course, if someone was dressed entirely in black from head to toe, with nothing but a few shiny silver chains to give them away, it would be much easier to be overlooked in the darkness behind the stage.

Rebecca was about to voice her suspicions to her friends, but they were suddenly being shooed away by a visibly shaken Miss King. Wendy was gone, but the remnants of her accident still littered the stage, leaving behind an awful reminder. The fallen table, the broken mirror, the splattering of quickly drying blood. It all made Rebecca feel a little sick.

Mr. Russ appeared with a dustpan, a mop, and an angry scowl. Rebecca wondered if he had been waiting in the hallway all along for some kind of disaster to occur. She even thought for a moment that maybe *he* was the one behind the accident. But he had been in the doorway the whole time. It would have been impossible for him to trip Wendy with the wire.

The janitor mumbled to himself under his breath as he dragged his equipment up the aisle. But when he reached the top of the stage, he turned around, and very deliberately stared at them. No, it wasn't really *them* as a group that he was watching. He stared right at *Rebecca*. It only lasted for a minute, and then he was back to work as usual, but it was obvious and deliberate enough that everyone in her small party noticed it.

"What is *he* looking at?" Carmen asked. "Is he in love with you too, Becca? I swear, it's getting a little ridiculous the way every man who gets within five feet of you gets all weak in the knees."

Was it just her imagination or did Carmen sound just a little bit jealous? She certainly wasn't envious about the old janitor. But Tom had been as much of an unfilled fantasy for Carmen as he had been for Rebecca up until recently. She had thought her friend was happy for her, but there was an edge in Carmen's voice that she had never heard before. It made her wonder if she was really okay about her budding relationship with Tom. But as quickly as it came, the unhappy tone disappeared, and Carmen was back to her normal, talkative self. It was probably just the stress of the day that was making everyone a little edgy. And Rebecca always did have a tendency to read too much into things.

It was no surprise when Miss King canceled the rest of practice. Carmen invited herself to Rebecca's house so they could work on their science projects, which really translated to Rebecca doing the project while Carmen talked about boys and painted her nails. Debbie, of course, decided to tag along as well. Tom gave Rebecca a quick kiss on the cheek and left the girls to their business. He had decided to meet up with some of the guys from the basketball team, with Jay following behind him like an ever-present shadow.

Rebecca and her friends shuffled across the stage to grab their bags so they could leave. As she bent down, Rebecca noticed the crumbled paper that Wendy had tossed at her before practice had begun. She knew it wasn't a good idea. She knew she was only going to drive herself insane, but she picked it up anyway, smoothed it out, and read the quote again. This time the words took on a much darker meaning because she knew it was more than just a joke.

"I tell you, daroga—mirrors can kill."

How could anyone believe what happened to Wendy was just a coincidence? The note, coupled with the mysterious fall, was a prank worthy of the phantom himself. She would have thought the whole thing was suspicious even if she hadn't seen the wire. But who would have wanted to do something so terrible? Sure, Wendy wasn't the nicest person in the world, but she didn't deserve to be hurt. Could it have been Justyn? He couldn't possibly think that violence would be the way to her heart. But, then again, he knew how much she loved the story of Erik and Christine. It wasn't inconceivable that he could try to mimic their story. After all, he *was* always quoting lines from the book and the play.

"Becca, your face is as white as a ghost," Debbie said. She took hold of Rebecca's hand, and squeezed it reassuringly. "What's wrong?"

"This was no accident," Rebecca told her. "Someone did this to Wendy on purpose."

Debbie's face turned just as white as Rebecca's. "You don't really believe that, do you?"

"How can you think anything else? The note, the mirror . . . ."

"The paranoia," Carmen interjected. "It was just an accident, Becca. Wendy tripped over her own big feet."

Rebecca shook her head. She thought about telling them about the wire. But she knew that now that it was gone, she couldn't prove anything. It would only make her sound even more like a raving lunatic if they thought she was seeing things. So she dropped it altogether, and the three girls went out to her car.

The doors were unlocked, so Carmen and Debbie climbed in. But when Rebecca reached into her bag to get her keys to start the engine, they weren't there. She had to resist the urge to smack herself in the forehead. She figured they must have fallen out of her bag and into her locker. The last thing she wanted to do was to run back inside the deserted school alone to retrieve them. But she also couldn't stand the thought of her friends teasing her if she admitted she was afraid to go in alone because of an invisible stalker. So she fought back the unreasonable jitters and bravely walked up to the front doors on her own.

Once she was inside, and out of sight of Debbie and Carmen, Rebecca all but flew down the hallway to her locker. She rummaged through the unorganized bottom shelf until she found her heavy key chain. She had every intention of darting right back out the door, but of course that would have been too easy.

"Where are you running to in such a hurry?"

Rebecca jumped as Justyn came around the corner and stood between her and the exit. Her first reaction was annoyance. Why was Justyn always skulking around in the hallways after school was over?

"Do you even *have* a home?" She asked him in a huff. "Or do you just live in the rafters?"

Justyn actually flinched. "Ouch."

Rebecca immediately felt guilty. It wasn't like her to be so nasty. That was the kind of thing Wendy or Jay would say to him. Not Rebecca. She was supposed to be the nice one.

"I'm sorry; I'm just really stressed out over this thing with Wendy. And I really need to get out of here now, so if you don't mind . . . ."

"Are you late for a date with your hero?"

Now she was getting annoyed again. Her emotions always ran a strange gamut whenever Justyn was in her presence, though for once the flustered feeling was absent. The jibe about Tom made her think again about her suspicions, and she had to wonder if she was safe being alone with Justyn. When she spoke again, she knew her voice was a little shaky, even though she tried to hold her ground.

"Not that it's any of your business, but Carmen and Debbie are waiting for me outside."

She felt another twinge of guilt at the crestfallen look on his face when he heard the harshness in her voice. But her suspicions were overshadowing any guilt, and Rebecca tried to squeeze past him through the door. He stepped out of her way, but he looked confused.

"Is something wrong, Becca?" he asked, just as she put her hand on the door push. "I feel like you're angry with me."

Rebecca sighed and turned back around. She knew she wasn't being fair. She had no proof that Justyn was the one who tried to hurt Wendy. He had never been anything but nice to her, not to mention open and up-front. And he obviously liked her, even though she was being a total jerk to him. She did her best to pull herself together and give him the benefit of the doubt.

"No, I'm not mad," she told him. She tried to sound more relaxed, but her voice was still strained. "It's just that . . . ."

"Just that you think I had something to do with Wendy's accident," Justyn concluded.

Rebecca had to stop and pick her mouth up off the floor. "Why . . . why would you say that?"

He laughed, just a little bitterly. "Because you're practically jumping out of your skin. And because whenever something bad happens, the first person to get blamed is either the new guy or the person who's a little different. In this case, I happen to be both. Who else *would* you blame?"

She swallowed hard. His voice wasn't exactly belligerent, but it certainly wasn't docile either. She couldn't help but wonder why he would think it was anything more than an accident at all. No one, aside from Rebecca, seemed to think so. It made him seem even guiltier. But Rebecca decided that if he *had* done it, the last thing she should be doing was trying to make him angry. So she tried to be nonchalant.

"It's not you. I just . . . I have a lot of homework to do." *That was so incredibly lame*, she thought.

Justyn studied her, his dark eyes sad and brooding, for what seemed like a long time before he finally spoke. "Well, I wouldn't want to be the reason why you didn't make the honor roll this semester."

"Okay then. I'll see you tomorrow at practice."

She pushed open the door to walk out, but his lyrical voice stopped her in her tracks, so overflowing with all the misery and melancholy, all the heartbreak of the world, that she couldn't help but listen. This time she didn't swoon. Although he obviously meant the words as a testimony to his innocence, the fact that he was again quoting the same book as her real life phantom only made her doubt him even more.

"You are afraid of me and I am not really wicked. Love me and you shall see! . . . If you loved me I would be as gentle as a lamb, and you could do anything with me that you pleased."

Rebecca didn't respond. She couldn't. Instead, she walked out the door and into the parking lot without looking back.

Chapter Eleven

The week flew by as they tended to do when things were insanely busy. Between schoolwork and rehearsals, there wasn't much time for anything else. Before Rebecca knew it, it was Friday, Halloween, the night of the dance. It was going to be her first real date with Tom. It was also the first life goal she could cross off her to-do list. Even all the craziness going on around her couldn't diminish her excitement. In fact, she hadn't heard from her stalker all week and therefore hadn't thought much about him since Wendy's return to school.

Wendy had been absent for only one day after her accident. Then she was back and just as determined as ever to make Rebecca's life miserable. There was one deep gash on her cheek and another across her forehead that needed stitches, and multiple smaller scratches. But Rebecca had heard through the grapevine that the doctors didn't think there would be any serious scarring. Still, she was cut up pretty badly, and it was impossible for high school kids not to stop and stare when she walked by. But she didn't let it affect her performance. She returned to her role of Carlotta with a confidence and grace that made Rebecca admire her despite their personal issues.

Wendy didn't come right out and say that she blamed Rebecca for her accident. But the unspoken accusation was there, making her understand a little better why Justyn had been able to pick up so well on her own suspicions. Every time Wendy glared at her, Rebecca felt like she was waiting for the inevitable counter attack, however undeserving it might be. It wasn't a good feeling to think that someone blamed her for something she knew she didn't do, and it made her feel guilty about how she had treated Justyn.

As far as her co-star was concerned, Justyn had avoided her as much as possible. He moved through their mutual scenes with much less vigor than usual, and spent the rest of the time in the gloomy kind of melancholy that

Goths were stereotypically known for. Yet, Rebecca knew that was putting on a front. A part of her missed the teasing Justyn, the sarcastic Justyn, and most of all, the sensual Justyn that could hold her enthralled with his hypnotic eyes and angelic voice. Still, she had to admit, there was a small part of her that was worried he might be the one who was causing the strange incidents. When days past without him speaking to her, she thought it was probably for the best if he moved on to other conquests.

She kept *telling* herself it was for the best, but she was having trouble actually *convincing* herself. She found that she missed his unique way of flirting. She was even thinking about seeking him out to apologize as she packed her books up after school. Miss King had canceled play practice so they could get ready for the dance, but she was sure he was still around somewhere. As it turned out, Rebecca didn't need to seek Justyn out. He found her.

"Hello, Becca."

At first, when she heard his soft voice speaking so close to her ear, she was startled. She actually felt the hairs on her neck rise as his breath teased her skin. She was so flustered that she dropped the book she was just about to put into her backpack. Nevertheless, she was secretly a little pleased that he hadn't given up on her after all.

He gave her a crooked, sarcastic smile as he handed her the book she had dropped. "You know, you don't have to worry. I wouldn't attack you in front of all these witnesses." He gestured to the still crowded hallway. School had just let out, and the students were shuffling around as they prepared for the weekend.

"Do you really believe that's what I was thinking?"

He shrugged. "Only you know what you're thinking."

Rebecca blushed. "Well, I'm not worried about you attacking me. Even if we didn't have an audience."

"Really?" he asked. "Does that mean you've taken me off the Mainland Regional Most Wanted List?"

Rebecca had to laugh. He was taking her accusations fairly well. If he was willing to forgive her after the way she had treated him, the least she could do was apologize for it.

"I overreacted the other day. It wasn't fair of me to blame you."

"It's okay. I'm used to being the scapegoat."

"It still wasn't fair."

"No, but I forgive you. I even brought you a present."

Justyn extracted a round stone, about the size of an egg, from one of his large baggy pockets, and made a grand gesture of presenting it to her. He smiled at her as he held it out, a real smile, with no sarcasm behind it. It transformed his face. Black clothes, black makeup and all, he still managed to look innocent and sweet. Like a little boy giving someone a special gift he had made in art class. Rebecca couldn't help but smile back, even though she was a little confused by his present.

"A rock?" She teased. "Really, Lord Justyn, you shouldn't have."

The innocent look faded and turned playfully conspirative. "Sometimes, Becca, things are more than what they appear. Something can seem a little rough around the edges." He flipped over his little stone, revealing an inner cavern that sparkled with a layer of blue and white crystals. "But when you take the time to look a little closer, you might find something there that you never expected."

"It's . . . it's beautiful."

She accepted the gift hesitantly. She was almost afraid to touch it, worried that her clumsy hands would shatter its delicate perfection. It was surprisingly sturdy despite its fragile appearance. She ran her fingers along the shining crystals, and swore that the stone hummed with energy all its own.

"It's a geode," Justyn explained. "The crystals promote healing and creativity, and offer protection."

"Is this your subtle way of telling me my acting needs work?"

He rolled his eyes. "Well, it can't hurt. But I was more concerned with keeping you safe, especially after what happened to Wendy."

It was only with great effort that Rebecca managed to keep the conversation light after the reference to Wendy's accident. But she didn't want the conversation to end badly when things were going so well, so she just played off her nervousness.

"Make me a better actor *and* keep me from falling off the stage. That's a tall order. You really believe this one little rock can do all that?"

"There's amazing power and beauty in everything in nature. You just need to take the time to look for it and understand it. Which brings to me my second gift."

"Wow, I feel like it's my birthday."

"Well, Samhain, Halloween, is a special holiday at my house. It's one of the most important and powerful days of the year for a Wiccan. My family always likes to exchange little gifts."

Rebecca was having visions of Justyn and two black clad parental figures standing in the middle of the cemetery, chanting strange invocations in an effort to raise the dead. He must have noticed the look on her face. He rolled his eyes again, good-naturedly, and handed her a small paperback.

"This book will explain things. Wicca probably isn't what you think it is. But Samhain is a day when the veil between worlds is the thinnest. I always feel my father's spirit is close by on Samhain."

"Your father is . . . ." She paused, not wanting to sound rude.

"On the other side," Justyn finished. "I call it the Summerland. It's a place where your soul waits to be reincarnated."

"I'm sorry about your father," Rebecca said. "What happened to him?"

Justyn shrugged, trying to appear nonchalant, but she noticed he had to clear his throat before he spoke again. "Cancer. It was a long time ago, though. I was barely walking."

"So your mom raised you alone?"

"Pretty much. She got married again a few years ago. Matt's cool, but he doesn't really understand me."

"I can't imagine why. I mean—you're such an open book."

Justyn rolled his eyes. "Yeah, well, as long as my mother's happy, it's all the same to me. Matt gives me my space."

"Well, I'm going to make a point of reading this book over the weekend." Rebecca promised. "I'm sure it will be . . . very enlightening. But right now, I really need to get home and get my costume together. Will you be coming to the dance tonight? Or will you be too busy exchanging Halloween gifts and communing with the dead?"

"I'll do my best to work it all into my schedule, but I can't make any promises."

It didn't seem right that she should feel so disappointed when she was going to the dance with someone else, but still she felt her hopes drop. "All right. Maybe I'll see you later."

"Yeah, maybe. Have a good time with Tom."

It was hard to miss the hint of contempt in his voice when he spat Tom's name in only barely contained disgust. Rebecca was relieved when she was able to slip away before he could take it any further. The last thing she wanted to talk about with Justyn was her date with Tom.

Rebecca drove home, and immediately jumped into the shower. After she blow dried her hair, she rolled it in hot curlers. Then she fixed her makeup as she waited for the curls to set. It took her a few times to get the sparkling false eyelashes to stick, but when they finally did, she added glitter eye shadow and a deep pink blush. She didn't normally wear much makeup, but for Halloween, which had always been one of her favorite holidays, she made an exception. Her own life was so boring, it was fun to pretend to be someone a little more exiting, or adventurous, or in this case magical. This year, Rebecca had chosen a wood fairy as her costume.

After she was done with her makeup and removed the curlers, she used a sparkling lotion to cover her arms and legs in a very light, subtle shimmer before slipping into the costume. The flowing orange, gold and green gossamer top stopped just above her belly button. The matching skirt was a little shorter than she expected, but she had to admit, it was sexy. She completed the outfit with a pair of golden leg laces that tied just below her knees, a set of over-sized wings, and a ring of orange flowers that she placed on top of her hair. The whole ensemble was covered in a splattering of leaves, giving it an earthy, fall look. The colors complimented her olive skin tone, and overall, she was pleased with the final results. She just hoped she wouldn't have to turn sideways to get her wings through the door.

Rebecca was always the one oddball female who was done getting dressed way before she had to leave. She had at least another half hour before Tom would arrive to pick her up. On a spur of the moment, she picked up Justyn's book, and looked at the cover.

"Wicca Revealed," she read aloud. "A glimpse into the peaceful life of pagans."

She opened up to the first chapter and found that just the first few lines enchanted her. She had known witchcraft wasn't really a bunch of big-nosed women with warts who flew around on broomsticks. But she had never known much about the principles of the practice. She didn't think it was anything more than casting spells and reading tarot cards. As she read the opening lines of the poetic "Wiccan Creed", which beautifully summed up the basic philosophy behind the religion, she learned that not only was it not evil, it was actually beautiful. She finished the entire first chapter and was just about half way through the second when her cell phone rang.

She stuck a piece of paper in the book to mark her page and picked the phone up off her desk. She noticed it said "unknown number" instead of a name, but she was worried Tom might be calling her to tell her that he had changed his mind about taking her to the dance after all. So she answered it on the second ring.

"Hello."

"Don't go to the dance with Tom tonight."

Rebecca just about dropped the phone when she heard the same garbled voice that had threatened her before, distorted by some of type of electronic gizmo. Even as her hand started to tremble she cursed the Internet for making it possible for some crazy person to obtain the device they were using to terrorize her.

"Who is this?" Rebecca demanded. "Why are you doing this to me?"

Instead of answering, the voice plagued her with a horrible tuneless verse. The same verse that the phantom sung not long before the chandelier was sent crashing down into an unsuspecting audience.

> *"Listen to the demands I make,*
> *Do it for your lover's sake.*
> *If you don't there's sure to be,*
> *Disaster, misfortune, a calamity!"*

The line went dead as soon as the last word was sung, leaving Rebecca to wonder if the Halloween dance could possibly go as well as she had hoped with such a horrible threat hanging over head.

Chapter Twelve

A horn was honking loudly and a little obnoxiously from her driveway. Rebecca peeked out her bedroom window and saw Tom's truck. As she ran down the stairs, she resolved not to think about the phone call. There was no point in letting it ruin her night. After all, what could possibly happen at a high school dance? There would be at least a dozen chaperones there. She would be fine.

Rebecca had expected that Tom would at least be gentlemanly enough to get out of his car and knock on her door. Maybe it was for the best—if he didn't come in, her father wouldn't try to grill him about his intentions toward his daughter. In fact, her parents barely looked up as she slipped through the living room and out the door. They probably assumed she was going to the dance stag and riding with a group of girls, the way she normally did.

When she first walked up to the truck, she couldn't see Tom through the tinted windows. She wasn't sure if he planned on getting out of the truck at all. She was just about to reach for the handle when the passenger side door suddenly flung open. Before Rebecca could guess whether she was supposed to climb in, Tom stumbled out and fell onto his knees in the pebbled driveway. He burst into snorts of laughter as he pulled himself back to his feet. Rebecca was too surprised to even think about helping him up from the ground.

"Becca!" Tom shouted much louder than was necessary when she was standing only a few feet away. "Your captain has arrived!"

She assumed the captain pun was a reference to his pirate costume, complete with curly black wig, phony beard, and swashbuckling sword. He even had a colorful stuffed parrot attached to his shoulder. It was a great costume and more than appropriate for the resident surfer. Tom would have looked great except for the fact that he was still having trouble standing.

"What's wrong with you, Tom?"

Tom opened his mouth and scratched his fake hair like he was trying to think of an answer. But before he could, the horn blared again, and Jay's head popped out of the window.

"Dude, come on! We're going to be late. What are you doing?"

Tom rolled his eyes, reached for the door again, missed it, but somehow managed to maintain his wobbly footing. "Okay, okay." He dismissed Jay with a wave of his hand. Then he turned to Rebecca and whispered confidentially. "Jay's just mad because it's his turn to be designated driver."

"You're drunk?"

Rebecca was a little shocked, even though she knew it was a common practice for a large majority of the kids to get trashed before the dances. She just hadn't realized that Tom was one of them. She had expected more from him.

"You, ho, ho, and a bottle of Captain Morgan." Tom laughed again and used all fours to climb back into the truck. "Drunk. Crunk. Smashed. Hammered. Sauce money!"

Rebecca seriously considered turning right around and stomping back into her house. She took a few seconds to process everything, and she finally told herself that it really wasn't such a big deal. Tom would probably calm down once the effects of the alcohol wore off a little. She had been looking forward to the dance for too long to just walk away. At least Tom was responsible enough to have someone else drive when he was obviously impaired. So even though she was still annoyed, she squeezed into the cramped two-seater next to Tom.

"You look purty, Becca," Tom slurred.

Rebecca fought the urge to roll her eyes as she put her folded fairy wings on her lap. Jay pulled out of the driveway almost before she had time to pull the door shut, and certainly before she had a chance to buckle her seat belt. His driving was reckless; she had to wonder if he had snuck a few drinks as well. Other than that, the point of Tom's plastic sword was poking her in the back the whole way there. Luckily, it was only a ten-minute drive from her house to the school, and somehow they made it there in one piece. Rebecca's legs were trembling as she slid back down onto solid ground, and she felt the urge to drop to her knees and kiss the concrete parking lot in gratitude for having survived the crazy joy ride.

They waited for Jay as he pulled his costume out of the back of the truck. Rebecca watched curiously as he draped a large red and silver magnet around his shoulders. It wasn't a real magnet, of course. It was made of Styrofoam. About a dozen little, yellow birds were attached to it with Velcro.

"What are you supposed to be?" Rebecca asked as she strapped her wings back around her shoulders.

"Isn't it obvious?" He appeared disappointed that she hadn't figured it out. "I'm a chick magnet."

Rebecca couldn't help but chuckle as the three of them walked towards the doors of the cafeteria where the dances were always held. There was a line leading to the entrance where the student council was checking IDs before allowing anyone in the building. Tom fumbled in his pocket to find his, and then dropped it at least ten times before he finally managed to hand it to the underclassman manning the door. It wasn't a good start to the night, and Rebecca knew things were only going to go from bad to worse when Wendy came up behind them.

"Well, well, Tom. You've really lowered your standards, haven't you? Last year you came to the Halloween dance with *me*. This year you've resorted to traveling with geeks and freaks." Tom stuck his tongue out at her even as Jay flipped the middle finger, but she was too busy glaring at Rebecca to notice. "What are *you* supposed to be anyway, Becca?"

Rebecca sighed. The last thing she wanted was to start a word war with Wendy. "A wood fairy."

Wendy sneered. "A fairy? How cute. I hear that's the most popular choice for kindergarteners this year."

Rebecca felt her face turn beet red. She certainly couldn't think of any snappy comebacks, especially when Wendy was walking perfection in her sexy hippie costume. The short paisley print dress had a dramatic plunging neckline that showed off her figure to full advantage. Her straight blonde hair was parted down the center, and accented by large, dangling peace sign earrings. Hot pink, vinyl go-go boots completed the outfit, and even the healing cuts on her face didn't take away from the stunning look. It really did make Rebecca's costume seem childish in comparison.

"Shut up, Wendy." Tom draped his arm around Rebecca's shoulders so heavily that she almost fell over under his weight. "Why you gotta be such a *be-atch* all the time. Leave Becca alone."

Tom started to drag her away, but he was slow, and Wendy was able to lean over and whisper a not so veiled threat. "It's not over between us, Becca. I'm going to get you back for what you did."

Wendy stormed off in one direction, and Tom gratefully led her in another. They squeezed through the cafeteria doors and into a maze of flickering strobe lights, orange and black streamers, and fake spider webs. They were instantly blasted by the loud, blaring rock music, and even if Tom said something, she probably wouldn't have been able to hear him.

Somewhere along the way, they lost Jay in the crowd as they blended in on the dance floor. Tom was hardly coordinated enough to match even Rebecca's pathetic attempts at dancing. Instead, he dragged her over to a dark corner where they sat silently for a few minutes while Rebecca watched the disco ball bathe the dancers in circlets of sparkling lights. Monster masks and creepy costumes swirled around and blended together until the scary faces started to look almost real. She wondered if somewhere among them the mysterious caller was lurking. The thought made her shudder.

Rebecca tore her eyes away from the dizzying scene when Tom inched a little closer to her. He put one hand on her knee, a little awkwardly, and used the other to lift her face to meet his still slightly glazed eyes. Then he leaned down to kiss her.

It was hardly romantic. Not at all the way she had dreamed her first real intimate kiss with Tom would be. He tasted of alcohol, and was almost rough as he forced his tongue into her mouth. It was so unlike the times he had gently brushed her lips when he was sober and more himself. Then he had been sweet and tender, not clumsy and awkward. Rebecca realized that she didn't like Tom very much when he was drunk. When he clipped her lip with his teeth and she tasted the irony bitterness of blood in her mouth, she finally had to pull away.

Tom pouted. "What's wrong, Becca?"

"You're drunk."

"So what? Everybody's drunk."

Rebecca crossed her arms and huffed. "Well, *I'm* not drunk. And I don't really feel like making out with someone who is."

Tom sighed and put his head in his hands. He seemed a little more sober than he had been just seconds before. "I'm sorry. I guess I was trying a little too hard to be cool. But I really like you, Becca. And I . . . ." Tom paused and was quiet for a lot longer than he should have been. Then he suddenly groaned and clutched his stomach. "I . . . I think I'm going to be sick."

Rebecca didn't have time to ask if he was all right. He jumped down from the table and flew across the dance floor, very nearly knocking over a few dancers in his haste. He ran toward the bathroom with his hand over his mouth and never looked back. Before long he was out of sight, and Rebecca found herself groaning as well. Her dream date had officially turned into a nightmare.

Rebecca slid down from the table, and scanned the crowd for a friendly face. She spotted Debbie and Carmen at the small concession stand, buying a couple of sodas. She weaved her way through mummies, witches, and what appeared to be the entire cast of *The Wizard of Oz* before finally joining them just as they stepped away from the line with their drinks in their hands.

Rebecca's mouth fell open when she saw Carmen's sexy prep girl school costume. It had to be only marginally dress code appropriate. The plaid skirt was so short that if she wasn't wearing white ruffled bloomers underneath, there would have been very little left to the imagination. The white tie top displayed her dark olive skin and newly pierced belly button. Her thick black hair was pulled back into two big ponytails, and she completed the look with white, nylon knee-highs and black Mary Jane's. Once again, Rebecca was left feeling juvenile in comparison.

At least Debbie's choice was a little less revealing. She had chosen a cute gray fifties skirt with a white poodle embroidered along the hemline and a sequin trim. On any other girl, it probably would have fallen just below the knee, but on the six foot tall Debbie, it had landed just above. Her blonde hair was too short to put in a ponytail, but the pink tie looked just as nice as a scarf around her neck.

Both Debbie and Carmen looked up as she approached, and they both took a moment and examined her costume with the same curiosity with which Rebecca had examined theirs. Not far behind them, she noticed Mr. Russ was mopping up a spilled soda on the floor. She wondered why the strange old man suddenly seemed to be popping up everywhere she went. Did he ever go home? Or did he live in the basement of the school in the same way that the phantom had once lived in the cellars of the opera house?

"Where's Tom?" Carmen asked. "Shouldn't you two be swapping spit or something?"

Rebecca couldn't help but to roll her eyes. "I'm sure that's the last thing on his mind right now."

"What do you mean?" Debbie asked.

"He drank too much and now he's puking his guts up in the bathroom."

"Yuck." Carmen crinkled her nose in distaste. "Well, forget him then. Come out and dance with us."

Even if she wanted to decline the invitation, Carmen didn't give her the chance. She pulled her out onto the dance floor, along with Debbie. She refused to let them leave, even when an embarrassing line dance caused Rebecca to make a complete fool of herself. Despite her lack of coordination, she was having a good time, and she even forgot about her disappointment for a few minutes. But when the music slowed to the stereotypical boy band love song, and everyone broke off into pairs, Rebecca lost track of her friends.

She found herself standing alone in a corner, watching dozens of couples cuddling and kissing. The fact that she was, once again, not a part of that romantic scene left her with the sudden urge to burst into tears. She leaned her head back against the wall and closed her eyes, hoping that shutting out everything would make the ache in her heart go away. Instead, she heard a sweet, delicate voice that whispered words that were clear despite the loud music. The same words that she had heard sung by the chorus many times as they rehearsed the dance scene from the masquerade ball. They seemed only fitting considering their setting.

> *"Masks and hidden faces dance*
> *Each one waiting for their chance.*
> *To reveal the secrets hidden within*
> *Revealing truth, revealing sin.*
> *When all masks are stripped away,*
> *Will you find love or only dismay?"*

Chapter Thirteen

Rebecca opened her eyes and smiled when she saw the darkly dressed figure beside her. She was never happier to see Justyn than she was at that moment. She knew her wide smile revealed that happiness. She saw her own feelings reflected in Justyn's eyes, even though he tried to keep his face emotionless.

"So, you made it."

"It would appear that way."

"No ghosts in the mood to chat with you tonight?"

"Who needs spirits when I just walked through the mists into the world of fairy," he whispered, and ran a hand along her sparkling fairy wings. "You look beautiful tonight, Becca."

While she wasn't exactly sure what he meant about walking through mists, she somehow knew he was paying her a compliment. It was beyond a compliment. It was just like when he was reciting poetry. Once again she felt herself blushing. She was so flustered that she couldn't look him in the eyes.

"Ummm . . . thanks."

"So, where's your date? If I had the pleasure of being your escort, I wouldn't leave your side for a second."

The moment of dreaminess passed as she thought about Tom. Rebecca snorted, annoyed. "I would imagine he's on his knees worshipping the porcelain god."

Justyn chuckled. "Can't hold his liquor, eh?"

Rebecca couldn't help but smile, too. Justyn was really cute when he smiled. She wished he would do it more often. "I guess not. And what about you? How many beers have you had tonight?"

"None." He admitted. "I don't drink."

"Really? Not at all?" She couldn't hide her surprise.

"I don't believe in poisoning my body." She must have looked as shocked as she felt because Justyn shook his head, half amused, but also slightly irritated. "I don't shoot heroine either, in case you were wondering. Just because I'm Goth doesn't mean I'm a lush or a drug addict."

"I didn't mean to imply that you *were*. I just thought that *I* was the only sober person here." She tried to think of a way to lighten the mood. "Where's your costume?"

He was dressed in his normal, everyday clothes. He had on a black t-shirt with fishnet sleeves and decorative silver d-rings and silver zippers on the shoulders. His black, tight cut jeans were adorned with ornate bondage straps. His heavy black boots were silver tipped and had multiple silver buckles. And of course, his pentacle was clearly visible around his neck. It was exotic enough, but not at all out of the ordinary for Justyn, and could hardly be called a costume. But when he lifted up his upper lip in a feigned snarl that revealed pointed canine teeth, she realized he had added an extra touch for the evening. The fangs looked so natural, that for a second Rebecca found herself wondering if they might be real. It was a ridiculous thought, but she still had to clear her throat before she could speak again.

"A vampire?" she asked. "Are you serious?"

"What can I say? I enjoy irony."

Rebecca laughed. "Obviously. But is that *all*? Just the fangs? No cape? No freaky contacts? No blood dripping down from the corner of your lip? If Halloween is really your favorite holiday, I'd think you'd do a little better than *that*."

"Well, there is this."

Justyn lifted his right index finger, revealing a large, full-fingered silver ring. It had an intricate skull design on the knuckle and a dangerous looking point on the tip. It was fashioned to look like a claw, and appeared to be capable of doing some serious damage.

"Yeah, I'd say that's sufficiently freaky." Rebecca admitted with a small shudder. "I stand corrected."

She could see that he was amused by her reaction. "It's just for effect. It isn't sharp at all. See?"

Justyn ran the tip of the ring teasingly along her cheek. Then he continued, following a path from her neck to her bare shoulders, all the way down to the very tips of her own fingers. He was right. The point was completely dulled. Yet, her skin was suddenly covered with gooseflesh. She found herself shivering even though her face was burning, and she knew it was his simple touch that was making her tremble more than his vampire accessories.

Rebecca wasn't sure how long they would have stood that way, their fingers touching, staring into each other's eyes, barely hearing the thumping of the music around them. They might have stood frozen forever, maybe even drifted off into the fairy world that Justyn had mentioned. It certainly seemed in that moment that he was capable of anything, even transcending into a fantasy dimension. The magical imagery quickly dissolved when Jay appeared, ruining the perfect moment. He danced his way over to them, completely out of beat with the music, but hardly seeming to care.

"Hey, Becca. Hey, vampire." He added casually. Justyn gave him a dirty look but stayed silent. "Where did Tom disappear to?"

"He wasn't feeling well," Rebecca told him. She was a little nervous. What would Tom think if he knew she was spending time with Justyn while he was indisposed?

Jay slapped himself in the forehead and shook his head. "I *told* him Captain Morgan and beer don't mix. But did he listen to me? Noooo. Of course not. He *never* listens to me."

"He's been gone for a while now. Maybe you should go check on him," Rebecca suggested.

She really *was* concerned about Tom, but she also wanted to get rid of Jay as quickly as possible. She admitted to herself, with a little guilt, that it was because she wanted more time alone with Justyn. On Halloween night, of all nights, it was hard not be entranced by his odd charm.

"Great! Now I have to be designated driver *and* play nursemaid?" Jay complained. "Sheesh!"

He wandered off, shaking his head and mumbling under his breath. Rebecca turned back to Justyn, who was watching Jay walk away with a raised eyebrow.

"What is Jay supposed to be?"

"I've asked myself that question every day since freshman year."

Justyn grinned. "I meant his costume."

"Oh, that. He's a chick magnet."

"Hmmm. I see that Jay enjoys irony as well."

The laughter died on Rebecca's lips as the blaring base eased into a gentle ballad. She found herself examining her shoes. Justyn wasn't shy at all; he reached out his hand to her.

"Since your date is otherwise engaged, do you suppose I might have the pleasure of this dance?"

At first Rebecca thought she should say no. After all, she had come to the dance with Tom. It seemed inappropriate for her to be dancing with someone else, especially someone who had so obviously set out to be Tom's rival from the start. But before she knew what she was doing, Rebecca found herself accepting the offered hand, albeit somewhat timidly. She almost expected to find his skin as cold as any real vampire's, and was a little surprised when his hand was warm to the touch.

They *glided* onto the dance floor. She ignored Carmen's shocked stare. Other people were watching them as well. Among them was Wendy, who would probably waste no time telling Tom all about Rebecca's disloyalty. It was impossible for people *not* to take notice. Justyn didn't lead her in the modern, traditional slow dance where two people moved around in boring circles. Instead, he lifted her left hand with his right, draped his other arm around her waist, and began to lead her in the steps of a graceful waltz.

He spun her and dipped her, and guided her in movements she didn't know she was capable of with her two left feet. She thought briefly that she should have been embarrassed and self-conscious. She knew that people were openly gawking at them and some were even hiding their snickers behind their hands. But Rebecca didn't care. It somehow felt perfectly natural to be waltzing with Justyn. In fact, she really couldn't imagine him dancing in any other way.

They turned and swirled to the slow love song, but Rebecca didn't even hear the words. In her mind, she heard Mozart and Bach. In her mind's eye, the room filled with teenagers and corny Halloween decorations faded away and were replaced with an elegant ballroom and beautiful people in swishing Victorian gowns and tuxedos with tailcoats. It somehow seemed like more than just a fantasy. It was like a long forgotten memory or a distant dream. Some part of her felt like she and Justyn had waltzed before, in some other time, in some other place. It made her feel almost giddy with excitement and longing.

The music ended much too quickly, and Justyn's hands fell away. Immediately the spell was broken and Rebecca was back in the school cafeteria. A new slow song with a hip-hop beat had begun to play. Rebecca hoped for an encore, but Justyn had already started to walk away.

"Where . . . where are you going?" Boy, did she sound pathetic. Why didn't she just get on her knees and beg him to stay?

Justyn gave her a small half-smile. "I'm afraid I must take my leave."

"Time for you to get back to conjuring spirits?"

"Time for *you* to get back to your date. Thank you for the dance, my lady."

Justyn was lost in the crowd before she even remembered to breathe. But she could still feel his arms around her waist; still smell his woodsy scent against her skin. She was left standing alone in the middle of the dance floor looking for a small glimpse of his shadow. She realized with a little wonder that she was trembling, gaping, swooning all over again. Every time she was around Justyn she turned into a weak-kneed mess. It really *was* getting ridiculous.

"Becca?"

Rebecca jumped at the sound of her name. She turned around and understood why Justyn had left so suddenly. She found a white-faced Tom standing behind her. His black pirate wig and beard had been lost somewhere during the course of the evening, and his blonde hair was a matted mess beneath it. Besides looking pale, he also looked embarrassed. Rebecca wanted to be mad at him for ruining their night together but she didn't have the heart. After all, the dance hadn't been a total loss, at least not for her. Not that she was going to admit that to Tom any time soon.

"Hi, Tom. Are you feeling any better?"

Rebecca actually thought he might cry with relief when she didn't yell at him. "Yeah. A little. Listen, Becca. I . . . I'm really sorry about tonight. I was a total jerk."

"It's okay."

He shook his head. "No, it's not okay. And it wasn't even the real me. I don't usually drink that much. I only did it because I was nervous and I wanted to impress you. I wanted you to like me, and instead I wound up making a total ass out of myself. Now you probably hate me."

He looked so crestfallen that Rebecca wouldn't help but take pity on him. "I already liked you, Tom. You just needed to be yourself."

"Does that mean you'll give me another chance?"

"Sure . . . why not?"

Rebecca was in a generous mood. She reached out to take Tom's hand and lead him onto the dance floor. She was only slightly worried that his stomach might not be able to handle it. But it didn't matter because they never made it that far. A couple of boys came running from the hallway. They were screaming so loudly it was impossible not to hear them, even over the blasting music. One of them screamed over and over again in an eerie monotone, the same desperate exclamation.

"He's dead! He's dead!"

The other one was a little more rational. He found the nearest chaperone, who happened to be standing just a few feet away from Rebecca and Tom. They were able to overhear every terrifying word—words that very nearly made Rebecca's legs give out from under her.

"Come quick! Some man in a cape and a mask just *killed* Mr. Russ!"

Chapter Fourteen

Rebecca came very close to skipping school on Monday morning. She had barely slept the whole weekend, and she hated the thought of dragging herself through an endless routine of boring classes. But after giving it some thought, she decided that facing assignments was better than spending the day alone in an empty house, jumping at every sound.

Every time she closed her eyes, she saw Mr. Russ's face. What little sleep she did manage to get, she spent dreaming of him hanging from the rafters of the stage, with the phantom's voice laughing in the background. Sometimes that phantom sounded like Justyn, but other times she was sure it was Tom. And sometimes it was the nameless, faceless monster that was stalking her waking nightmares. Those nightmares were the predominant thoughts on her mind when she joined her friends at their lunch table on Monday afternoon. Even the fact that Tom chose to sit with them didn't cheer her up. In fact, he and his annoying sidekick, Jay, were only making the day that much worse with their inconsiderate and uncouth topic of conversation.

"I heard he hung himself in the bathroom stall."

Tom made exaggerated gagging noises as he strung his own neck with an invisible noose. The others at the table laughed, but Rebecca grunted in disgust. Not that anyone noticed.

"I heard he was strangled," Carmen added. "They say when they found him, he had huge red hand prints around his neck."

Carmen was quick to chime in whenever anyone was talking about anything dramatic. She couldn't stand being left out, so Rebecca expected no less from her. But she was surprised when even quiet Debbie starting to take part in the morbid talk. It wasn't like her at all.

"The guys who found his body swear they saw a man in a cape and a mask running from the bathroom," Debbie whispered. "They're sure it was the killer."

Jay always wanted the last word. "I heard he drowned in the toilet bowl."

Rebecca had enough. With an outraged huff, she tossed her spoon down onto her lunch tray, so hard that remnants of yogurt shot across the table and splashed Carmen in the face.

"Hey, what's *your* problem?" Carmen wiped yogurt off her nose with the sleeve of her shirt and gave Rebecca a dirty look.

"My *problem* is that someone is dead! A human being is gone forever. It would be nice if *someone* would show a little respect, maybe an *ounce* of compassion, instead of treating his death like one big joke!"

Debbie was quick to agree and looked embarrassed. "You're right, Becca. We shouldn't be making jokes when someone was killed."

"Old Russ bit the big one. He kicked the can," Jay said with a snicker. "He's pushing up daisies. What do you want us to do? Cry like a bunch of babies?"

Rebecca lost what little was left of her composure. She stood from the table and grabbed her lunch tray, prepared to stomp away. Tom grabbed her arm and gently pulled her back into the seat. She didn't have the energy to fight him and she didn't even realize she was crying until he used his napkin to wipe away her tears.

"I had no idea you had such a soft spot for poor old Mr. Russ," Tom said gently. "I'm sorry if we upset you."

"No . . . I'm sorry," Rebecca said through a hiccup. "I had no right to yell at you guys. It's just that I . . . that I feel . . . *responsible* for what happened."

"What?" Carmen exclaimed. "How could *you* possibly be to blame for what happened to that creepy old man?"

"The same way I'm responsible for what happened to Wendy." Rebecca sighed and put her head in her hands. "Someone called me before the dance.

They warned me that if I went with Tom, something horrible would happen. And now Mr. Russ is *dead*. He's dead because of *me*!"

Tom was skeptical. They all were, but he was the only one brave enough to address her when she was apparently having a nervous breakdown. "Becca, I don't doubt that someone is trying to scare you. But don't you think that killing someone would be taking the joke a little too far? Not even that Gothic freak would do something like that."

"*I* don't think it's a joke."

Rebecca crossed her arms and glared at him. Tom's statement had been condescending. It was the remark about Justyn that had annoyed her the most, even though she didn't mention it.

"I actually have to agree with Tom," Debbie said. "Whatever happened to Mr. Russ, it couldn't have anything to do with you, Becca. Of all the people to target, why would anyone choose him? He had nothing to do with you. There's no motive."

"I have no idea why they picked him. But we can't deny that he's dead, that he was *murdered*."

"Dude, Mr. Russ was a schizophrenic nut job," Jay told her. "He probably really *did* drown himself in the toilet. Let it go already."

Rebecca did let it go. At least, she made the conscious effort not to bring it up again for the rest of the lunch period. Her friends were careful not to mention the janitor either. It became obvious by the strained silence and nervous glances that they all wondered if *she* was a schizophrenic nut job as well. And maybe she was. Maybe she *was* crazy, plain and simple. The notes and phone calls could be irrational delusions. Maybe she was trying so hard to play the part of Christine that she was tricking herself into believing she had become her on a deeper level. That would certainly explain her strange fascination with the mysterious Lord Justyn.

Even as she thought about Justyn, she reached into her handbag and stroked the crystal geode he had given her. She had tossed it into her bag as an afterthought that morning when she left for school. It did somehow comfort her when she felt its smooth surface between her fingers. It was ironic; the person who had given it to her should have been her number one suspect. Not even the magic of the geode could keep her thoughts from straying back to poor Mr. Russ and his unfortunate end. She kept seeing his accusing face all throughout her afternoon classes. She almost expected to see him glaring at her every time she turned a corner.

Once she arrived at rehearsal, her irrational worries continued to plague her and hindered her performance. More than once, she hit a sour note, and every time she did she was painfully aware of Wendy's laughter on the side of the stage. Her thoughts kept her from noticing the tension growing around her between Tom and Justyn—tensions that finally came to a head during the sword-fighting scene.

The fighting scene was one of only a few that Justyn and Tom shared. It was also the first time they had seen each other since the disastrous Halloween dance. Tom had apparently heard rumors of her waltz with Justyn because it was plainly obvious that he was unhappy. It was obvious to everyone but Rebecca, who was in her own unpleasant little world. She watched the fight scene unwind with glazed eyes. Her character was supposed to be watching in horror. Instead, Rebecca was staring off into space with her arms crossed while the two boys exchanged blows with their plastic swords in her name. It wasn't until Tom had Justyn pinned to the ground in feigned defeat that Rebecca realized it wasn't just pretending anymore.

"Do you think you're going to move in on my girlfriend?" Tom poked Justyn in the ribs with the plastic sword just a little harder than was necessary. "Stay away from Becca!"

Rebecca saw Justyn's eyes flash dangerously. Even though his voice was calm, there was clearly a threat in his words. "What if Becca doesn't *want* me to stay away from her?"

Rebecca immediately came to her senses and ran over to break up the duel. Other people were watching too, with more attention than usual. It was obvious that the scene had strayed from the normal act. As she moved closer, and Justyn rose to his feet, phony sword forgotten, she had to wonder if she was going to be able to stop the inevitable.

"Cease this folly!
End this mad game!
No more violence.
In the angel's name!"

Rebecca desperately wrung her hands. Both Justyn and Tom were as oblivious to her as she had been to them just a moment earlier. They didn't hear her melodic pleas for restraint, and they both seemed to forget their own lines as they continued to glare at one another. Rebecca scanned the crowd for Miss King, but the useless moderator was too busy flirting with the orchestra's bandmaster to pay any attention to what was happening between the actors on the stage.

"I'm sick and tired of you always getting in my way, vampire!"

"And I'm tired of your juvenile comments. Is talking the only thing you can do?"

That was the challenge Tom needed. He threw his sword to the ground and moved in closer. "Why don't I show you what I *can* do?"

Rebecca saw Tom's arm preparing to swing, and she knew she had to intercede. She couldn't let anyone else get hurt because her. Even as she jumped between the boys, she knew it was more than just the fight that was going to come to an end. She'd had it with everything. It wasn't worth the fear, the threats, or the fighting. As much as she had once loved the story of the phantom, at that moment she hated it to the very core of her being.

"Stop it! Just *stop* it! Both of you!"

Tom's arm immediately fell to his side when Rebecca blocked his target, but his fists were still balled in frustration. Each word was enunciated through his clenched teeth. "Move out of the way, Becca."

"Yes, Becca, go ahead. Move out of his way." Justyn agreed. His musical voice was still irritatingly calm.

"No, I won't get out of the way unless the two of you promise to stop acting like Neanderthals!"

Justyn huffed. "There's only one Neanderthal here."

Rebecca was getting more and more aggravated. Her anger didn't seem to faze Tom or Justyn. Luckily, Miss King had finally noticed what was happening and came over to break things up. It was a good thing too, because Rebecca was done trying to keep the peace. She was done acting the part of the damsel. She had made a decision. To the horror of Miss King and the rest of the cast, Rebecca threw up her arms in defeat and stomped off the stage.

"That's it!" she declared. "I'm done. I'm quitting the play!"

Chapter Fifteen

"Becca, wait!"

Rebecca ignored Justyn even though she was completely aware that he was following her. She had no intention of stopping or turning around. She fought the childish urge to burst into tears as she ran down the deserted hallway towards her locker. The last thing she wanted was for him to see her acting like a blubbering weakling. For some reason, that would be just too awful to bear.

"Becca, come on!"

This time it was Tom's voice, almost echoing Justyn's, and making the whole situation ten times worse. The fact that the two of them were apparently coming up behind her at the same time was enough to finally make her give in and turn around to face them, if only to make sure they weren't going to kill each other. She already had Mr. Russ's death on her conscience. She couldn't handle the possibility of adding another body to the head count. But she was still furious with them both, and she knew her flashing brown eyes revealed it.

"What do you want?" Rebecca demanded.

Her voice was so sharp that they both turned to look at each other and exchanged nervous glances.

"Becca, you can't quit the play!" Tom said bravely. "We need you!"

Justyn nodded his head in agreement. "Tom's right."

Justyn was agreeing with Tom? That was something that Rebecca *never* thought she would hear. What made the situation even more bizarre was that Tom and Justyn were presenting a united front. It really wasn't fair. They were double teaming her. How was she supposed to hold her ground?

"It isn't fair to everyone else in the cast who's worked so hard" Justyn continued. "We need you, Becca."

On some level, she knew they were right. The whole production would fall apart if she quit now. Weeks of memorizing lines and long rehearsals would have been for nothing. The price of the tickets that had already been sold would have to be refunded. But Rebecca wasn't ready to back down. It would serve them right if she really did quit.

"Let Wendy take the role." She huffed. "That will solve all my problems at once. It'll get Wendy off my back, and I won't have to deal with you two fighting over me like a . . . like a piece of meat."

"Becca, I never meant to make you feel . . . ."

"No, wait." Justyn interrupted Tom, which resulted in a glare and a barely contained string of curses. He apparently realized that fighting wasn't going to solve anything, so he bit his tongue and didn't say more. "Becca's right." Justyn continued. "Instead of acting like testosterone driven animals, why don't we act like gentlemen? Let Becca make the choice between us."

That was almost too much for Tom to take. "What makes you think she *needs* to make a choice?" he asked through gritted teeth.

Rebecca sighed in resignation and took her accustomed spot in between them. "I *have* made a choice. I don't want anything to do with *either* of you. I'm not going to be the reason that you rip each other's heads off. So, I'm done with both of you, and with the play."

When she was reasonably sure that they weren't going to start swinging, she moved to her locker and turned the combination.

"You can't mean that!"

Tom's voice sounded almost pathetically desperate, though whether it was over the play or their relationship, she had no way to tell. Justyn, on the other hand, was annoyingly confident when he spoke.

"She *doesn't* mean it. Becca can't walk away from the phantom, any more than Christine could."

She wasn't about to admit he was right. Even after all the accidents, the threats, the fighting, she was still drawn to the beauty of the music. Just as she was still drawn to him, despite the fact that she sometimes wondered if he was the one behind all the dangerous games. She was so frustrated with her own self-betrayal that she refused to look at them. She yanked open her locker violently and shoved her books into her bag. When he realized she had no intention of responding, Justyn turned to Tom, and actually stuck out his hand.

"I propose a truce."

Tom scowled at the offered hand like it was a giant insect. "*I* propose you go back to whatever circus freak show you came from."

Justyn didn't lose his composure for a second. "If you really care about Becca, you'll give her the chance to choose between us civilly. She's obviously drawn to us both."

Tom snorted. "You're living in a dream world."

"Am I?" Justyn raised an eyebrow and turned to Rebecca. "Becca, am I living in a dream world? If you tell me honestly that you aren't interested, I'll walk away and never look back."

The thought of Justyn walking out of her life forever was enough to make her choke back a gasp of horror. That was the last thing she wanted. But of course she wasn't going to admit that. She was too annoyed at his audacity to be overly civil, so she snorted and glared at him instead.

"Oh, do *I* actually get to take part in this conversation about what *I* want? I thought the two of you would just decide for me."

Her sarcasm was completely lost on Tom. "You don't actually *like* this guy, do you Becca?"

"I don't know. I mean . . . ." Rebecca let out a cry of frustration and actually banged her head against her locker. She decided that it wasn't worth trying to deny it anymore. Not to Tom. Not to Justyn. And especially not to herself. "Yes. I can't explain it . . . but I am drawn to him."

Justyn didn't say anything, but his expression was undeniably smug. Tom, on the other hand, looked so crestfallen that she wished she could take it back as soon as she had said it.

"What about *me?*"

"I like you, too, Tom. I like you *both*." Rebecca sighed. "Which is why I need to just walk away. I don't want to hurt anyone. And I don't want you two to hurt each other because of *me*. It's the best thing for everyone involved if I just quit the play and go back to being invisible."

"I don't think it's necessary for you to quit the play, Becca. Tom, don't you think that we can control ourselves long enough for Becca to make up her mind?" When Tom nodded grudgingly, Justyn turned back to Rebecca. "One date with each of us. Then you have to make your decision, once and for all. The loser bows out gracefully. No fighting. Tom, are you game?"

Tom was frowning, but he still agreed. "If that's what Becca wants, I guess I'll have to go along with it. But *I* get to go first."

Justyn gave him a cocky smirk. "Technically, you've already had one date with her."

"That doesn't count. I was sick!"

"You mean you were *drunk*."

"*Aghhh!*" Rebecca shrieked and slammed her locker door shut. The boys had taken one step closer to each other, their fists balled. "Obviously, this isn't going to work. You can't even make the agreement to stop fighting *without* fighting!"

"No, this will work. I secede," Justyn told Tom. Rebecca was fairly certain he had no idea what 'secede' meant, judging by the dumbfounded look on his face. "I mean . . . you can go first. I've waited this long. What are a few more days?"

"You might wind up waiting forever." Tom promised. "After I take Becca out, she won't even remember your name."

Justyn was unfazed. "That's a chance I'm willing to take. So, how about it, Becca? Are you coming back in to rehearsal?"

Rebecca shook her head. She was far from convinced that an open competition was a good idea; she didn't like the idea of being the trophy in that competition, either. Nevertheless, they were both behaving themselves, and looking at her so imploringly that it was hard to stay angry with them.

"Diva, we need you!" Justyn exclaimed.

Once again he was spouting lines from the play. He cleared his throat; waiting for Tom to pick up his cue, but he was oblivious until Justyn elbowed him in the ribs. Tom looked annoyed until his face lit up with understanding and he realized what Justyn was trying to do.

"Oh, umm." Tom stuttered for a minute, trying to remember a line that wasn't his own. "Your audience awaits!"

Before Rebecca could decide whether to walk away or start laughing, the mismatched pair broke into an unseemly duet.

> "Beautiful diva step into the light.
> The opera house awaits your appearance tonight.
> Wave to the crowd; break their hearts with your song.
> Sing for us diva, sing loud and sing strong."

In the play, the managers sang the song to Carlotta to try to coerce her into performing after she had been upstaged. But they had all been through the scenes enough that they had the whole play memorized. The two of them, the black-haired Goth and the blue-eyed surfer, were polar opposites of one another, yet they managed to sing in perfect harmony. For the first time, and most likely the last time, they were fighting for a common goal—to get her to return to the play. Rebecca couldn't help but smile at their performance. They noticed the change in her demeanor right away, and she could tell by both sets of gloating eyes that they knew they were winning; she was about to give in.

"What are you guys doing out here?" Carmen demanded from the auditorium doors. "Miss King is just about ready to have a heart attack. Becca, you aren't really going to quit, are you?"

Rebecca was quiet for a minute. Justyn and Tom were both waiting, looking at her pathetically. Justyn looked a little more confident about what her answer was going to be, even before she knew for sure herself.

"No, I'm not quitting," Rebecca told Carmen. "Come on. Let's get back to practice."

Chapter Sixteen

"I can't believe you're letting them fight over you like this." Carmen made a face as she picked through Rebecca's minimal nail polish selection. She finally settled on a dark shade of maroon. "It's completely degrading. Not just to you, but to the entire female gender as a whole."

Rebecca rolled her eyes. "I think you're exaggerating a little."

"*I* think its romantic, watching them vie for your affection," Debbie added in her defense. "They must both *really* like you."

"Everyone *loves* Becca," Carmen said, not without some bitterness. "And she won't let us forget it."

Rebecca stopped painting her nails long enough to look up at Carmen in surprise. She was a little peeved by her attitude, but she couldn't think of a quick enough comeback. She let the comment pass altogether. Besides, the last thing she wanted was to fight with her friends. She didn't really understand what Carmen was so upset about. They were supposed to be having a relaxing Friday night, free from the drama of her feuding co-stars.

Carmen had come by after school, and Debbie had shown up not long afterwards for a girl's night out. After a small amount of deliberation, they decided to catch a movie. They had a few hours before the film was going to start, so they broke out the beauty supplies and started on one of their favorite pastimes—makeovers. Once they had played around with their makeup, they moved on to manicures. It was peaceful and calming. Rebecca was hoping that the night would pass without any male influences, but Carmen and Debbie couldn't talk about anything else.

"So Becca, do you seriously like Justyn?" Debbie asked. "Or are you just curious about what's underneath the black makeup?"

Rebecca felt herself blush. "I think Justyn is . . . interesting. He's artistic. Dramatic. You know, he's not like other guys."

"He's not like other *human beings*." Carmen crinkled her nose in distaste. "I can't believe you would even consider dating him when you have a hottie like Tom interested in you. I mean *really*, you've been fawning over Tom for years, and now that you have him . . . what? It's not a big enough challenge anymore?"

"It's not like that." Rebecca insisted. "I never meant for things to happen this way. Believe me, the last thing I ever wanted was to be attracted to Justyn, especially since he scares me a little sometimes. But I can't help the way I feel."

"No one can choose who they love." Debbie mused with faraway look in her eyes. "If we could, no one would ever have to get hurt."

The statement was true enough to make them drift into a few moments of thoughtful silence as they waited for their nails to dry. Rebecca leaned back into the pillows of her twin bed and closed her eyes. Instantly, an image of Justyn popped unbidden into her mind. He was dark and mysterious. But did she like *him* as a person, or the rebelliousness that he represented? Was she tired of always being stereotyped as the good girl, always playing it safe? Maybe for once she wanted to see what it was like to walk on the edge of the precipice. Or at the very least, peek over it.

"Aren't you a little worried that Justyn might not be safe?" Carmen asked. "I would think a scaredy cat like you would want to keep your distance from someone like him."

Rebecca felt a little indignant, and her annoyance was obvious in the angry tone of her voice. "What do you mean by 'someone like him'? You know, you shouldn't judge a book by its cover."

Carmen shrugged, and suddenly became uninterested. "You're the one who was worried that someone was stalking you. And if you're going to eliminate Wendy because of her *accident*—" She made quotation marks with her fingertips. "Then Justyn would be the only logical suspect."

"Not really," Debbie said. "Tom's motive is just as strong as Justyn's."

"We've known Tom since junior high. Do you really think he'd be capable of killing Mr. Russ?" Carmen asked. "Assuming that Mr. Russ *was* murdered."

Rebecca shuddered. She had managed to forget about the janitor in the last few ordinary days. True to their words, Justyn and Tom were on their best behavior, both making a valiant effort to avoid each other. And even Wendy had stayed quiet and caused no trouble. Nothing out of the ordinary had happened since the Halloween dance. Still, there were occasional reminders, such as the new janitor she had seen whistling happily in the hallway after school.

No one had officially said that Mr. Russ's death was anything but an accident. Rebecca had noticed a few men around the school, talking to teachers and students, who could have easily passed for plain-clothes policemen. She had to wonder how much, if anything, they knew about what had happened to Mr. Russ. She almost expected one of them to show up at her locker with a string of questions. But so far, no one had involved her. It made her feel a little better. If she were somehow connected to his death, surely the police would have figured it out by now.

"I don't believe that either one of them killed Mr. Russ," Rebecca said with more confidence than she felt. "And I have no intention of living my life in a bubble because of a few random notes and phone calls. Like you guys said before, it's probably just one big coincidence."

Debbie cheered her on. "That a girl, Becca! Don't let this nut job scare you away from what you want. Love is worth fighting for. There's nothing else in the world that matters more than love."

Carmen rolled her eyes. "Whatever. You're being yanked around like a rope in a tug of war between two barbarians. If you call that love, then go for it. As for me, I'd rather stay single."

When she put in that way, Rebecca wondered if she would be better off single, too. But she figured she had to at least fulfill her end of the bargain and give both guys a chance. Maybe when it was over, she would decide she didn't want either one of them. And that would be okay. In fact, it would make everything much easier. The trouble was that she was afraid she might still find herself drawn to both of them. If that happened, she wasn't sure how she was going to make a decision without hurting them—or herself. But she would cross that bridge when she came to it. Right now, she was more concerned with heading to the chick flick they were planning to watch.

"Come on," Rebecca told her friends. "Let's get out of here. I don't know about you two, but I'm sick of talking about my love life. Let's go wrap ourselves up in someone else's love story for a few hours."

"Sounds good to me," Debbie said as she slipped into her shoes.

The three girls jogged down the steps, making as much noise as a herd of elephants. They grabbed their lightweight jackets as they came closer to the door. They were all giggling as Carmen told them about Jay's most recent escapade. He had released a dozen mice during gym class, sending their female teacher into near hysterics. Rebecca was so busy laughing that she didn't even notice the box on the steps when she went to open the door until she practically tripped over it.

"The queen of klutzes strikes again!" Carmen teased.

Rebecca was a good sport and laughed at herself as she bent down to pick up the culprit. It was a long white box, wrapped with an elaborate black velvet bow. A little note in a small square envelope had her name emblazoned across it in beautiful, calligraphy-style handwriting.

"Ohhh." Debbie gushed. "It looks like one of the guys is trying to score a few extra points."

"Do you think so?" Rebecca smiled, secretly pleased at the prospect.

"Duh, it's a flower box," Carmen said. "Of course it's from one of the guys. Well, come on. Read the card already. Don't leave us in suspense."

Rebecca felt her heart flutter in anticipation as she slipped the small note from the envelope. The same fancy handwriting greeted her, with a few poetic lines that she read aloud for the girls. It was a quote from one of her favorite and most exciting parts of the play. The phantom brings Christine down to his lair the second time, and gives her the choice of loving him, or having the entire opera house blown to pieces by the trap he's set. As twisted as it was, it was strangely appealing to think of someone loving anyone so much.

> *"The beauty of your soul is matched by your voice*
> *I am your master, but to love me is your choice.*
> *Sing with me angel. Join me this night.*
> *And never again look upon my face with fright."*

Rebecca read the words a few times, and she wasn't sure whether to swoon or panic. Justyn always had a way of making the lines from the play seem personal—so did whoever was trying to scare her. She didn't know who had left the package on her doorstep. Maybe the two were one and the same. Either way, she wasn't sure that she wanted to open the box.

Carmen had no such qualms, and was already pulling off the fancy black bow. She ripped the top off the box with equal enthusiasm, but the glimmer of amusement and humor in her eyes quickly faded as the lid slipped from her trembling fingers and fell forgotten onto the floor. The smile died on her lips, her face turned white, and she put a hand over her mouth to stifle a gag.

"Oh . . . gross . . . ."

"That's disgusting," Debbie echoed.

Rebecca didn't say anything at all. Her churning stomach had a lot more to do with fear than with the awful smell or the sight that greeted her from the depths of the flower box.

They were roses, or at least they had been at one time. Now they were slimy and rotten, and only barely resembled the thing of beauty they had once been. Squirming white maggots wrapped themselves around the decaying stems. As Rebecca struggled to keep down the greasy pizza she'd eaten for dinner, she began to realize that the phantom's ways had a lot more to do with obsession than they did with love. The verse, which she read one last time, lost all their appeal.

Chapter Seventeen

When Saturday night finally arrived, Rebecca refused to let the awful gift—which she had tossed into the nearest dumpster—ruin her evening. She was turning over a new leaf. No longer would she play the role of the helpless victim. No longer was she going be a twenty-first century Christine, falling to pieces at the first sign of trouble. She was a modern, independent woman. She was going to proceed with confidence, with her head held high. She wasn't going to spend a single minute worrying about the maggoty flowers or whoever was twisted enough to leave them on her doorstep. If the stalker had meant to scare her enough to ruin her evening with Tom, they had not succeeded. There was only one person who might ruin the night, and that was Tom himself. Rebecca was a little worried that their second date might not go any smoother than their first.

She dressed with extra care even though Tom told her he was going to keep their evening casual. She didn't mind. She was never one for excess, and anything other than casual would have been unlike him. After all, he was an all-American, blue jean sporting kind of guy. So Rebecca wore her jeans as well, along with a lightweight sweater. They were having an Indian summer in South Jersey; even though it was the beginning of November, it was still warm enough to go outside without a jacket in the early evening. She applied her makeup and brushed her hair. When she checked her reflection in the mirror, she was pleased with the results.

Once she was dressed, there was nothing left to do but wait. It was nearly six and Tom would be arriving at any moment. She kept expecting the nervous jitters to begin. It was strange. She should have been a complete wreck. A month ago she would have been hyperventilating. Now, she was surprisingly calm, hardly even excited at all. Yet, when she thought ahead to the next weekend with Justyn, she felt her heart begin to flutter.

Rebecca wandered over to her nightstand and picked up the book Justyn had given her. She had forgotten about it after the excitement of the Halloween dance, but that afternoon, she had read more than half of the paperback. She was surprised by how interesting it was. The more she read about the pagan deities, the guardian elements, and all the amazing magical practices that Justyn believed in, the more familiar it seemed to her. It was like she was reading a book that she had already read years before and it was all coming back to her as she flipped through the pages. Yet, she knew for a fact that she had never read anything about Wicca before. So why did the strange feeling of familiarity persist?

Rebecca dropped the book onto the table when she heard the doorbell ring. She finally started to get the nervous jitters, but it was more because she was worried that her father would make it to the door before she did and begin the type of interrogation usually reserved for hardened criminals. Luckily, Rebecca moved a lot faster than her middle-aged father. She yelled out her goodbyes before her parents could even stick their heads out of the kitchen, and slipped out of the door before they had a chance to open their mouths. She found Tom waiting on the porch steps looking twice as nervous as she felt. A month ago, she would never have believed his demeanor possible.

"Hey," he said.

"Hey."

There was a moment of awkward silence, and he scratched his head. "So, are you ready?"

She smiled. "Ready as I'll ever be."

"Cool, then I guess we should get going."

"Sounds like a plan."

Rebecca followed him to his truck. She was incredibly relieved to see that Jay wasn't waiting inside. Tom was much more gentlemanly than he had been on their first disaster of a date. Of course, he was sober this time. He opened the passenger side door, and even took her hand as she stepped up into the seat—probably a good idea considering her reputation for tripping and/or falling. It was a sweet gesture, and Rebecca felt her heart warm up just a little.

"So," Tom said once they had pulled out of the driveway. "I thought we'd grab something to eat and maybe catch a movie or something."

"Sounds good to me."

It also sounded ordinary. It was the all-American date with the all-American boy. Why did that suddenly seem so boring? All her life she had settled for the simplest, the easiest, and the most normal course of action. When did that change? When did she start longing for something more, something different, something more exciting? In the back of her mind, she pondered that Justyn Patko would have thought of something much more interesting than your basic dinner and a movie.

When they arrived at the restaurant, Rebecca was hardly surprised to find it was the typical Italian chain complete with the never-ending pasta bowl, and their famous salad and bread sticks combo. The walls were covered with paintings of Venice, the counters were lined with wine bottles, and every waiter and waitress recited the same greeting as they walked up to their tables.

It was a nice place with a decent menu, but Rebecca was watching her waistline, so she stuck with just a salad. She needed to be sure she would be able to get into her costume, which the cast of the play had already been fitted for. Tom wasn't worried about his weight. He ate so much lasagna, meatballs, sausage, bread sticks, and even dessert, that she was a little concerned they might have a repeat of the Halloween dance, with him spending half the night with his head in the toilet bowl. But he did manage to keep the conversation pleasant and flowing, asking her just as many questions about the things that she enjoyed as he spent talking about his love of surfing and basketball. It all seemed to be going well, and Rebecca was pretty much over her pessimistic thoughts. She was even starting to remember why she had liked him for so long. That is, until they got to the movie theater. Then she was reminded that Tom worried too much about what everyone else thought about him.

They pulled up to the little theater about twenty minutes before the movie was supposed to start. Tom bought tickets for some thriller flick without even asking Rebecca whether she wanted to see it. But that wasn't the worst of it. As they were standing in line to get popcorn and sodas, Jay and several other members of his posse came up behind them, slapping Tom on the shoulder.

"Dude!" Jay shouted. "You didn't tell me you were going to be here tonight."

"There's a reason for that, Jay. I'm on a *date*."

"I can see that. Hey, Becca. Mind if we join you?"

Tom was annoyed. "Of *course* we mind. Like I said, this is a *date*. We're supposed to be *alone*."

"Aw, come on. I don't mind a little PDA, you know, public displays of affection. You can make out all you want. Just expect me and the guys to be watching every second of it."

Now Rebecca was annoyed. The last thing she wanted was to spend the rest of her evening with Jay spying on their every move. "Tom," she whispered. "I would really like it if we had some time alone."

Jay heard her and he crinkled his nose in distaste. "Dude, are you gonna let some chick tell you how to spend your Saturday night?"

Tom looked torn for a minute. Then he made the choice that any self-respecting guy in the popular crowd would make. "Oh, come on Bec, it won't be so bad to sit with the guys. The more the merrier, right?"

There was absolutely nothing merry about the situation at all, but Rebecca knew it wasn't worth fighting about. There was no escaping Tom's faithful sidekick and his string of minions. But she wasn't happy about it, and she came very close to pulling away from him when Tom took her hand to lead her into the movie theater with Jay and the others in tow. It wasn't in her nature to be argumentative, so she let him have his way.

She spent the next ninety minutes being hit in the head with popcorn kernels and listening to a wide array of strange and almost musical bodily functions. Even when Tom tried to slip his arm around her, Jay had to make his presence known by moving to the other side and laying his head on her shoulder, *oohing* and *awwing* like the juvenile moron that he was, and in general making a complete nuisance of himself. The crowd was so rowdy that Rebecca could barely follow the storyline of the movie. She was surprised that they made it through the whole picture without getting kicked out. Strangers shot them icy stares and there was more than one loud "*shhh*". When the credits finally started to roll, Rebecca heaved a sigh of relief. It couldn't have come soon enough.

Tom was quiet and obviously embarrassed on the ride home. Rebecca felt a little sorry for him. He had planned a nice normal evening. It wasn't his fault that Jay had shown up uninvited and ruined things. She understood why he had given in to their demands. Adolescent male teasing could be a brutal force to reckon with. And she really did have a nice time with him at dinner. All in all, the evening hadn't been a total loss.

Tom pulled into the driveway and shifted his truck into neutral, still looking grim. "I guess there's not much hope that there's going be a third date, huh?"

When he turned those sad blue eyes on her, any lingering sense of annoyance melted completely away. "I wouldn't jump to conclusions just yet."

He smiled a huge bright smile and was visibly relieved. "I'm sorry about Jay. He's . . . you know . . . he's Jay."

She did know. There were few non-vulgar words that could be used to describe Jay Kopp. "It's okay. I won't hold you accountable for his actions." She would have thought it impossible, but Tom's smile widened. "Good. Because I'd hate to think I'd blown it with you, Becca. I . . . I really like you. You're smart and pretty . . . and not like the other girls. You know, you're special."

Rebecca blushed. "I . . . I like you too, Tom."

If he wanted to ask if she liked him more than Justyn, he restrained himself. And she was glad. She wasn't ready to answer that question just yet.

"I'm glad to hear that."

He leaned over the armrest and pressed his lips against hers. The kiss wasn't at all rough this time, and she found herself returning it with much more willingness than she had on Halloween. It was a nice kiss, and she waited for the warm fluttery feeling in her chest to finally come back. She waited for that sudden burst of inspiration where she would realize that he was the one. But as sweet as the kiss was, there were no fireworks. No breathlessness. No yearning for something more. Maybe she had just read too many romance novels. Or maybe Tom wasn't the one that she really wanted to be kissing.

Chapter Eighteen

"Hi, Becca!"

Justyn buzzed past her on his black bike, which was a perfect match to his black silver-chained pants and metal-tipped boots. He came to a screeching halt just a few feet away from her with a huge smile on his face. She didn't think twice before jogging to catch up with him. She couldn't deny that she was happy to see him. And she was even happier when the two of them walked side by side to the bike rack, where he locked his bike up securely.

"So, will I be riding on your handle bars on Saturday night?"

Justyn smirked. "Don't worry. I have a car. I just prefer to be out in the fresh air whenever possible."

It *was* a beautiful day. Groups of students were loitering in the walkways, putting off the inevitable for as long as possible. It was a shame that it was a Monday and they were going to be stuck inside all day. It was warm and mild, without a cloud in the sky.

The sky? That reminded Rebecca of something interesting she had read that weekend. She pulled Justyn's book out of her backpack, and handed him the small paperback.

"I finished reading your book," she told him.

He raised a pierced eyebrow. "And?"

"Skyclad, huh?"

"Ritual nudity is completely optional."

Now it was Rebecca's turn to raise *her* eyebrow. "And do *you* opt for it?"

He shrugged. "I guess you'll have to tag along to one of our get-togethers and find out for yourself."

"Is that what we'll be doing this weekend? Dancing naked in the woods with a bunch of witches?"

"Maybe . . . I guess you'll have to wait and see."

Justyn wasn't about to give up any information. Rebecca had a feeling that trying to get him to change his mind would have been a pointless endeavor. If he had his mind set on keeping their date a surprise, nothing could drag the secret from him. But it was certainly going to make the next five days go unbelievably slow for Rebecca while she waited in suspense.

As they walked toward the school entrance, Justyn explained some of the symbolism in Wicca. Rebecca asked one question after another, hungry for as much information as possible. The more she heard about Wicca, the more fascinating she found the religion. Before she knew it, Justyn was planning a whole reading list for her, which she found herself more than willing to accept.

Justyn held the door open as they slipped into the hallway. She noticed a few kids were pointing and snickering in her direction as they moved towards her locker. She assumed it was because of Justyn and his fashion sense. He still had a strange effect on most of their classmates. But he didn't seem to be bothered by people staring at him, so Rebecca didn't see any reason to let it bother her either.

Their lockers were in different directions, and Rebecca was just about to say goodbye to him when Carmen and Debbie swooped down on her like a pair of whirling dervishes. They each grabbed one arm in an almost eerie synchronization, and started pulling her down the hall toward the girls' bathroom before she knew what was happening. She didn't even have time to look back over her shoulder to see if Justyn was surprised by her sudden and unintended departure.

"What's going on?" Rebecca demanded. "I know you guys aren't crazy about the idea of me and Justyn, but don't you think this is a little extreme? What's next, a chastity belt?"

"Shhh." Carmen hissed. "This has nothing to do with your freaky Gothic boy toy."

She locked the bathroom doors even as Debbie was checking under the stalls to make sure they were alone. Rebecca was getting nervous. She had never seen her friends act so strangely. It seemed like hours passed before they were sure the bathroom was secure and even then they stood there in silence, surrounded by the smell of bathroom disinfectant. She waited for her friends to explain themselves, but they just stared at each other stupidly, each one waiting—no *hoping*, that the other would begin.

"Is someone going to tell me why I've been abducted?"

Debbie was twitching nervously as she ran her hands through her short hair. "We wanted to get to you before you saw it."

"Saw *what?*" Apparently they needed some prompting.

Carmen shook her head. "Girl, you don't even want to know. You should just go down to the nurse's office right now and beg to be sent home for the day."

"What are you *talking* about?"

Debbie took a folded newspaper out of her backpack, and handed it to Rebecca, which only added to her confusion. She shook her head in exasperation as she flipped it over to the front page. She stared down at the familiar face on the cover, and it all started to fall into place. The pointing and the laughter when she had come in the door had nothing to do with Justyn. They were laughing at *her* because she had made front-page news.

It was only the school newspaper. A thin, four page printout that was handed out every Monday morning by the mousy little editor-in-chief. Normally, the articles were the typical boring stories that were found in high school papers across the country. Like which sports team was heading to the championships or who was most likely to be elected class president. Never before had anything so blatantly scandalous been splashed across the front page. Rebecca had to wonder how it had made it past the teacher who was the newspaper's moderator.

"Phantom Star Rebecca Hope Named Number One Suspect in Russ Murder"

That one line was horrible enough. But the humiliation didn't end with the headline. It only got worse as she skimmed through the whole article. A little further down, right under an old yearbook photo of Mr. Russ, a disgusting question was raised in large bold print.

"Russ & Hope—were they involved in a secret love affair?"

The very thought made Rebecca a little sick to her stomach. Mr. Russ had been old enough to be her grandfather. He had been dirty, and about as unattractive as humanely possible. She wanted to die from the shame of the whole thing. As soon as she thought that, she felt guilty, because poor Mr. Russ *was* dead, and possibly murdered. Even pity for the old janitor couldn't overshadow the complete *humiliation* of having such horrible lies printed about her for the entire school to see. It didn't even matter than everyone knew it wasn't true. This was high school. They were going to use this against her anyway. Who could have printed it? Who hated her this much?

"Becca, are you all right?" Debbie asked.

She and Carmen were both standing at a careful distance in case she decided to start throwing things. They were right to be cautious. Rebecca was furious—angrier than she had ever been before. Angrier than she knew she was capable of. She crumpled the newspaper into a ball, and with a cry of outraged fury, she sent it hurtling across the linoleum.

"*Who* did this?" she demanded. "*Who?*"

She didn't wait for them to answer. She already knew who was responsible. There was only one person nasty and vindictive enough to pull off this kind of stunt. There was only one person in the whole school who hated Rebecca enough to try to tarnish her reputation this way. And she was going to find that person and straighten her out once and for all.

Rebecca unlocked the bathroom door and burst into the crowded hallway without waiting to see if Carmen and Debbie would follow her. Anyone who dared to look at her and giggle was immediately silenced by her smoldering glare. Most of them probably started to wonder if she really *was* capable of murder. At that moment, she was starting to wonder herself, because only one fantasy kept playing through her head. That fantasy involved wrapping her hands around Wendy Wright's neck and squeezing it until she turned blue. When she spotted her at her locker, laughing with her friends as she held up the offensive newspaper, that fantasy very nearly became a reality.

Wendy saw her coming, and the hearty laughter settled into a pleased smirk. Rebecca had always thought she was pretty, but her personality was really bringing out her ugly side, and it had nothing to do with the fading cuts on her face. Rebecca felt the last of her self-control slipping away.

"How *could* you do this to me?" She grabbed the newspaper from Wendy's hands and tossed it haphazardly to the ground.

"Do what, Becca? I don't know what you're talking about."

The feigned wide-eyed innocence was ten times worse than the open sarcasm. It pushed Rebecca right over the edge. She took both Wendy and herself completely by surprise when she shoved the blonde against her locker with all her strength. Nevertheless, Wendy knew how to play a better game, and she was a good actress. The innocent look quickly changed to startled fear, and the people around them probably thought Rebecca was as crazy as Wendy tried to make her out to be in her article.

"Becca, please don't hurt me!"

Wendy put her arms up to make it look like she was defending herself. Rebecca noticed a few teachers peeking out their doors to see what was happening, and she let her arms fall down to her side, defeated. There wasn't anything she could do about the newspaper article. There wasn't anything she could do about Wendy in general. She had won this round. Wendy knew it, and she smiled.

"I warned you," Wendy whispered, just loud enough for Rebecca to hear her. "I told you I'd get you back for the mirror."

Rebecca started to shake her head, when she had a sudden realization. Denials hadn't worked. Peace talks hadn't worked. Maybe the only type of conversation that *would* work with Wendy was threats. Maybe that was the only language that she understood. Maybe Rebecca needed to jump on board and threaten her right back.

"You better be careful, Wendy," Rebecca told her. "The next time someone throws you into a mirror, maybe you won't survive."

Chapter Nineteen

"Watch out! There's the psycho killer!"

A group of underclassman snickered as they passed by Rebecca and her friends. Rebecca felt her face turn crimson for what must have been the millionth time that week. She had to wonder when the childishness was going to end—if it was *ever* going to end. Maybe she would just spend the rest of her senior year in exile.

"Wendy is the only psycho in this school," Carmen called out loudly from their corner of the stage. Her voice carried pretty far, and a few people turned to stare at her, including Wendy. The look she gave them was anything but friendly. Wendy had the masses on her side, as the popular crowd always did.

"Really, Becca, you shouldn't let her bother you anymore," Debbie told her. "Everyone will have forgotten about this stupid joke by the end of the weekend. They'll have moved on to another victim."

Rebecca would have loved to believe that. But five days had passed and it hadn't been enough to make anyone forget about the newspaper article yet. In fact, the rumors had gotten even more twisted as they were passed from one gossipy teenager to the next. The last she had heard, she was having Mr. Russ's love child. The stigma didn't end with her. Carmen and Debbie had become outcasts by association. Rebecca never appreciated them more than she did that week. They stood by her through every taunt and sneer, and had truly proven themselves loyal friends. It only gave Rebecca one more thing to feel guilty about. She sat down on the edge of the stage and put her head in her hands.

"I'm so sorry that you guys got dragged into this mess."

Carmen shrugged. "What are friends for?"

"After all, we're *The Three Musketeers*, right?"

"That is *sooo* corny, Deb," Carmen complained with a roll of her brown eyes.

Practice was about to begin and they all moved to their allotted spots, promising to get together when they were done. The rehearsal proceeded without any problems. Rebecca noticed, not for the first time, that Tom seemed to be avoiding her. He called her every night, but in school he was always conveniently unavailable during the times when they would normally run into each other. Justyn, on the other hand, seemed to be lurking around every corner, and took her new leper status as further proof that they were destined to be together. He never came right out and said that he found the whole thing amusing. He didn't have to. She could sense that he enjoyed the fact that Tom, and every other available male, was staying away from her. This left the door wide open for him to make his move. That might have been the one bright side of the whole ridiculous situation.

"So, are you ready for tomorrow night?" Justyn asked as they packed up to leave after practice.

"Do I need to wear a black cloak?"

He laughed good-naturedly. "You could wear a burlap sack if you wanted and I wouldn't care. You'd still be beautiful."

Rebecca felt her cheeks grow warm, and that fluttery feeling had finally returned with a vengeance. "You still aren't going to tell me where we're going, are you?"

"Not a chance. But trust me; you're going to love it. I'll be at your house around six tomorrow," he told her with a secretive wink. "See you then."

He headed out to his bike, leaving Rebecca slightly breathless and completely flustered in his wake. *Trust me*, he had said. And strangely enough, though she had plenty of reasons not to, she *did* trust him. She remained nervous about their date. What kind of places did Gothic Wiccans take their would-be girlfriends? She kept having visions of a candle-lit dinner in a cemetery. But she knew that was silly. She had read Justyn's book. While it had left her with just as many questions as it did answers, she knew she had nothing to worry about. If he were going to take her someplace witchy, it would probably be a drum circle in the woods. Such a gathering might actually be fun, as long as everyone in attendance kept their clothes on.

Rebecca was still daydreaming when Tom came out from behind the auditorium doors. Carmen and Debbie were right behind him and were quick to run interference. They knew Tom had been avoiding her, and they weren't happy about it. They both shot him dirty looks as he walked towards them with his shoulders slouched, his hands shoved in his pockets, and a pathetically guilty look on his face.

Good. He should feel guilty, Rebecca thought. Even though he was coming to talk to her, she wasn't about to forgive him. He was only willing to be seen with her now that the hallway was empty.

"Hey, Bec," he said. "How ya doing?"

"Not bad, considering I'm the laughing stock of the whole school," Rebecca told him. "So, what gives me the honor of *your* presence today, Tom?"

He flinched at the cold tone of her voice, but he knew very well that he deserved it, and probably a lot more. "I've kind of been a jerk, haven't I?" Rebecca only snorted.

"Jerk doesn't begin to describe you," Carmen said with a frown.

Debbie continued to glare at him. Since she was significantly bigger than him, it was threat enough. Tom cleared his throat nervously. He knew he was outnumbered three to one.

"Yeah, well, I think I found a way to make it up to you."

"Not likely," Carmen muttered.

Rebecca was inclined to agree with her best friend—especially when Tom pulled out a copy of the school newspaper and handed it to her. She came very close to tearing it into pieces and tossing it back in his face. The last thing she wanted was to see that horrible article again. But when she tried to shred it, Tom reached out and placed a hand on her shoulder.

"It's *next* week's edition. I got you an advance copy," he explained. "Wendy isn't the only one who has pull with the nerds. Remember, Jay is my best friend."

That got a small smile out of her, but her friends still narrowed their eyes suspiciously. Rebecca took a deep breath, and pulled open the newspaper. It *was* a different edition. Emblazoned across the front page was a very unflattering photo of Wendy. Above the photo was the simple headline:

"Wendy Wright's Lies Revealed, by Tom Rittenhouse"

Rebecca went on to read the surprisingly well-written article that outlined out all the events that had taken place between Rebecca and Wendy. It began with Wendy's jealous reaction to the play casting and ended with her nasty article. It cast Wendy in a very bad, though extremely accurate, light. Tom was putting his head on the chopping block, and he knew it. He was taking the risk and doing it all for Rebecca.

"Tom I . . . I don't know what to say . . . ."

"Say thank you!" Debbie told her. She was reading every word over Rebecca's shoulder.

"Or say rest in peace," Carmen added. "Because when Wendy sees this, your ass is toast."

Tom heaved a heavy sigh. "She already knows. I asked her nicely more than once to admit what she did and have the article rescinded. But she wouldn't back down. So this is the price she has to pay. Someone needs to teach her that she can't treat people this way and pay no consequences."

"And how is *she* going to make *you* pay?" Debbie asked.

It was a good question. Where Wendy was concerned there were always consequences, and this time they wouldn't be good for Tom.

"Don't worry about me. I can handle Wendy."

Rebecca was truly touched, and felt a lump rise in her throat. "I can't believe you did this for me. You're a good friend."

Tom seemed disappointed. "Just a friend? Does that mean I'm too late to win you back from *Lord* Justyn?"

Debbie grunted. "She isn't a prize, you know."

Tom nodded. "I know that. And I'm going to be fair. Go on your date tomorrow night. But remember, I'll be thinking about you the whole time."

"Dude, that is so sweet. It brings a tear to my eye. Seriously." Jay had arrived on the scene. He pretended to wipe away phony tears with all his classic charm. "How's it hanging, Becca? Amazon? And you, sexy Latina lady, how's about you and me catch a movie or something tomorrow night?"

Jay brushed up against Carmen in an attempt at being provocative. But she sidestepped him just in time. Jay only stopped himself from falling by slamming face-first into the nearest locker.

Carmen smiled sweetly. "I would rather stick bamboo splinters up my finger nails than go anywhere with you, Jay."

Jay was unfazed by the rebuff. "Whatever. Your loss, babe," he told her once he had regained his footing. "I got a date tomorrow night already anyway." He turned to Tom and put his hands together in an exaggerated begging motion. "Dude, can I *please* borrow your truck tomorrow night? I can't pick up this classy chick on my bike."

"Sure, I don't have any plans anyway."

Tom shrugged and turned his sad eyes on Rebecca, making her feel just a little bit guilty. After all, he was practically signing away his reputation for her sake, and she was going out with another guy. But she didn't get a chance to say anything because the last group of stragglers was walking out of the auditorium doors. And one of them was Wendy. She did *not* look happy. Not one little bit. She stomped over to Tom and her cheeks were red and blotchy with barely controlled fury. The still healing scars on her face made her look that much scarier.

"Tom, if you go through with this, you're finished. You realize that, right?"

Tom huffed. "Whatever, Wendy. Your threats don't scare me."

"Maybe they should scare you. Because if I have my way, your life will be over. You can count on that." She turned to glare at each member of the small group in turn. "*All* of your lives will be over."

Chapter Twenty

The sun and the clouds fought for dominance over the sky when the day of Rebecca's date with Justyn finally arrived. Raindrops dripped sporadically. The sun would burst back onto the scene, drying up the rain almost before it had time to hit the ground. The air stayed damp, leaving Rebecca's hair flat and lifeless. As she examined her reflection in the mirror, she wondered why the forces of nature were always working against her.

Besides having a bad hair day, she also had no idea what she was supposed to wear for this date. Since Justyn wouldn't even give her a tiny hint about where they were going, she wasn't sure whether to go with a casual or a semi-casual look. The burlap sack he had mentioned was starting to seem like a good idea. That might teach him not to mess with a girl and her wardrobe. She finally decided on a brown skirt and a lightweight, slightly low-cut, tan blouse. If she could get her hair to come to life, she would be fine.

Rebecca was already nervous, and she practically jumped out of her skin when she heard the sudden sputter and groan of an old clunker pulling up to her house. Strange and unfamiliar noises were coming from her driveway. Rebecca peeked out her window just in time to see Justyn put an ancient black *Mustang* in park. And once again she made a mad dash down the stairs in order to beat her father to the door. If her parents saw Justyn's dark make-up and facial piercings, an interrogation would be the least of their problems. Her father would probably flat out forbid her from going out with him at all. And that wasn't something she had any intention of putting up with.

Rebecca yanked open the front door just as Justyn was stretching his arm out to ring the doorbell. She immediately clicked the door shut behind her, taking a moment to notice he was dressed in his everyday black attire. It made her wonder if she was overdressed. But he was quick to quell her worries. He looked her over with an approving smile.

"You look lovely, Becca."

"Thanks. So, I'm all ready. Let's get going."

She tried to hasten him away before her parents decided to spy on them through the window curtains. He narrowed his eyes at her suspiciously.

"Are you ashamed to let me meet your parents?"

"Yes." She admitted, and had to laugh when she saw his face fall. "Ashamed of *them*, not of *you*. Now, come on. I've been waiting all week to see what kind of surprise you've cooked up for me."

"It won't be long now. Come along, my lady." He bowed and reached out his hand to her. "Your chariot awaits."

Rebecca rolled her eyes as she climbed into the passenger seat, and noted the torn leather seats and faded black vinyl. "Some chariot." She teased, after he tried three times to coax the ignition to life. "I think we might have been better off on your bike."

"Don't listen to her, baby. She needs to learn to have respect for her elders." He patted the cracked dashboard and was rewarded for the pep talk when the car finally sputtered to life. "If I were you, Becca, I would send only positive thoughts out to this car. She is going to carry us all the way to Atlantic City."

"Atlantic City?" Rebecca swallowed hard. If her parents had any idea she was headed to the city, they would have a coronary. "What are we going to do there? We're not old enough to gamble."

"There are much more interesting places than casinos in the city. Just wait. You'll see. Hey, don't look so scared." He joked. "I promise to get you there safely."

"What if we break down on the expressway?" Rebecca fretted.

Being stuck on a road outside of Atlantic City was a scary thought—almost as scary as the idea of being lost *inside* the city. Certain areas of the town were known for their less than friendly occupants and dangerous side streets.

"You don't have to worry about that." Justyn promised. "I know my way around an engine."

Surprisingly, she felt reassured—at least a little bit. "Is there anything you *don't* know?"

"I don't know how I finally managed to get you to come out on a date with me."

Rebecca found herself blushing again, but she certainly couldn't explain it. She had no idea what strange magnetic pull kept leading her back towards Justyn. She tried not to think about it, and instead focus on the fall foliage that lined the road in breathtaking shades of red, orange and yellow.

It was only a twenty-minute drive to Atlantic City from her house, but Rebecca was still a little uneasy as they began the treacherous journey. The traffic started to pick up as soon as Justyn got on the expressway, and Rebecca was glad she wasn't the one driving. When his speedometer inched past sixty, she had to wonder if the vehicle would make it there in one piece at all. The entire car started to tremble from the exertion, and pieces of rust were falling down from the ceiling. Still, Justyn was true to his word, and soon the large, brightly lit casinos were looming overhead. But when he drove past all the huge parking lots and pulled down a shady looking back road, she had to wonder how long they were going to stay in one piece.

"We're going to a pawn shop?"

That seemed to be the only type of store that lined the back road they were on. Justyn smiled secretly as he dropped a handful of quarters in the meter.

"You really have no patience whatsoever, do you?"

Rebecca shrugged. "Patience isn't a virtue I've been overly endowed with."

"Well, you're going to learn to have patience today. Because we still have to walk a few blocks to get our destination."

Rebecca had wanted to break away from the ordinary. Well, walking through the streets of Atlantic City certainly wasn't ordinary for a goody-goody high school senior like her. And it *was* much more exciting than dinner and a movie—maybe a little *too* exciting. Maybe she would be better off with the all-American Tom instead of the risk-taking Gothic after all. Or maybe she was just no closer to choosing between them than she was when they made their ridiculous bargain.

"Come on. The boardwalk is this way."

Justyn took hold of her hand. She immediately felt a surge of energy shoot up her arm, and she wondered if he felt the same thing. If he did, he gave no indication of it. It made her think that the electricity between them was only her imagination, and not a real life manifestation of chemistry.

They crossed a few streets and came to the front of the large, multi-story casinos. Justyn led her through one of the packed parking lots and they soon found themselves facing the deep blue ocean. Even over the noise of the slot machines and drunken patrons, she could still hear the calming crash of the waves breaking against the shore. She found that it calmed her frazzled nerves. They both paused at exactly the same moment to admire the awesome beauty. Then it started to drizzle again.

"You don't mind getting a little wet, do you?" Justyn asked.

"Hey, you're the witch. Are you sure you aren't going to melt?"

He smiled and squeezed her hand. "I think I'll take my chances. Hey, look!" He pointed up to the sky, and his face lit up like a little boy with a big present to open. "It's a rainbow!"

Rebecca saw it too. It stretched over the patchy clouds in luminescent blues, reds, and purples, reaching down into the water on one end, and into the vast unknown on the other. It was completely breathtaking, and it filled her with a sense of wonder. It also made her heart swell with emotions she didn't quite understand.

"It's beautiful," Rebecca whispered.

"Rainbows are a sign of new beginnings," Justyn told her. "It means something wonderful is starting, right here, right now."

"And what might that be?"

She expected some kind of poetic, romantic response. But she should have known by now that Justyn never did what she was expecting. He shrugged his shoulders, suddenly feigning disinterest. He just loved to annoy her.

"I don't know. Maybe someone just hit the big jackpot in one of the casinos. Now, come on." He pulled her across the boards. "We have reservations and we're going to be late."

They walked only a few more blocks before Justyn led her down a ramp and back onto another small side street. This road was dotted with a few different ethnic storefronts, and Justyn was guiding her towards one of them. It was a Middle Eastern restaurant called the Kairo Cafe. The front of the building had a fantastic mural painted to look like exotic castle doors. Again Rebecca felt a little nervous as she walked through those majestic doors and into a cloud of strange smelling smoke.

She coughed. "I thought smoking was outlawed in restaurants in New Jersey."

"Not at a smoking bar."

Justyn gestured to the line of colorful glass hookahs and the dark skinned men who sat with the braided tubes protruding from their mouths. Each blew a stream of smoke from their noses or mouths. Some even managed to blow circles with the smoke. Rebecca didn't really see the appeal to the smoking. But the blown glass hookahs were elaborate and lovely, each a different color with carvings and engravings in silver and golden tones.

"Don't worry." Justyn continued. "We're going into the dining room, and there isn't any smoking allowed in there."

Rebecca felt decidedly out of place as they were led to their table and handed their menus. But she couldn't deny the ethnic charm of the small dining room. The candlelit chandeliers and a single flickering candle at each of the high tables cast the room in a delicate, romantic glow. Each one of those high tables, complete with matching bar stools, were filled with a wide array of people of every age, race, color, and creed. Apparently the Kairo Cafe was a hot spot in Atlantic City.

The walls were covered in colorful tapestries with delicate stitch work, and large oil paintings of far off lands. In the corner of the room was a small stage, complete with a dancing pole. It was all very charming, but Rebecca noticed that they were by far the youngest couple in the crowd. And when she stared down at the strange and unfamiliar menu choices, she felt even more anxious.

"Do you actually eat this stuff?"

Justyn had the nerve to look offended. "Of course. The food here is excellent."

"Do you know what any of this means? Chicken Shawarma? Shish Tawook? Kafta Kabbob? Don't they have any good veggie burgers here?"

He smiled; apparently impressed that she remembered he was a vegetarian. "I'll be getting the Veggie Tabsi Falafel. That's a shish kabbob made with all vegetables. Do you like chicken?" Rebecca nodded. "Then try the Shish Tawook. That's just chicken in a garlic sauce. It's not too spicy but has a really good flavor."

"I'll have to take your word for that."

The waiter came and took their orders. Justyn laughed and the waiter looked at her like she had three heads when she asked for a soda to drink. With a blush, she settled for a glass of water, and sat back to wait for the mystery meal to arrive. When it did, it actually smelled pretty good. She picked up her fork, and was just about to ask Justyn what had made him choose such a little place for their date when the lights on the stage sprang to life. An older man walked up to the little podium, and spoke into a crackling microphone. He had a long, graying beard, and a colorful turban covered his head. His wide smile lit up the stage more than the lights.

"Ladies and gentlemen." The man spoke in a thick Middle Eastern accent, each word rolling off his tongue like a purr or a growl. With only a few words, he had the whole crowd anticipating a great show. "Tonight for your viewing pleasure, we bring you a remarkable seductress. Let her entrance and mesmerize you with her breathtaking fusion of modern and traditional belly dance. I present to *you* . . . the amazing . . . the extraordinary . . . the alluring . . . *Tempest!*"

The old man disappeared around a corner taking the microphone with him, and Rebecca waited for someone to step onto the stage from behind the small curtain. A slow, deep, rhythmic drumming and the gentle flow of a wooden flute began to play, followed by a stringed, guitar-like instrument Justyn identified as a sitar. She was surprised when she heard a sudden jingling that beat in time with the music coming from behind her. She turned around and saw one of the most beautiful creatures she had ever laid eyes on standing in the dining room entrance way.

The woman sparkled and glimmered from head to toe. Even her eyes, the only part of her visible behind the long blue veil, were outlined in deep glittery make up, enhancing the already hypnotic stare of her deep, nearly black pupils. Long black curls cascaded down her bare back, moving in time to the music along with her gently shaking and pulsating torso.

Her costume was spectacular. The skirt was a rich blue that was fitted around her shapely hips and hung loosely down to her ankles. It reminded Rebecca of a mermaid fin; it fit her curves so perfectly. Both the skirt and the bra top were covered in silver coins and diamond cut glass that jingled and shimmered with every fluid movement. Her smooth perfect belly, bejeweled with large dangling blue gemstones, was so dazzling it might have been part of the costume instead of her own skin.

Rebecca was entranced as she watched the veiled woman weave her way through the crowd. Her face was still covered, giving her an air of mystery. She moved with a slow, practiced grace until she reached the center of the stage. Then the veils fell away, revealing her highly painted cheeks and lips. Her hips swayed to the music, her arms moved like snakes through the air. With each motion, the coins around her waist jingled in time to the slow moving music. Then the tempo changed. The new age ballad blended effortlessly into a faster paced mix, and the movements of the dancer became more intense. She wrapped her legs and arms around the dancing pole like she was gripping her lover in the throes of passion. Around them, the men in the room started to hiss.

"Why are they hissing at her?" Rebecca was a little shocked. How could anyone think she was anything but perfect?

"That's a sign of appreciation in the middle east," Justyn explained. "It's like clapping, only not as noisy."

Rebecca nodded, appeased, and went back to watching as the belly dancer twirled at an incredible pace, shaking and shaking, faster and faster, until Rebecca was sure she would fall to the ground in exhaustion. But when she did hit the ground, she inched her way along the stage, sliding on her belly like a graceful cat about to pounce on its prey, all the while sensually licking her lips. Then when the audience least expected it, she jumped back into a standing position, again without missing a beat, shaking her ornamented bosom in a way that would have been obscene if anyone else dared to try it. Yet on her it was only beautiful and feminine. She continued a complex mixture of shakes, twists and shimmies that were truly poetry in motion. Rebecca couldn't tear her eyes away. She didn't even blink. She was too afraid of missing even one impressive, fluid movement.

"Do you like it?" Justyn whispered beside her.

Like it? He was an artist. How could he possibly think a word as simple as 'like' could express the way she felt as she watched the dance continue. She had to swallow past a lump in her throat so that she could speak.

"It's the most beautiful thing I've ever seen in my life."

Justyn was undeniably smug and pleased with his accomplishment. "I'm glad you think so. I knew you would appreciate it."

They watched in silence for the next half hour as the performer finished her routine. Rebecca's dinner sat untouched, growing cold on her plate, because she refused to tear her eyes away from the dancing for even a moment. Only when there was an intermission did she even consider picking up her fork. But she quickly dropped it again when the beautiful, dark-haired woman waltzed up to their table, and without a word leaned over and kissed Justyn on the cheek. Rebecca knew her mouth fell open, and she had to stifle the ridiculous twinge of jealousy she felt. The woman had to be at least thirty, and hardly interested in a seventeen-year-old boy.

"Justyn, what a wonderful surprise." Her voice was just as fluid as her movements. "I was wondering when you'd finally come to see my show."

Justyn shrugged, completely nonchalant. "I told you I'd make it eventually."

She nodded and looked Rebecca over appraisingly. "Aren't you going to introduce me to your friend?"

"Darlene, this is Becca. Becca, Darlene."

"It's wonderful to meet you," Rebecca told her honestly. "I really enjoyed your show. It was amazing."

Darlene smiled broadly at the sincere compliment. Rebecca would have thought it was impossible, but it made her look even more beautiful. "Thank you. Well, I have to freshen up before I get back up there. It was very nice to meet you, Becca. I hope to see you again."

"Great job tonight, Darlene."

"Thanks, honey." She patted Justyn's shoulder, and again Rebecca felt inadequate. How could she possibly compete with perfection, even if she was at least ten years younger?

"I can't believe you know the dancer," Rebecca said, once she was gone. "How long have you known her?"

She tried to make the question sound casual, but Justyn was too perceptive not to pick up the hint of jealousy in her voice. It only infuriated her even more when he looked amused by it. She tried to mask her frown by picking up her water glass.

"Hmm, how long have I known Darlene? Well, only since the day I was born." He smirked. "She's my mother."

Rebecca very nearly spit out the water she had just sipped. She actually did start choking on it. "Your . . . your mother," she sputtered between coughs. "Are you kidding me?"

"Why would that be funny?" He seemed honestly confused.

"But she's so . . . so . . . ."

"Beautiful? Exotic? Sexy? Yeah, I know. It's a little weird sometimes. But she's more than just a belly dancer, you know. She's an EMT, an artist, and a Wiccan high priestess. She's an amazing teacher, and an even more amazing mother. Besides, she doesn't dress that way at home."

Rebecca couldn't help but giggle, just as much at her own silly jealousy than anything else. "Why do you call her Darlene?"

"Because that's her name."

"Do you always call her that?"

"No. Sometimes I call her Tempest. That's her stage name, and the name she uses in the circle during her Wiccan rituals. She was the leader of a huge coven back in Vegas. Here, it's just the two of us, until we meet some other pagans. And no, we don't practice skyclad. I don't want to see my mom naked even if she *is* more attractive than average."

That was an understatement. Rebecca's own mother was a plump, middle-aged matron who spent her nights playing bridge with her friends or watching reality television with her father. She would never be able to pull off that costume, and would probably wind up in traction if she even attempted any of those outrageous bends and twists.

"Wow, you certainly are full of surprises."

"I try not to be boring."

Rebecca laughed. Boring was not a word that could ever be associated with Justyn. And apparently it ran in the family.

They sat through the second half of the show, which was just as amazing as the first half. It was dark when they finally decided to leave. But Rebecca didn't feel nearly as jumpy on the walk back to the car. In fact, she wasn't nervous at all. The excitement of the night left her yearning for more. She waited with sweet anticipation for the goodnight kiss she was sure would come when he dropped her off at her front door. When Justyn led her to a bench so they could look out at the water, she thought perhaps the moment would arrive sooner.

It was the perfect romantic setting. The nearly full moon was large and bright in the sky, and its reflection shimmered across the calm water of the ocean. The earlier clouds had dissipated, but the temperature outside had dropped and Rebecca didn't have a jacket. Justyn noticed right away when she started to shiver, and wrapped a protective arm around her shoulders.

"Are you cold? Do you want to leave?"

"Not yet. It's so beautiful here. I could look out at the water forever."

Rebecca sighed and leaned back against his chest. He lifted her chin, and his dark eyes met hers. She found it impossible to look away as he ran his hand along her check and started to sing. It was just a few short lines from the play, but the words had meaning in their real life situation.

> *"Beauty is the sound of your voice.*
> *Tell me angel, have you made your choice?*
> *Is it I or is it him?*
> *I wait here to obey your whim."*

He moved in closer as he spoke, and Rebecca could feel his sweet breath on her lips. But right when she was certain those lips would touch hers, right when her body ached and yearned to feel that touch and her lips parted in anticipation, Justyn pulled away.

"I won't kiss you, Becca. Not until you've made your choice. Not until I know I have you completely, body, and soul."

Chapter Twenty-One

"Of all the frustrating, aggravating, annoying, impossible . . . Justyn Patko is just completely . . . *aghhh*!"

Rebecca stalked into her bedroom and tossed her handbag across the floor in her agitation. It landed on the ground in a small heap and all its contents spilled out onto the carpet, including the crystalline geode that she had gotten into the habit of carrying with her everywhere. It rolled to her feet, sparkling brighter than any diamond, and making dozens of little rainbows flash across the wall as it glittered in the brilliance of the overhead lights. The colorful rainbows reminded her that earlier that night she had experienced the most perfect and magical date of her life. She picked up the stone and caressed it lovingly.

"Justyn you are . . . the most romantic, sweet, amazing, wonderful . . . *moron* . . . that I have ever met!"

Rebecca heaved a sigh. There weren't enough adjectives, positive or negative, in the entire English vocabulary to sum up exactly the way she felt about Justyn at that moment. She was frustrated with him, yet she wanted him in a way she had never wanted any other man. She was angry, yet resentfully respectful of his methods. No other man alive had the power to attract and annoy her in the way that he could. No man alive had ever had this kind of effect on her at all.

It was ridiculous, really. One minute she was fuming, and then the next she was daydreaming about him. She just couldn't believe that Justyn hadn't kissed her. It made her feel slighted. Yet, at the same time, the fact that he hadn't kissed her and had wanted to wait until the moment was true and sincere, had permanently tipped the scales in his favor. It could only mean one thing—something that Rebecca was no longer able to deny or push to the side. She was falling in love with Justyn. Maybe she was *already* in love with him. And this was no schoolgirl crush like what she had—and it was past tense—felt for Tom. This was the real deal. The once in a lifetime connection that some people waited their whole lives to experience. Rebecca knew without a doubt that there was only one man for her. And that man was Justyn Patko. *Lord* Justyn. It was an exciting but also a terrifying revelation.

Every touch sent fire through her veins. Every word left her hanging on breathlessly, waiting for more. All she wanted was the chance to hear him speak. It didn't even matter what he said as long as she could hear the sweet sound of his voice. All she longed for was his gentle touch. It didn't matter where he touched her as long as his hands were on her body somewhere. This was the kind of connection where she felt his presence all the time, even when they were apart. Whether she wanted to admit it or not, this was the thing that she, that every human being on the face of the earth, longed for, and waited for all of their lives.

She had never given herself over to anyone so completely, and Rebecca was more than a little afraid. The old proverb that no one could choose who to love was certainly a true one. She had never fantasized about a dark Gothic prince carrying her off on his ebony stallion. She had only ever seen white knights in her dreams, just like every other teenage girl who had been weaned on stories of fairytale princesses. The fact that Justyn not only broke the white knight's mold, but also seemed to ridicule it with his very existence was a little disturbing. Yet still, he made her feel every bit as beautiful as a princess. And more than that, he made her feel like a grown woman, with all the wants and yearnings that a girl blossoming into womanhood should be feeling. She wasn't a fairytale princess longing for love's first kiss. She yearned for *more*— so much more that the very thought of it brought a ferocious blush to her cheeks.

Riiiiinnnnggggg.

The sudden jarring ring of her cell phone startled her from her deep thoughts. She jumped and dropped the crystal geode she was still holding. It rolled under her white dust ruffle and she forgot about it as she reached down to pick her handbag up off the floor. She pulled the phone from the bag so she could rid herself of the obtrusive noise that dared to take her thoughts away from her daydreams. But then again, the thoughts she was having were frightening and unfamiliar. So maybe it was better that they were disrupted after all.

She glanced down at the number display as the phone rang for the third time. "Unknown number" flashed threateningly across the brightly lit screen. Rebecca immediately forgot all thoughts of romance as she felt her rebellious heart begin to pound.

She had sworn up and down that she wasn't going to let her mystery stalker terrorize her anymore. She had vowed to herself again and again that she would *not* live in fear of some unknown psychopath. But as the phone continued to pulse and vibrate in her open palm, she found that she didn't have the courage to flip back the cover. On the fourth and final ring, she was so overcome with panic that she flung the phone across the room with all her strength. It slammed against the far wall, making a dent in the plaster, before falling silently to the ground.

Rebecca left it there, staring at it in wide-eyed horror, half expecting it to come to life and fly back into her hand of its own accord. But it remained still and silent for several long moments. Long moments in which Rebecca held her breath to the point of turning blue. Then, just as she had recovered a little bit of her sensibility and allowed herself to breathe again, a few musical beeps declared that whoever had called had left a message. Rebecca found herself frozen in place once again.

Chicken. Chicken. Chicken. Rebecca chided herself silently. *It's just a stupid phone. What are you so afraid of?*

It wasn't a question that could be answered rationally. All she knew was that she was suddenly filled with a terrible sense of foreboding, an indescribable feeling of dread. She had never considered herself even remotely psychic; in that moment, she clearly saw a future heralding death. The feeling of doom was so strong that she thought she might choke on her own overwhelming fear. Terror was gagging her, paralyzing her. She didn't want to listen to that message. She didn't want to prove herself right. But she couldn't control herself. She inched closer and closer to the phone, drawn to it by some sort of morbid fascination.

She approached the phone with such exaggerated caution; it might as well have been a tarantula or a cobra. She was sneaking up on it, like a cat preparing to pounce on a helpless mouse, even though she knew she was behaving like a complete and total fool. She was grateful there was no one there to witness this lapse in sanity.

When she finally bent down to pick the phone up from the ground, her fingers trembled with a terror that was impossible to contain, and the fear deepened to out and out horror when she saw that she really did have a new message and it wasn't just her imagination or some waking nightmare.

It took an incredible amount of willpower for her to hit the button that dialed into the voicemail system. Her shaking hands hit the wrong button more than once before she was able to retrieve the message she didn't really want to hear. She fought the urge to hang up just as strongly as she fought the urge to hyperventilate. But when she heard the voice she had come to know so well begin its gently broken recitation, she came very close to having a panic attack despite all her best efforts to remain calm. These were words she knew well—words of the phantom. Words she had heard Justyn speak every day at rehearsal. Words that sounded eerily melodic despite the machine that distorted the voice beyond recognition.

> *"Joseph Buquet could not hold his tongue.*
> *So his neck had to be wrung.*
> *Now his silence I guarantee.*
> *As his soul drifts into eternity."*

So many times she had heard Justyn say those words. So many times she watched as his face twisted in feigned anger. She thought it was only the brilliance of his acting ability. But could there be a real darkness, a real *evil*, lurking below the surface of the man she was falling in love with? Perhaps there a side of him she didn't know. Could the voice on the message belong to Justyn? And if it *was* Justyn, could she possibly stop herself from feeling these emotions she had never wanted to feel in the first place?

Either way, she had to know. She listened to the message again, and again. Three times. Five times. Ten times. Maybe more. Before she had played it for the final time, before she had given herself a moment to think beyond who the caller was and to consider the implications of the words, her call waiting announced that another call was coming through the line.

There was a moment of dread before she realized that this time a name flashed across the small screen. It was a name she knew well and was even relieved to see. She needed a friend, someone she could talk to about all this before she drove herself completely over the edge to the brink of insanity. She switched lines without even taking the time to delete the message.

"Carmen?" she whispered.

"Becca? Becca, it's so horrible!"

Carmen was crying, hysterically sobbing. She heard it in the tremble of her voice. Fear paralyzed Rebecca. Carmen never cried. Never once, not even in kindergarten, had she ever seen her friend shed a tear. She knew something horrible must have happened. Something unthinkable. And something, she realized with that ever-growing sense of eerie premonition, that was directly related to the awful message.

"Carmen, what is it? What's wrong?"

She knew what her answer was going to be even before she said it. Rebecca didn't need to be psychic to figure it out. It only made sense once she thought about it with a strange and sudden calm. The mystery caller had spoken of the murder of Joseph Buquet. Jay played the part of Joseph in the show. Another scene from *Phantom* was about to turn into reality. Rebecca felt her stomach churn as her friend verified her worst fears.

"It's Jay," Carmen sobbed. "There was a terrible accident. And Jay . . . Oh Becca, Jay is *dead!*"

Chapter Twenty-Two

"Is Tom home?"

Mrs. Rittenhouse stood in the doorway pale-faced and serious, and looked Rebecca over with a little uncertainty. After all, hers was not a face that she was used to seeing on her porch steps under any circumstances. It must have seemed odd for her to show up unannounced when their whole family was obviously grieving over the loss of a close friend. She put her hands on her wide hips and pursed her lips together in annoyance.

"I don't think Tom wants to see anyone right now."

"Can you just tell him that Becca's here? If he doesn't want to see me, I promise I'll leave. No questions asked. But just please let him know I'm here."

Tom's mother still appeared a little suspicious. But Rebecca wasn't above begging, and her desperate pleading was too hard to ignore. Mrs. Rittenhouse disappeared up the stairs with a shrug of her shoulders.

Rebecca tried not to pace impatiently in the foyer as she waited for her to return. She was worried about Tom. She had called his cell phone more times than she could count. She had left voice messages, sent text messages, and emailed him like crazy from the second Carmen had told her the news. Tom seemed to be avoiding all forms of communication with the outside world. And he had every reason. His best friend, his confidant, his ever faithful sidekick was gone. Jay was *dead*. They had been two halves of a strangely fitting whole all through high school. One existing without the other seemed almost impossible.

Rebecca knew that concern for Tom's emotional well being was only part of the reason why she had driven halfway across town to his house. It was his physical well being that really concerned her. She hadn't slept all night, thinking about the message, wondering who might be next on the would-be killer's hit list. Rebecca wanted to warn Tom. Even if he thought she was crazy, even if it was an unnecessary precaution, she thought that he had to know about the call.

"Hey, Becca."

Rebecca jumped at the sound of her name. She was surprised to turn and find Tom standing at the bottom of the stairway. She hadn't really expected him to come down. She immediately forgot the real reason why she had come. She forgot everything when she saw how utterly wretched he looked. All she knew was that she felt obliged to make some kind of effort at comforting him.

Tom had aged ten years since she had seen just days ago. She didn't think it was possible for someone to look so different after just two days. His once youthful, carefree face was lined with grief. His blue eyes had lost all their sparkle, and were red and swollen. He was so pale that he could have actually given Justyn competition for the role of school vampire. Rebecca couldn't look at that kind of torment and just turn away. She was propelled forward by her compassion. It didn't matter that she wasn't in love with him or that she was pretty sure she *was* in love with his arch nemesis. It didn't even matter anymore that she was afraid there might be a murderer on the loose. Tom needed comfort and she couldn't deny it. Rebecca flung her arms around him with reckless abandon.

He seemed surprised at first. His arms stayed limp at his sides for a full minute, even as Rebecca pulled him close against her. Then finally, he woke from his half trance and returned the embrace. His arms wrapped around her waist, squeezing her so tightly in his desperation that she could barely breathe. She could feel him trembling in her arms, and before long she felt his tears soak through the thin layer of her sweater as his body racked in silent sobs.

"Becca, I . . . I just can't believe he's gone."

There wasn't really anything she could say. Telling him that Jay was in a better place was ridiculous when all Tom wanted was for his friend to be alive again. Saying that everything happened for a reason was equally mundane and cliché. What reason could there possible be for a seventeen-year-old boy to have his life cut so dramatically short? And what words could possibly ease the pain that Tom must be feeling? Instead of saying meaningless words, Rebecca just let him cry. All the while she patted his back, and ran her fingers through his hair soothingly. It seemed to help calm him down. Eventually the heart wrenching sobs settled into gentle hiccups. When Tom finally lifted his red-rimmed eyes, he even managed to give her the smallest hint of a smile.

"Wow, not much of a tough guy, am I?"

"Grieving for your friend doesn't make you any less of a man, Tom. It's okay to be sad."

He nodded. "I know that. But I guarantee you that wherever Jay is right now, he's looking down on me, rolling his eyes, and calling me a whole bunch of unflattering names."

Rebecca had to smile. Knowing Jay, that was probably true.

Tom did this best to collect himself. He wiped his eyes and nose on the sleeve of his shirt before leading Rebecca into the kitchen. He poured a couple of glasses of ice tea, both of which sat untouched and glistening with moisture on the table as they stared off into space, each lost in their own thoughts. After several minutes of deafening silence had passed, Tom finally spoke.

"So, how did you find out? I didn't expect the news to spread so quickly."

Tom wasn't taking into account that besides living in a small town where everyone knew everyone else's business, Rebecca also happened to be best friends with the queen of gossip. If there were news, good or bad, exciting or mediocre, Carmen would be the first to find out. And ultimately Rebecca was the next to find out whether she wanted to or not.

"Carmen called me last night. Debbie's dad owns the tow truck company that . . . um . . . ." She had to clear her throat. "That took the car away."

Tom nodded. He voice was controlled but his face had turned a few different shades of green. "So you know what happened?"

"I know there was an accident."

"An accident?" He laughed, just a little bitterly. "Stupid, reckless moron. Jay was always driving like a maniac. I should have known that eventually he would drive my truck straight into a telephone poll. You know, it's funny. I can almost hear his voice in my head, giving me a whole bunch of lame excuses about how it wasn't his fault. Like, 'Dude, an entire family of cattle ran out in front of me'. Or, 'I was blinded by the lights of this giant UFO.' Sure, I would have been angry as hell at him for totaling my truck, at least at first. But I would have forgiven him eventually—especially once it hit me how lucky he would have been to be alive. I mean, who really cares about some stupid car, right? I'd never drive again if it meant that Jay . . . that he was still . . . ."

Tom lost it again. All trace of the composure he had fought so hard for was gone. He buried his head in his hands to hide the tears he had thought had finally run dry. Rebecca reached across the table to gingerly touch his hand, unsure that he even remembered that she was still there or if he wanted her to touch him. She didn't even realize that tears were trickling down her cheeks as well until she watched them slip onto the table and absorb against the cloth mat.

"Tom, I'm so . . . so sorry."

"It was *my* truck. It should have been *me*."

Rebecca was horrified by the thought. "Don't say that! This wasn't your fault. None of this was your fault. It wasn't you . . . it was . . . ."

Tom looked up at her with grateful, watery eyes, and Rebecca couldn't finish the sentence. She couldn't tell him whose fault she thought it was. She couldn't tell him the main reason she had come was because she suspected that Jay's accident might not have been an accident at all. And it wasn't only because she was unsure of the killer's secret identity that she held her tongue. She couldn't give Tom anything else to torture himself about. He had enough to deal with.

Besides, maybe she was wrong. Maybe it was another coincidence in a long line of coincidences. Maybe the caller had heard about Jay's accident through the grapevine and had worked in into their threats to make it scarier.

Surely if there had been foul play involved, the police would have realized it. Right? There would have to be some trace of tampering or some proof that someone had run Jay off the road. Didn't they always find a dozen clues to lead them to the perpetrators on detective shows like *CSI?* Real life crime scenes couldn't be any different. It must have been nothing but an accident. A horrible, horrible, accident.

It seemed like the logical conclusion. But there was nothing logical about the panic stricken tightening in her chest every time she remembered the threatening voice. There was nothing logical about the pain Tom was feeling over the loss of his best friend. The whole thing was a terrible situation, whether Jay's death had been intentional or not.

"It really means a lot to me that you came here today," Tom told her.

He squeezed her hand. Then suddenly and without warning, he leaned over the table and kissed her. It took her by surprise, and she knew she should have pulled away. She knew she was giving him false hope. But he was already hurting. How could she deny him this small bit of human comfort? How could she hurt him even more by turning away from him in his time of need? The answer was that she couldn't. Rebecca let him kiss her, and told herself it would be for the last time.

Chapter Twenty-Three

It was strange how life just went on, even when it seemed only natural for the world to stop spinning on its axis. It didn't seem right for things to continue like nothing had happened—for schools bells to ring, for people to laugh in the halls, for play practice to continue as scheduled. Yet, things did go on just like it was any other day, even though Jay was no longer a part of their lives. Life went back to its normal routine as soon as everyone dried their eyes after the memorial service. Even Rebecca was falling back into the daily humdrum of classes, and was surprised when she found herself looking forward to seeing Justyn. She hadn't talked to him since their date, and she missed him. As the day wound down, she couldn't help feeling a little excited flutter, even though she was still sad about Jay.

It was also strange how quickly her thoughts about Justyn kept running the gamut from the romantic to the somewhat disturbing. Talk about an emotional roller coaster. One minute she was sure he was a cold—blooded killer, and she was terrified of him. The next, she was imagining herself walking down the aisle at their wedding. Both scenarios were equally ridiculous. She decided she wasn't going to let her irrational fears or her silly fantasies get the better of her. Instead, she was going to try to take the blossoming relationship one day at a time. Starting, hopefully, that afternoon when she would tell him that she had made her decision once and for all. She would just have to leave out the part about how she sometimes doubted his sanity and thought he was a murderer. That *might* ruin the moment.

There were only a few weeks left until opening night. The props had come a long way in the last week. The stage crew had truly outdone themselves with their amazing backdrops, from the graveyard scene to the phantom's underground lair. Rebecca found it much easier to move through the scenes surrounded by the artwork and antique style furniture. It gave the play more realism. She was especially impressed with the scene shifting for the *Don Juan* scene.

The *Don Juan* act was one of Rebecca's favorites. Not only because it was the climax of the play, but also because the duet was the most beautiful song that she and Justyn shared. In the scene, the phantom kills the lead baritone of the opera house and takes his place on the stage. Christine realizes instantly who he is and what he must have done, but she's still drawn to him by his passionate singing. They come close to sharing a forbidden kiss. But instead, at the last moment, she removes his mask, revealing his deformity to the horrified audience. More than once, especially with Justyn in the role of the phantom, Rebecca was tempted to rewrite history and have Christine run away with Erik, leaving Raoul behind.

The scene called for a high platform with a stairway on either side. Erik and Christine would each climb one end of the stairway as they inched their way closer and closer to one another, finally coming together in the center of the high bridge. Beneath them were half a dozen large wooden cutouts, cut and painted into the shape of red and orange flames to represent the blazing inferno of *Don Juan's* territory.

It was the first time they had the fancy platform available, and Rebecca was a little nervous about making the treacherous journey up the narrow wooden steps. She had never been very good with heights. She looked up at the platform, and thought that fifteen feet suddenly seemed dangerously high. Just looking up made her feel a little woozy, but she did her best to overcome her irrational fears. What could possibly happen?

Because of the new props, and because the scene involved an elaborate dance routine with the chorus, Miss King had decided to focus on that scene for the better part of the afternoon. Of course, after the events of the weekend, no one was overly enthusiastic about performing at all. Even the teacher seemed a little less animated than usual as the stagehands moved the backdrops into place.

"I realize that this is a difficult time. We'll all miss Jay, especially his unquenchable sense of humor." Miss King had to stop to wipe a tear from her eye. "But as cliché as it might sound, the show must go on. So let's make this play the best performance this school has ever seen! And let's dedicate it to the memory of our friend and co-star, Jay Kopp."

If Miss King expected a hearty round of applause or exuberant shouts of agreement, she must have been disappointed. Most of the cast barely lifted their eyes during the speech, and a few even snickered at the melodrama.

Rebecca stole a glance at the front row of chairs where Tom was sitting with his arms crossed. His face had gone eerily blank. She somehow found that empty, zombie-like stare much more disturbing than the open emotion she had seen him display just the day before. Rebecca decided she had to go see if he was all right before they started. After all, despite what he had been through that weekend, he had still made sure the newspaper article about Wendy had been released. He had cleared Rebecca's name and bravely faced the wrath of Wendy, who didn't spare him out of sympathy for the loss of his friend. For the first time in Mainland Regional history, people were too busy laughing at Wendy to pay any attention to anything that she said. For once, her malicious plans had backfired.

Rebecca jogged over and plopped down in the empty seat beside Tom. He didn't even notice her until she cleared her throat, and even then he didn't look up in acknowledgment.

"How are you?" she asked.

He shrugged, but didn't say anything.

"That good, huh?" Rebecca felt decidedly awkward, and struggled to think of something appropriate to say. "I was surprised to see you at school today."

"It's better to stay occupied than to sit home alone feeling sorry for myself."

Rebecca nodded, and was about to comment that she understood when she suddenly felt eyes on her, burning into her with an intensity that was impossible to ignore. She looked up to the stage, and saw Justyn watching her from a corner by the curtain. He didn't look angry, but he certainly didn't look happy either. She realized that to him it must have appeared that she had chosen Tom after all. Rebecca knew she had to get Justyn alone so she could explain the circumstances. She had to let him know that Tom was just a friend in need, and would never be any more than that ever again.

Justyn wasn't going to make it easy for her. Miss King ordered them into position and she had to leave Tom alone with his sullenness. Along the way, she tried to grab Justyn's arm as they crossed paths before the scene began, but he pulled away. He wouldn't even look her in the eyes as he spoke.

"I told you I would bow out gracefully when you made your choice. Be happy with your hero."

"Justyn, wait . . . ."

She tried to stop him, but like the mystical creature of the night that he was, Justyn all but disappeared into the darkness backstage. The music was starting and Rebecca was forced to wait behind the scenes for her queue while Wendy and the chorus began the ballet routine. She watched with a little envy as Carmen and the other chorus girls swirled effortlessly around the dance floor. She was a little relieved that Miss King had foreseen her inability to be even remotely graceful and had made sure she had very little dancing to do.

Soon the ballerinas slowed, and one by one, they slipped out of sight. The music deepened emotionally as the choreography came to an end. Rebecca began to inch her way out onto the empty stage with a basket of silk flowers in her hands.

It was a challenging scene, especially when her mind was already moving in a dozen different directions. She was an actress playing the role of an actress. Her character, Christine, was portraying an innocent maiden about to be carried away by the darkly handsome *Don Juan*—carried away to the corruption of her innocence.

How close to reality art really was. When Justyn stepped onto the stage, wearing the black mask of the opera ghost, Rebecca caught her breath at his dark beauty. He was so unbelievably sensual, so hypnotically captivating. She wanted to throw herself at his feet and offer herself up to him, body and soul. And that was before he opened his mouth and the sweet beauty of his voice enveloped her in its silky embrace. She felt her knees tremble like any virgin maiden's would have trembled at the feet of the irresistible rogue who was *Don Juan*.

> *"In all your innocence you have come to me here.*
> *Release your doubts and shed not one tear.*
> *There's no going back the way that you came.*
> *You will know passion but feel no shame."*

Rebecca was wrapped in the caressing shroud of his melodic voice. They stood on opposite ends of the stage. It seemed like a never-ending chasm was between them. She trembled with unspoken longing as she watched him glide towards the wooden steps of the platform. She was drowning in that longing, sinking into his voice. She struggled to make her weak knees carry her to her own stairway, casting aside the forgotten flowers of innocence.

It was only through the direct unspoken order of his dark eyes that she was able to find the strength to release her own voice in a strong soprano that matched his perfect baritone. She admitted in the words of her song, in the radiance of her voice, how much she longed for his embrace. Justyn had to know it wasn't just a duet between Christine and Erik anymore. They had somehow transcended from fantasy to reality, and the words she sang were meant for him and him alone.

> *"A strange fire burns within my breast.*
> *Is this passion real or merely a test?*
> *Will the burning be quenched when our bodies unite?*
> *Will we become one on this dark, moonless night."*

They had reached the center of the platform. Rebecca was both grateful and a little afraid to find him suddenly at her side. Her heart pounded furiously as Justyn took her hand, spun her around, and then mercifully steadied her dizzied body with the firm grip of his hands around her waist. She sank into his arms, letting her head rest lightly against his firm chest.

When they began the final verse, their voices met in an almost elemental clash that rung in perfect, sweet harmony—a harmony that went beyond the aspects of music and into the harmony of the spirit. As their voices became one, so did their souls. It was a beauty that even the most untrained ear in the room suddenly became aware of. It was an art form that could not be ignored.

"All barriers have been crossed.
All innocence has been lost.
The seeds of passion have been sown.
From this crossing there is no return."

Rebecca waited with closed eyes, in both the real and imagined throes of passion as Justyn's hands caressed and explored her waist, her arms, and ran gently across her shoulders. Such a simple touch, yet it set her blood on fire. His breath was warm and sweet as he nuzzled against the soft skin of her neck. His hands shifted as he used them to brush her long hair out of the way so that his lips could trace a path from her neck to her burning cheeks, making her entire body tingle with pleasure and her breath come in short gasps.

Rebecca knew what she was supposed to be doing. She knew her role was to remove the mask, to betray the phantom once and for all, thus proving her devotion to Raoul and sending Erik into a murderous rage. But this Christine had no desire to betray her phantom. *This* Christine felt no fear, at least not in that perfect moment, of what was hiding beneath the mask. This Christine wanted the phantom to finally have the happy ending that so many fans had dreamed of.

She felt Justyn pull her toward him, and she finally opened her eyes. He looked confused. He was waiting for the scene to continue. He didn't realize that in her mind, the play had merged with reality. She met his sad gaze, and with a small smile, she reached out her hand to gently touch his cheek. She wanted to tell him that she had made her choice. That she had chosen *him*. But the words stuck in a throat swollen with emotion. Nevertheless, she was almost certain that he had read her mind, and knew all her unspoken thoughts.

Even through the dark mask, she was sure she saw his eyes light up just a little as it dawned on him. His entire demeanor was magically transformed.

Justyn leaned down, unable to resist the urge any longer. Rebecca thought that finally, *finally* she would know the ecstasy of his kiss. Finally, she would know what it was like to be truly complete in his arms. She closed her eyes in anticipation. But just as she sensed the parting of his lips as they neared hers, something snapped him violently from her grasp.

Shocked and startled, Rebecca's eyes popped open just in time to see Tom swing his fist squarely into the unprepared face of an even more shocked and startled Justyn. Justyn staggered back in surprise, and put a hand against his lip. Rebecca gasped in horror as she saw blood ooze from the broken skin. Tom only sneered, apparently pleased with himself and his unsportsmanlike attack.

"Look, the vampire bleeds."

Rebecca hardly recognized Tom, his face was so twisted, his voice so harsh and bitter. How had he gotten there, anyway? When and where had he come from? She hadn't even heard him coming up the steps.

"Tom, what are you doing?" Rebecca exclaimed.

"You aren't going to take Becca away from me!"

He was practically spitting in Justyn's face, and Rebecca knew the Goth well enough to know he wasn't going to just stand there and take it. His silence was only a testament to his rage.

"Tom, you have to stop this!"

Tom didn't listen or even acknowledge Rebecca. Even Justyn seemed to have forgotten her presence. He lunged back at Tom with uncontrollable fury, despite her startled cries of protest. There was nothing she could do to stop them. It had been too long coming.

Tom was too quick for Justyn. He easily sidestepped Justyn's counterattack, and before he could come at him a second time, Tom shoved him backwards as hard as he could, sending him sprawling backwards into the railing.

Rebecca saw what was happening. She even made a desperate grab for Justyn's hand as she saw him go down. But someone so uncoordinated never stood a chance. She heard a high-pitched scream, and was shocked to realize it had come from her own mouth. But even that sound was overpowered by the sickening crack of wood splintering as the railing of the platform gave way under Justyn's heavy weight.

She saw Justyn tip over the edge. She could see the horrified guilty look on Tom's face as he realized what was happening. Time moved so slowly that she even noticed a dusting of sawdust on the ground as she fell to her knees. She saw everything in terrible, vivid detail, including the fact that one side of the railing had cracked, but the other had been cleanly sawed through. She gasped when she heard the awful crash of Justyn's body slamming into the painted, wooden flames, shattering several of them to pieces. She watched it all unfold in eerie slow motion. Then she saw nothing but a blur of tears as she ran down the platform steps to Justyn's side.

Chapter Twenty-Four

The next few seconds were terrible. They were filled with a sudden and awesome silence in which it seemed that every single person in the auditorium had turned to stone—had stopped even the necessary intake of breath as they waited in paralyzed shock. It was a silence in which the resonating crack of Justyn's body hitting the ground seemed to echo over and over in her ears.

Rebecca was the only person in the room who was moving—or more appropriately, flying—down the platform stairs. All thoughts of her own clumsiness were forgotten as she rushed to Justyn's side, even when she tripped near the bottom. She hardly noticed the bruises on her knees as she pulled herself back to her feet, only to fall back down beside the shattered remnants of the wooden flames next to Justyn's body—Justyn's still, unmoving body. Rebecca pressed her hand against her mouth and gasped, terrified.

"Justyn? Justyn, are you all right?"

The voice she heard was so tight and scratchy; she could hardly believe it was her own. Around her, other people were repeating the same question, but she was having trouble focusing on them. All she could see was Justyn. All she could hear was her own heart pounding in her chest as she waited. She wanted to touch him, to roll him over. But some small part of her brain that was still functioning rationally knew it wasn't a good idea to move people who had fallen, especially from a large height. The less rational side of her was afraid that if she dared to try, she would find him impaled by the splintered wood. Afraid he might turn to dust before her very eyes, thus fulfilling the fate of a vampire once and for all.

"Justyn . . . please . . . ."

Why wasn't he moving? Was he even breathing? He couldn't be . . . couldn't be . . . *No!* She wouldn't even think it. It was too terrible. Justyn was fine. He had to be fine. Fate wouldn't be so cruel as to take him away from her when they only just found each other. She had never spent much time thinking about divinity, but Justyn's Goddess would never be so cruel.

"Someone . . . someone call 911." Miss King's voice cracked the order from the sidelines, and all at once at least half a dozen cell phones were flipped open and started beeping as a multitude of trembling fingers fumbled to press the three simple digits.

"No, no don't . . . ." The muffled reply came from the crumpled black heap on the floor. It was a voice she would know anywhere. Justyn's voice, sweet and melodic even though it was strained, and he seemed short of breath.

"Justyn . . . ?"

Unbelievable relief flooded through her when he rolled over, and with a small groan managed to pull himself, somewhat unsteadily, to his feet. "I'm fine. Just winded," he croaked.

Rebecca immediately reached out a hand to help him up, as did several of the stagehands, but he brushed them all away, looking undeniably annoyed by their efforts. Rebecca could understand him wanting to play the tough guy when his ego had been so horribly bruised. But she would have thought he would have accepted at least *her* help, even if it were only to get back at Tom.

Tom had at some point climbed back down the stairs as well, and was visibly relieved to see Justyn on his feet. Justyn glared at him from across the stage. But for once, neither of them took it any further. She didn't think they *could* have started fighting again, even if they wanted to. She wasn't quite sure which one of them looked more wobbly-legged. She could still sense as much as see the anger radiating from Justyn, a wave of dangerous heat that might drown them all in its intensity if she didn't intervene.

"Justyn, are you hurt?"

Miss King was fretting around him like a typical nervous Nelly. What kind of stupid question was that to ask anyway? *Obviously* he was hurt. He had just fallen fifteen feet. Already Rebecca could see an ugly black and purple bruise appearing on his left temple. And blood was running down his chin where Tom had split open his lip. But when she watched him close his eyes and grimace, and was pretty certain she saw him sway just a little, she echoed the same rhetorical question as the teacher.

"Are you okay?"

Justyn turned, and seemed to notice her there for the first time. The blind fury had faded from his eyes, but he remained silent. He looked like he wanted to say something. His mouth even opened and closed a few times. But instead of talking, he nodded his head and climbed down the stage steps, albeit very slowly and with some difficultly. He didn't acknowledge the shocked stares of his cast mates as he walked out the door without a backward glance.

Rebecca was probably the most shocked of all, staring at his retreating back with her jaw very nearly touching the floor. But then she collected herself, and without taking a moment to wonder what anyone thought about it, she moved forward to dart after him. She hadn't even made it to the steps before Tom stepped in front of her and blocked her path.

She wanted to yell at him. She wanted to scream every nasty four-letter word she had ever heard while she pummeled him with her bare hands. But she only wanted to do that for about a millisecond. Then she looked at his face which had already been a mask of pain and grief before the incident, but which now had the added lines of deep regret. How could she scream at him when she knew he was already berating himself for what he had done? Besides, she knew in her heart that Tom had never had any intention of doing any more than throwing a few punches. And even though *someone* obviously had worse intentions when they sawed the platform railing, she couldn't for a second imagine that person had been Tom.

"Becca, I'm so sorry. But you have to know . . . I mean, you understand . . . I didn't mean for him to *fall*. You *do* believe that, don't you?"

"I know, Tom," Rebecca told him. "I know it was an accident, but I can't talk about it now. I have to go."

"You're going after him?"

It was half question and half accusation, but Rebecca didn't have time to explain things to him. Even though she hated the hurt look she saw in his eyes, she brushed past Tom and was down the stairs in a flash.

She heard Carmen calling, saw Debbie watching tight-lipped and shaking her head in the shadows behind the curtain. She even noticed Wendy scowling at her as she ran past her. She ignored them all as she followed the path that Justyn had taken. It didn't take her long to find him. He was at his locker, leaning his bruised head against the cool metal. One hand was clutching his side. Rebecca felt an immediate rush of concern that bordered on sheer terror. Justyn, her mystical, beautiful creature of darkness, couldn't be hurt. It just didn't seem possible that a fairytale creature could get hurt.

She approached him with caution, like she would a wounded animal. But she was certainly not very stealthy because even though she tried to inch up on him slowly and quietly, he heard her soft footsteps. He knew immediately who it was without turning around or even opening his eyes, giving even more credence to what she truly believed were supernatural abilities of perception.

"I'm fine, Becca." She didn't need to see his eyes to know that on some level they were rolling. She heard the exasperation in his voice. "You don't need to worry about me. Go back to Tom. I'm sure he's not going to be happy that you came after me."

Rebecca felt the ridiculous urge to stomp her foot, to have an all-out tantrum. How could he be so stupid, so blind, so downright annoying? For someone that she knew for a fact was highly intelligent, he sure had a strange habit of acting like a moron.

"I don't want to go back to Tom," she informed him as she crossed her arms defiantly.

"Really?"

He turned his head around so he could cock his eyebrow, but he still leaned heavily on the lockers. She wouldn't have thought it was possible for him to be any paler than his normal shade, but his face was a ghastly white, except for the areas that were bruised and bloodied. Yet, although she knew he had to be hurting physically, the pain, the *yearning*, in his eyes was so much more intense. It made her heart swell with emotion. That stupid lump was back. She had to clear her throat.

"Look at you. You're a mess." She gestured towards his face. "You're bleeding."

Justyn looked confused at first, like he hadn't even realized he was hurt at all until she pointed it out to him. He flinched a little as he gingerly fingered his broken lip. When he lifted his hand away and saw the bright red stain on his fingers, his already chalk white face turned an awful combination of gray and green. Rebecca only barely caught hold of his arm as his legs gave way beneath him. She did her best to gently ease him to the ground, even though he was almost twice her size.

"Justyn!" She exclaimed.

She was already digging into her handbag for her cell phone, sure that she was going to have to call for help after all. For a split second, she imagined him completely passing out, slipping into a coma, and never waking up again. She pulled the phone out of its casing, and was just about to start dialing. He stopped her before she hit the first digit. Then he gently pulled the phone free from her fingers, closed it back up and handed it to her.

"I'm okay. Really."

Was it her imagination or did he actually sound a little sheepish? Well, it didn't matter. She wasn't falling for it.

"I don't believe you."

"I swear that I'm fine. It's just that I'm . . . ." He looked like he was fighting back the urge to gag as he looked at the blood on his fingers again. "I'm not really good around . . . blood."

If he wasn't so pale, he might have blushed. Rebecca felt a little relieved, and had to smile, even though he was completely mortified by his confession. She couldn't resist the urge to tease him just a little.

"You're afraid of blood? What kind of vampire are you?"

Now there was no denying the fact that he looked sheepish. He was even pouting a little. "The kind that's a vegetarian."

She actually laughed out loud which coaxed the smallest of smiles out of him. "Okay, tough guy, stay here. I'll get something to clean this up before you go and pass out on me."

Rebecca ran across the hallway to the nearest ladies' room, grabbed a few paper towels, and wet them under the sink before emerging to play Florence Nightingale. Justyn was sitting on the hallway floor, with his head between his knees. Somehow seeing him so wretchedly human for the first time since they had met made her want him that much more. She smiled as she knelt down by his side, and gently lifted his chin. He grimaced a little as the cold water stung the open wound.

Rebecca gave an exaggerated huff. "Come on, now. Don't be a big baby."

He certainly would have smirked if it wouldn't have made the bleeding worse. She noted with slight humor that he actually kept his eyes closed while she dabbed the blood away, and didn't open them again until he knew the stained paper towels were disposed of. After tossing them into the nearest wastebasket, she gave him the go ahead to open his eyes.

"There now. All better?"

Justyn notably grimaced as she helped him to his feet. She felt his hands tremble, so she knew he was a far cry from better. But he didn't complain as he tossed a few textbooks into his bag. Rebecca chewed her lower lip nervously as she watched him. Actually, *studied* him would be a better way to describe it.

"Can I drive you home?" Rebecca asked when he headed toward the door without another word. She wasn't sure what to make of his attitude. She liked it better when he was talking, even if it was sarcastically.

"I've got my bike."

Rebecca felt her mouth fall back open and wondered if it might be possible for it to get stuck that way. "You can't ride a bike home. You're hurt."

He shook his head. "I'm fine."

"You hit your head pretty hard. What if you have a concussion? What if you pass out or something?"

"I *said* I'm fine."

He actually had the nerve to sound annoyed about her concern. That of course made Rebecca annoyed, and she considered leaving the stubborn jerk to his bike and going back to practice. She even stopped dead in her tracks for all of thirty seconds. But then her feelings for him overwhelmed her pride and she started following him again, feeling like a lovesick puppy dog following a grumpy master that might just kick her to the side. But she was glad that she held her ground. Because when Justyn bent down to unchain his bike and than made a valiant effort to climb up onto the seat, he couldn't deny anymore that he was hurt worse than he was letting on. The bike fell to the ground with a loud clank, and he very nearly doubled over, clutching his side and gasping for breath.

"Justyn!"

Rebecca ran up and put her arm gently around his waist, careful not to hurt him worse as she helped him to stand upright. He didn't fight her. In fact, he leaned heavily against her as he tried to even his breathing. But he still wasn't ready to completely let go of his stubborn pride.

"I'm . . . fine." He insisted.

"The fact that you're normally extensive vocabulary has been reduced to two words is all the proof I need that you're *not* fine. Now let me see."

At any other time, Rebecca would have been just as shocked as Justyn at her own audacity as she pulled his black t-shirt up to see his injured side. But she was too startled by the awful skin discoloration she saw to feel any shyness. She was pretty sure her own face turned as gray as his, and she found it almost funny that he was suddenly trying to comfort her.

"It's okay," he said soothingly. "Really. It's not a big deal."

"So you're a doctor now?" she asked, once she had recovered the use of her vocal cords.

"It's . . . *aghhh* . . . ." He bent over again. "It's . . . nothing."

"You're a little off on your acting today. You're not convincing me." She gave him a hard stare. "I think you need to go the ER."

He shook his head firmly. "No."

"No?" If she weren't afraid that she might have hurt him worse, she would have slapped him silly.

"No," he repeated. "Just take me home. Remember, I told you my mom's an EMT. She'll know what to do. I don't need to go spend hours sitting in the ER."

Rebecca was a little appeased, but only a little. She still thought a doctor was better than an EMT. But he wasn't giving her a choice, so she had to agree. "All right. But I'm staying with you until she assures me that you're all right."

He smiled a little, even though his face was still shadowed with pain. "Is that a threat or a promise?"

Rebecca smiled back. "Maybe a little of both."

She wanted to help him to the car, which was all the way on the other side of the parking lot, but he insisted he could walk on his own. It seemed that Lord Justyn, for all his pretty poetic talk, had just as much pride as any other guy his age. But once they got in the car and pulled away, she saw him close his eyes and try to fight back a spasm of pain when he thought she wasn't looking. It was almost more than she could bear to know that he was hurting, and that she was helpless to stop it. She did the only thing she could, and reached across the driver's seat to take his hand. He accepted her small offering. Every time they went over a pothole, he squeezed her fingers so hard that she thought he might break them. She didn't care as long as it gave him some comfort. She focused her thoughts on cursing whatever idiot had paved the stupid, uneven roads.

Justyn gave Rebecca directions to his house, and she was pleasantly surprised to find that they lived only a few blocks apart. What she found even more surprising was that Justyn's mother was pacing frantically up and down the driveway with a phone to her ear.

Even without the elaborate belly dance costume, it was impossible to mistake her. Her long black hair was pulled back in a ponytail, and her navy blue EMT uniform didn't make her look any less like a super model than she had when she was dancing. How weird was it to feel plain next to her boyfriend's—well *almost* her boyfriend's—mother? It was hard not be feel a little envious of her perfect figure and strange, exotic charm.

When Darlene saw Justyn in the passenger seat of the unfamiliar car, her face lightened with visible relief. She looked anxious as she ran up to the car. That anxiety deepened as she watched her son struggle to step onto the pavement.

"Justyn! What happened? I knew something was wrong. I *sensed* it. I always know when you're in trouble. Oh, Goddess, look at your face! Look at your beautiful face! Tell me who did this to you and I'll make sure he knows all about karma and everything coming back three times." Darlene gave new meaning to speed talking by giving that entire speech in a single, agitated breath.

"Calm down, Darlene. I'm fine."

Rebecca felt like an outsider in an alien world as she stepped out of the driver's seat and turned to Darlene. Maybe Justyn was going to make light of the situation, but Rebecca was going to make sure his mother had all the facts.

"He fell off the platform on the stage."

"*Fell*, huh?" She gave Justyn a suspicious look. Then she turned back to Rebecca as though she knew questioning him would be pointless. "How high up?"

"Maybe fifteen feet."

Darlene frowned. "Follow my finger with your eyes." Justyn moved his eyes back and forth, following the path of Darlene's hand, though he did it grudgingly. "Did you hit anything other than your head?"

It was obvious that Justyn had no intention of admitting to anything, so once again Rebecca found herself answering for him. "He hurt his side."

Darlene heaved a heavy sigh. "Better come in the house and let me take a look at it. You come in too, Becca. I can use your help."

Rebecca didn't think it was really possible that the darkly beautiful woman could need help with anything, especially not from someone as blasé as she was. She followed them inside just the same. She needed to know Justyn was going to be all right before she even considered leaving.

Inside the house, it was easy for her to lose track of her thoughts. She might not have noticed as much if she hadn't read Justyn's Wiccan book. She saw evidence of witchcraft everywhere. There was a broom hanging on the door. Above the door was a plaque that announced "Blessed Be", which was a typical Wiccan greeting. There were statues of the Goddess, displayed on shelves, in many different shapes and forms, and pentacles hanging from the walls. A black cat twirled around her ankles. But in contrast, there was an everyday sofa and loveseat combination in the family room. There was a television, too. There was no bubbling cauldron hanging in the fireplace. But there was still no way Rebecca could have walked into the house and not have known that someone unconventional lived there.

"What's all the commotion?" The new voice came from somewhere in the kitchen.

"I *told* you, Matt. Didn't I tell you something happened to him? I *knew* something had happened. And of course he never answers his phone."

Justyn shrugged nonchalantly. "I forgot to charge it."

"You're always right about your premonitions, Darlene. But he can't be hurt too badly if he still has a smart comeback."

A smiling, good-natured man walked out into the living room. He looked like a strange match to the Gothic mother and son duo with his shoulder length blond dread locks, hemp jewelry, and Guatemalan pants. He couldn't have been more than twenty-five, and even that was pushing it. So Rebecca was a little surprised when he walked up to Darlene and kissed her on the cheek. She realized that the young hippie must be Justyn's stepfather.

Matt stepped away from his wife and circled his stepson. He examined Justyn's bruises with concern. But when he spoke, he sounded more like an older brother than a father figure. "Got your butt kicked, huh?"

Justyn rolled his eyes. "Thanks for pointing it out, Matt."

"Well, you still got the girl to come home with you." He smiled at Rebecca and winked a green eye. "It doesn't matter if you win the fight as long as you still get the girl."

Darlene punched his arm. "Keep your words of wisdom to yourself, buddy. I guarantee Becca isn't going to be as easy a conquest as I was."

Rebecca's mind was whirling from the unorthodox conversation. She still hadn't quite gotten past the part where Justyn's mother had realized something was wrong before they had even got there. It was a little creepy, but at the same time, kind of amazing. It made her really start to believe that magic—at least magic by Wiccan standards—really did exist.

Darlene shooed Matt away and led them into Justyn's room. She instructed her son to remove his shirt, which he did obligingly. He had no idea the effect his perfect, muscular chest had on Rebecca's fluctuating heartbeat. Every muscle in her seemed to ache with unfamiliar longing as she watched Darlene examine him. She had to turn her eyes away, and look around at the gargoyle and dragon statues at the other end of the room, so her cheeks would stop burning.

"Looks like we have a few broken ribs." Darlene observed. Then she sighed in exasperation. "Only a son of mine could choose the drama club over football and still come home with broken ribs."

"It that something serious?" Rebecca asked.

Darlene smiled at her concern. "It's not the end of the world. They're going to need to be wrapped. I know some doctors are against that now, but I still think it's the best thing. It will at least make it hurt a little less. Hold on one second. I'll be right back."

Darlene stood up and glided out of the room, leaving Rebecca alone with Justyn. He was trying exceptionally hard to play the tough guy, but it was one role he was having trouble mastering. His coloring was still pasty, and he grimaced almost every time he took a breath. Despite this, he was beautiful. His bare arms rippled with muscles; every sinew and curve of his chest was masculine perfection. Tom would have had a real fight on his hands if the railing hadn't helped him.

Justyn caught her staring, and raised an eyebrow. She walked a little closer, and sat down beside him on the edge of the bed. For the first time, she noticed the tribal tattoo laced around his upper arm in an exotic Celtic design. Rebecca was surprised. She didn't know many people under eighteen who actually had tattoos.

"Is that real?"

He rolled his eyes again. "No, I drew it myself with permanent marker."

Rebecca couldn't be angry about the obvious sarcasm. She heard the hint of laughter in the undertones. Besides, it really was a stupid question. She ran her fingers along the design, feeling that familiar jolt of energy run up her arm as soon as they made contact. She felt him shiver with unexpected pleasure, and was happy to see she could have the same dizzying effect on him that he always had on her.

"Your mom let you do that?"

He laughed, and then flinched because it apparently wasn't a smart thing to do when you had broken ribs. "She helped me pick it out. Darlene is encouraging of individuality and self-expression. She would never do anything to hold back my creativity."

"Are you in a lot of pain?" Rebecca was too worried about the flinching to think anymore about the tattoo, even though she had to admit it was kind of sexy.

"Only when I breathe." She must have looked completely stricken because he immediately softened his tone, and leaned over to squeeze her hand. "It's not *that* bad. Really. And it helps that you're here. To know that you care."

"I *do* care, Justyn," Rebecca whispered. "About a lot more than just your ribs."

He seemed surprised by her honestly, but if he was going to say anything—or perhaps declare his undying love, for example—the moment was ruined when his mother reappeared in the doorway with a roll of bandages in one hand and a steaming mug in the other.

"I made you some willow bark tea," Darlene explained as she placed the cup on his desk. "It will help with the pain. This will work better than any bottle of pills you can purchase at the drugstore. And it's all natural, one hundred percent organic herbs." She gently lifted Justyn's arm out the way, and started to wrap the bandages around the darkening bruises.

"What's willow bark?" Rebecca asked.

"Darlene's what some people would call a kitchen witch. She's into home remedies and old wives' tales," Justyn told her.

Darlene rolled her eyes. "Willow bark is just a plant. Mixed with feverfew and valerian and a few other choice herbs, it will help with whatever ails you. In this house, we're not real big on pumping our bodies full of drugs. Though, I have to tell you, Justyn, by tomorrow you might want to pop at least a couple aspirin. If you think you're hurting now, wait until you wake up in the morning. You'll be lucky if you can get out of bed at all."

Rebecca didn't like the sound of that. She didn't like that Justyn was in pain at all, especially when it was at least inadvertently her fault. Darlene finally finished wrapping his ribs and left them alone. Rebecca hesitantly reached over to run her fingers along Justyn's back, desperate to do something—anything—to ease his suffering.

He looked up at her with a sad expression of his face. It was a strange combination of loneliness and adoration. She had never seen him reveal quite so much of himself in such a simple glance. She discovered that she was even more drawn to him in the midst of his vulnerability. She wanted to kiss him, to touch him, to feel his arms around her. But she was afraid she was going to hurt him. Finally, he took the initiative and lifted up his hand to stroke her cheek. The simple touch sent a surge of electricity through her that ignited every part of her body with fire.

"So long I've lived in solitude.
Love is a joy that I always allude.
All that I ask if that your love will be true . . . ."

He stopped for a minute. It must have been hard to sing, even in such a sweet and delicate whisper. He took a shaky breath before continuing, replacing her name with Christine's in the final line.

"Becca, can I ask this of you?"

In the play, this was where she was supposed to pull off the mask, revealing the twisted horror beneath. But Justyn's mask had already been removed. The Gothic that everyone ridiculed and feared was gone. *Lord Justyn* was gone. And he was simply a boy, a boy falling in love with a girl. His face shown with the brightness of that newfound romance despite the physical pain he was feeling. No matter how hard he tried to hide it, Rebecca knew there was a lighter side to his dark personality.

This time, when he leaned down to kiss her, there were no interruptions. No one pulled away. No one resisted. She felt his lips touch hers and every last shred of doubt simply melted away as she found perfection in that one, gentle, loving kiss.

Chapter Twenty-Five

"Becca, get your skinny white butt over here."

Rebecca wasn't sure how many times Carmen had called her before she finally heard her. Probably a lot judging by the way she was glaring at her and tapping her foot impatiently. Even after she noticed Carmen, she wished she hadn't. She wasn't ready for her good mood to come to an end.

Rebecca had spent the better part of the day floating on her own personal cloud, barely aware of anything that was going on around her in the real world. More than once she had found herself smiling for no reason other than the fact that she caught a glimpse of Justyn in the hall. But the authoritative tone in Carmen's voice immediately wiped the smile from her face and stopped Rebecca in her tracks as she was bending down to deposit her backpack in a corner. She sounded way too serious. It could only mean something bad had happened. Of course, in Carmen's book, something bad could range from a pimple to a near-death experience.

The thought of death instantly sobered her. After all, it had been less than a week since Jay had died. She started to feel a little uneasy, and found herself coming down off the natural high that had kept her bouncing from class to class in a sort of half-dream. What right did she have to be so happy in the midst of so much sadness?

The grim faces of Carmen, Tom, and Debbie made her even more anxious. Tom was especially serious as she came closer, but he also had the grace to look a little sheepish. This was the first time he had dared to come within fifty feet of her since the fight. But the fact that he was full of apologies and looked so utterly pathetic made it hard to stay angry with him, especially considering the kind of week he was having.

"Becca," Tom said slowly. He had trouble meeting her steady, expectant gaze. "You know yesterday was just an . . . an accident." Rebecca raised an eyebrow, a habit she had picked up from Justyn. Tom worked on rewording his apology to make it a little more sincere. "I mean, I know it was wrong of me to sucker punch him the way I did. It wasn't a fair fight. But I was—you know—I was really pissed and I did something stupid. But you have to believe me when I tell you that I never meant for him to *fall*. I would never do something like that . . . not even to *Lord* Justyn."

Rebecca sighed. She knew that Tom wasn't capable of being that violent, but it didn't really change what had happened. Plus, she didn't like his tone of voice when he spoke Justyn's name; it dripped with such obvious loathing. Maybe he hadn't planned the accident, but she wasn't so sure anymore that Tom was actually sorry. Maybe he was sorry that there were witnesses, but she doubted he was sorry that it had happened.

"Don't you think you should be apologizing to Justyn instead of to me?" Her own words held a sharp edge to them. "After all, he's the one with broken bones."

Tom twisted his face into a scowl that could have been a cocky smirk in disguise. So much for his apology—obviously, his words didn't mean very much. Rebecca crossed her arms and huffed. She thought the conversation was over, and she was just about to leave and search out Justyn to see how he was feeling. She turned back in surprise when Debbie came to Tom's assistance, backing up his lack of enthusiasm over a real apology.

"Under the circumstances, I think its best that Tom and Justyn avoid each other as much as possible."

Rebecca couldn't argue as much as she would have liked to. "I guess you're right. We don't need more fist fights."

"It's more than just that, Becca," Carmen said. She didn't bother to elaborate, but the deep lines of worry on her face said more than words. "Tom, you need to tell her what you found out."

Tom appeared stricken. He swallowed hard. He didn't look like he was going to say anything at all without some prompting but, finally, he managed to choke out a few strained words.

"It's . . . it's about Jay."

Rebecca immediately felt her face soften. What right did she have to be so judgmental? She was far from a perfect human being. She had made more than her share of mistakes, including leading Tom on. If she hadn't done that, there wouldn't have been any reason for fighting to begin with.

"Something about the accident?" She put a hand on his shoulder in support.

"That's just it. It *wasn't* an accident," Carmen blurted out.

Rebecca's hand fell away from Tom's arm, at the same time that her mouth popped open in shock. Carmen had never been very good at breaking bad news gently, and this news was just a little more than Rebecca had been ready to hear. She felt her breath catch in her throat. Once again, she felt that now familiar sense of panic. The terrifying sensation of suffocation almost overwhelmed her. It was so much worse than when the curtain had fallen down on her during that first practice, so much more intense.

She thought she had put all thoughts of murder out of her head, especially after the last nearly perfect night with Justyn. She had assured herself it was just her own irrational paranoia and that it was impossible that someone she knew could have the motive, let alone the heart, to kill. She had even dismissed that last phone call as a mean joke. Now all the fears and doubts she had tried to bury in the darkest recesses of her mind were slinking their way back to the surface. In fact, they were front and center, waving giant red flags in front of her eyes. Just three simple words, "not an accident", and Rebecca was drowning in fear and indecision. She knew already who they were going to blame before they said another word.

"Someone cut the break lines in my truck." Tom's face was ten shades of pale as he spoke.

"Let's not beat around the bush," Carmen said, annoyed. "We all know who that *someone* had to be."

Rebecca wanted to yell to keep from having to listen to the words she was dreading to hear. Carmen was untouched by either her or Tom's plagued faces, and was about to continue when Debbie, bless her sweet, gentle soul, interrupted her.

"We can't possibly know anything for sure. Wendy was pretty angry last week. Maybe that newspaper article pushed her over the edge."

Carmen rolled her eyes. "Can you honestly see Wendy climbing underneath a truck? Besides, she doesn't know her way around an engine."

Rebecca was having a little trouble breathing. On some level, as much as she would have liked to have kept Wendy on the top of the suspect list, Rebecca knew how unrealistic it was that she would ever get her hands dirty, literally or figuratively. But it was more than the improbability of Wendy being a suspect that was causing her to feel dizzy and lightheaded. Carmen had reminded her of a conversation she'd had with Justyn on their date. She clearly heard Justyn's voice in her head as they had made their way to Atlantic City.

"I know my way around an engine." he had bragged matter-of-factly.

It hadn't seemed like a big deal at the time. Most guys did know a little something about cars. But now those innocent words were suddenly as harsh as any threat. The flashing red lights in Rebecca's eyes were blaring now, blinding her. Her throat was so constricted that even if she wanted to speak, to share her dark thoughts, it would have been impossible. But of course she didn't want to share them. She didn't want to admit to her friends that they might be right.

"But why would Justyn want to kill Jay? He had no reason to hurt him."

Thank goodness for Debbie. She was the voice of reason. She was Rebecca's own personal guardian angel, complete with fluffy wings and shining halo. Carmen, on the other hand, might as well have been carrying a pitchfork.

"Don't be such a moron, Debbie." she snorted. "It was *Tom's* truck. Jay only borrowed it. Obviously, Jay wasn't the intended target."

"No . . . I was."

Tom's voice sounded controlled, but Rebecca could sense the hysteria lurking under the surface. He was desperately trying to keep it under control, but at any moment, he was going to snap and fall into a million pieces—pieces that would be impossible to put back together again. Rebecca understood what he was feeling. She knew what it was like to be completely eaten alive with guilt. She was right there with him, on the very brink of madness as that guilt threatened to swallow her whole—guilt over the fact that she might have played a role in Jay's death.

The whole world was spinning. She really thought she was going to faint. She might have even welcomed blissful unconsciousness. It was better than letting in those dark thoughts, those horrible doubts. Doubts made her feel wretched with disloyalty, but they were impossible to ignore. It all made too much sense. The means, the motive, the opportunity—it was all there. But could Justyn really have wanted to eliminate his competition permanently? Was it total vanity for her to think *she*, of all people, was worth killing for? She knew Justyn had a dark side, but was he really capable of cold-blooded murder?

"There's no doubt about it, Becca." Carmen continued heartlessly. "Justyn is a psychotic freak. He probably killed Jay *and* Mr. Russ. You need to stay away from him or you're going to be next."

They were harsh words even though they were spoken with only sincere concern for her well-being. Rebecca knew she should agree with Carmen. But even if she was capable of moving her mouth to form a coherent sentence, she wasn't sure that the words would come out right. And that was probably because the thought of ending her relationship with Justyn was almost as horrible as the possibility of him being a murderer.

Her friends didn't understand her silence. They were giving each other strange, questioning glances. She was sure she could read their minds. *Does Becca get off on masochism? Does Becca really think that Justyn might be innocent? Does*

Becca have a death wish? Is Becca completely insane? All of them were valid questions that she didn't have answers to.

"There's more," Debbie said quietly. "Something we overheard Miss King say after you left on Friday."

Of *course* there was more. She hadn't fallen into a state of complete catatonia yet. There *had* to be more, just enough to finish the job. Then she could be on her way to get fitted for her straitjacket. She fought the urge to cover her ears with her hands.

"Someone sawed the railing on the platform," Tom told her. "That's the reason why Justyn fell."

Rebecca let out the breath she hadn't realized she was holding. That wasn't so bad. She had already figured that out by herself.

"Obviously, whoever did it had no idea that Tom was going to go ballistic," Carmen added. "Which can only mean one thing . . . ."

Rebecca had never once thought about the reasoning behind the sawed railing. She hadn't had time to think about it. She was too busy coddling Justyn over his injuries. Taking care of him was all that mattered at the time. She had never once thought about the danger the compromised prop had presented to *her.* Never considered for a second that *she* could have been the one to fall. And there would have only have been one person up there with her. Only one person who could have made the possibility become a harsh reality. Suddenly it seemed obvious. It was a bright neon danger sign flashing in her mind's eye. Rebecca didn't want to ask, didn't want to hear the words spoken aloud, but she couldn't resist. Morbid fascination was taking control again.

"What . . . what does it mean?"

"Whoever sawed that railing probably meant for *you* to fall, Becca," Debbie said softly, verifying Rebecca's own awful conclusions. "And it was probably *Justyn* that wanted you to fall."

Chapter Twenty-Six

Rebecca's gasp was drowned out by the sound of the rustling curtain. They were all startled by the interruption and fell silent as Justyn stepped out onto the stage. Why did he have to have the ability to move seemingly without sound? And why did he always have to sneak up on her at the most inopportune moments? It was obvious from the look on his face that he had heard every word her friends had said. Not even the large dark bruise that covered the left half of his forehead could take her attention away from the devastated look in his eyes.

She was so stupid, so disloyal, so easily influenced by other people's opinions. Why didn't she say something? She should have defended him. Or walked away. Or done something that might have made that pained look on his face disappear. The trouble was, she wasn't entirely sure that she didn't agree with Tom's conclusions. She wasn't one hundred percent certain that Justyn wasn't the one who had killed Jay—or more precisely, the one who had wanted to kill Tom.

Justyn didn't say a word. He didn't acknowledge the others at all. He only looked at her with such utter despair that it completely broke her heart. She couldn't stay silent any longer.

"Justyn . . . ." she began.

He shook his head and disappeared back the way he had come. She wanted to call him back and tell him she was sorry. She wanted to throw herself in his arms and make everything beautiful again, the way it had been the night before. She wondered if that was ever going to be possible. She suddenly knew exactly how Judas and Benedict Arnold must have felt when they came to realize the full extent of their treachery.

"Oh, God, what did I do . . . ?"

"What did *you* do?" Tom snorted. "*You* didn't do anything. Be glad if he stays away from you from now on. You'll be a lot safer."

Rebecca felt her cheeks flush hotly. What right did Tom, Carmen, and Debbie have to play judge and jury? She knew the person she was really angry with was herself, but it didn't stop her from taking that anger out on Tom.

"Safer? With *you*?" Rebecca huffed. "Maybe until you decide to toss *me* off the stage."

Tom flinched as though she had slapped him. Good. He should feel bad about what he had done. He should feel terrible.

"Come on, Becca. You know I didn't mean to hurt anyone."

"Do I, Tom? How do I know that? Maybe the person I should be staying away from is *you!*"

Rebecca stormed away, ignoring the gaping mouths of Carmen and Debbie. She tried to follow the path that Justyn had taken, but wasn't really surprised when she was unable to find him. He was probably hiding in the shadows somewhere, justifiably sulking.

He didn't reappear until it was time for his first scene, and even then, he refused to look her in the eyes and avoided touching her as much as possible. Only when they reached the scene where Christine removed the phantom's mask for the first time did she see any real emotion in his face. That emotion was pure fury. The terrifying sentiment was echoed clearly in the words on his song. There was no doubt in her mind that those words were directed at her.

> *"Temptress of lies with your unearthly wiles.*
> *A succubus hidden behind lovely smiles*
> *Shrew that was sent from the depths of hell*
> *If you meant to destroy me than you have done well."*

He knocked down multiple iron candle holders as he raged across the stage, all the while keeping the one side of his face hidden with his hand. Erik was trying to shield both Christine and himself from the horrible view of his malformation. Justyn was just trying to mask his pain.

If Rebecca hadn't already been cowering on the ground in her role, she might have wound up on her knees trembling anyway, so powerful was the extent of his performance. He sang each word with the passion of true agony. In that moment, he was the tortured man who lived in seclusion under the opera house—not really a phantom, but just a lonely, broken man who had known nothing but rejection and pain throughout the whole of his life. A man who was hurt and betrayed by the only woman he had shown his true face to. A woman who had shied away from that face in fear even though she knew better than anyone that the man beneath the mask wasn't really a monster.

In that moment, Rebecca hated herself more than ever, and wondered how she could have ever doubted Justyn. She was just as weak as Christine, just as treacherous. Just as foolish because she was throwing away the possibility of real love due to childish fears and doubts.

Rebecca was so lost in her own thoughts that she didn't even realize when Justyn stopped singing. The music continued to play, but he had fallen into silence. She knew something was wrong, even before she looked up. He was standing in front of one of the many mirrors, and in the reflection, she could see the grimace he was trying so hard to hide. He was bent over, clutching his side. It gave Rebecca even more reason to chide herself. She should have known that he would still be in pain. He had just broken his ribs. And even though his mother was a kitchen witch, she wasn't going to be able to magically heal broken bones over night. In fact, Darlene had said herself that he would be hurting a lot worse the day after the accident. Judging from the look on his face, he must have been in agony. And she had added insult to injury, hurting him in a much deeper way. What kind of person was she?

"Cut the music!" Miss King called out in disgust. She climbed up onto the stage with her hands on her hips. "Justyn, is there some sort of problem?"

Justyn made an effort to stand a little straighter as he turned to face the director, but he couldn't quite manage to drop his hand from his side. He whispered something to her, too softly for Rebecca to hear from the spot where she was still crouching in a huddle on the stage. The teacher's face softened considerably.

"All right. Go get some rest. Opening night is only ten days away. I need you fully recovered by then."

Justyn nodded and took a few tentative steps down from the stage. He was halfway to the door before Rebecca was finally over the shock of him cutting practice for the second day in a row and was spurred into action. She pulled herself up from the floor, and went over to Miss King, tapping her on the arm before she could go back to her regular seat in the front row.

"Miss King, is Justyn all right?"

She sighed, very heavily. "He wasn't feeling well, Rebecca. I told him he was excused."

Rebecca chewed her lower lip with worry. The teacher was watching her with a wary expression, waiting for the next drama to unfold in the never—ending string of dramas she'd been forced to endure since she had made her casting choices.

"If it's all right, I'd like to go with him. If he's not feeling well, someone should drive him home."

Miss King rolled her eyes. "Oh, Becca, I swear this love triangle of yours is going to drive me to an early retirement. But fine . . . go. What good is Christine without the phantom, anyway?"

"Thank you, Miss King!" Rebecca called back as she ran to grab her book bag. She had just swung it over her shoulder and was getting ready to dart back down the steps when Tom grabbed her arm.

"You aren't going after him, are you, Becca? Not again."

Rebecca sighed, even more deeply than Miss King had. "Yes, Tom, I am. He's hurt and he needs me."

"I'm getting a little tired of playing second to that freak show," Tom told her. She swore she could hear his teeth grinding. "If you go, that's it! We're through, Becca. For good."

Rebecca stopped for a minute. Four years of fantasies were coming to an end. Four years of imagining herself beside the school heartthrob. Tom had proven himself to be a lot less perfect than she had thought. He had his jealous side and he was showing that right now. He was squeezing her arm so tightly she was sure he would leave a bruise. How did she know he wasn't the person who had been terrorizing her? If she was truly the motive, didn't it reason that Tom could be just as guilty as Justyn? Maybe Jay's accident had been planned by them as a cover up, but got out of hand. Maybe Tom had even killed his friend on purpose to throw everyone off track. It was a stretch, but wasn't it possible that the roles of Erik and Raoul had been reversed in their real life play?

She pulled her arm away from Tom. "Then I guess we're through."

Rebecca ran down the stage, and out of the auditorium without a backward glance. She hoped she wasn't too late to catch up with him. Luckily, Justyn wasn't moving as quickly as he normally did. Taking the hallway at a sprint, she was able to reach him just as he was pushing open the main doors.

"Jus . . . Justyn . . . wait," she called out, still slightly breathless from running.

He paused for a millisecond, and she knew he heard her, but he kept walking straight through the door without turning around. What he didn't realize was that Rebecca had her stubborn side too, and she wasn't going to be put off that easily.

"Come on, Justyn," she said once she had caught up. She slowed her steps to walk in stride with him. "Don't be this way."

He grunted. "What way is that, Becca? I'm not in character for the crazed killer you apparently think I am? Would it help if I pulled out my ritual dagger and held it against your throat?"

The harsh tone in his voice made her flinch. "That isn't fair. I wasn't the one who said those things."

"But you didn't defend me either. I thought after last night . . . I thought you had realized."

He let the sentence trail off. Rebecca lifted the eyes she had lowered in shame, too curious not to ask. "Realized what?"

Justyn grimaced, sucked in a hard breath through his teeth, and sat down on the bench at the edge of the student walkway. "Nothing, forget it. I don't really feel up to convincing you that I'm not a murderer right now."

Rebecca sighed and sat down next to him. She wanted to touch him, to comfort him, not only physically but emotionally. But she didn't know what to say, and she was too afraid that he would push her away if she reached out to him.

"Are you okay?" That was the best she could manage.

"Considering the fact that your hero dumped me off a fifteen foot platform, I'd say I'm doing just fine."

Rebecca shook her head. "Tom isn't my hero. He's a jerk."

Justyn raised an eyebrow. "You're just figuring that out?"

Rebecca felt a little annoyed at his patronizing tone of voice. Here she was, swallowing her pride, pushing aside her doubts, just to make sure he was all right, and he was giving her his normal Gothic attitude. She felt like tossing him off another platform.

"You know what, Justyn, you're a jerk, too. The two of you have been treating me like some sort of prize in the macho wars since day one."

He sighed and put his head in his hands. "If you think I'm that much of a jerk, then why did you waste your time following me out here?"

His voice didn't have half the strength that it normally did, and she could see that it was hard for him to breathe without grimacing. He was making a valiant effort to hide it from her. It made her feel even guiltier.

"I'm the biggest jerk of all. I shouldn't be arguing with you when you're in pain. It's just that you're so frustrating sometimes."

"You just *can't* make it through a single statement without insulting me, can you?" He tried to smile but it turned into a grimace, and escalated into a moan. He put his head in his hands. "*Aghhh*, I should have listened to Darlene and stayed home today."

"Darlene *is* a pretty smart lady," Rebecca agreed. "Are your ribs hurting a lot?"

"My whole body feels like it's been hit by a truck. And my head feels like it's going to explode."

Rebecca reached out her hand and gingerly touched the darkening bruise on his forehead. Even that light touch made him flinch. "You really got your butt kicked, huh?"

He shrugged. "What can I say? I'm an artist. Not a jock."

"I suppose offering you a couple aspirin would be pointless."

"I told you before, I don't like to poison my body. Besides . . . ." He puffed his chest out to try to look tough. It wasn't very convincing. "It's not a big deal. I can take it."

"Well, I don't have any willow bark tea handy, but maybe I can help a little."

"How's that?"

"I don't suppose you're opposed to back rubs?" she asked shyly, and felt her cheeks flush.

He had to clear his throat to respond as he turned just as red as Rebecca had. "No, that's pretty holistic."

"Okay, then. Sit up a little."

Rebecca reached her hands around to touch his shoulders, rubbing them gently. He was tense at first, a little unsure. She could feel where his muscles were tight and cramped. She kneaded the tight spots, and before long she felt his body begin to relax. She was never as sure of her fingers as she was at that moment. A warm heat was running through them and she knew he must have felt that same electrical charge that she felt every time they made physical contact. It was a connection that went beyond the physical and into something much more intense.

They sat like that for what could have been five minutes or five hours. Rebecca had lost her concept of time. They were silent for a while, but then he tilted his head up to look at her. Dark eyes watched her, filled with their normal melancholy, but also tinged with doubt and a little confusion. He wasn't sure why she was there after the conversation he had overheard. She wasn't sure why she was there, either. She only knew it was an urge she couldn't deny, like the primal instinct to survive at all costs. Her instinct was to be with Justyn whatever the cost, however irrational and possibly dangerous it might turn out to be.

Justyn moved closer as he pushed a loose strand of hair out of her eyes and tucked it behind her ear. He moved his fingers down to stroke her cheek. He never broke eye contact, forcing her to look into the mirror of his soul. Rebecca felt her breath coming faster, her pulse starting to race. Her hands dropped from his shoulders to wrap around his waist, careful to avoid the area she knew was hurt. He moved closer to her lips, and she had no intention of denying him. She had no intention of denying him ever again.

"What is it about you that makes me feel like you've stolen not only my heart, but my soul," she whispered as she leaned her head on his shoulder.

He smiled sadly, and continued to caress her hair as he sang to her in his clear, beautiful tenor.

> *"Your soul is filled with a beauty so rare.*
> *With the power to bring both love and despair.*
> *Which will you bring me, my angel of song?*
> *A quick painful end or a love that's life long?"*

Beautiful words. Romantic lines from the play they both loved. Normally, those words coupled with his enchanting musical voice, would automatically make Rebecca swoon. But suddenly something occurred to her. It had never seemed quite as ominous as it did at that moment. Instantly her hands fell away from Justyn. She jolted back on the bench as far as was possible without falling off the edge.

Those words. They weren't exactly the same as the ones she had heard before in the muffled distorted voice of her twisted stalker. It wasn't the same verses as the ones written on the threatening notes. But both Justyn and the stalker used the same motis operandi. Could that really be a coincidence? The voice had a different tone. But could it have been Justyn's voice? She couldn't be sure. As the familiar sense of fear and mistrust slithered up her spine, she felt herself pulling further and further away from him, even as Justyn reached out to her.

"What's wrong?"

"What you just said, what you're always saying . . . it's just like the message, like the calls and the letters."

"What are you talking about?"

"The person who has been threatening me, the person who killed Jay and maybe even Mr. Russ. They always use lines from the play, just like . . . just like you. "

Justyn looked confused at first and then horrified as the realization of what she was saying truly sunk in. She knew he was a good actor. His reaction didn't really mean anything.

"Becca, it's just a coincidence." He swore to her. "I was just trying to be romantic. I thought you liked it when I quoted the play . . . I'm sorry if I scared you."

He tried to reach out to touch her hand, but Rebecca jumped up off the bench, nearly tripping over her forgotten book bag in her sudden, panic stricken desire to escape.

"No, no . . . don't touch me."

She was really starting to freak out. She couldn't control it. Hysteria was taking over. She was breathing hard, half crouched and ready to pounce. She was like a frightened, cornered animal.

"You really think I did all those things, don't you?" The misery in his voice was undeniable, but Rebecca was too overcome with her own fear to dwell on it. "Why, Becca? Because I dress in black? Because I wear a pentacle around my neck? I thought you were different. I thought you could see past the stereotypes. I thought you knew who I was on the *inside*. You say you love the story of Erik, but you do you really understand it? It's supposed to teach you that it isn't the way someone looks that makes him a monster, but the way he's treated that can turn him into one."

Rebecca couldn't meet his eyes. The way he was looking at her was too heartbreaking. His words made her ashamed. She wished she could tell him he was wrong, that she wasn't that superficial. But she knew that it would be a lie, at least partially. It wasn't just because all the evidence pointed to him, but because he seemed to fit. If there was a killer on the loose, it had to be the freaky Goth boy, right? That was the conclusion everyone else had made. And she was the one who always followed the crowd.

She couldn't deny it, not to him or to herself. She was afraid of him. Yet, something deeper inside of her was still drawn to him. She realized that despite her suspicions, she would never be complete without him, and she didn't really want to let him go. But she didn't have much of a choice in the matter.

A little gold Suzuki pulled up in front of the school and beeped the horn. Through the open window, Darlene smiled and waved at her cheerfully, completely oblivious to the nightmare that Rebecca and her son were living at that moment. Somehow, Rebecca managed to lift her own hand in response, but she couldn't even begin to force her lips into a smile. Darlene must have noticed her lack of enthusiasm because she frowned.

Justyn had picked up his bag, and started toward the car, moving slowly and with some difficulty, obviously in a great deal of pain. Rebecca watched him go, knowing she should be helping him, but afraid to move or even to speak because she knew that no matter what she said now, it was only going to come out wrong. Justyn always had a way of saying exactly what needed to be said.

"You were never a prize to me, Becca. From the first time I saw you on that stage, even before I heard your voice, I knew that I loved you. I thought I had found my soul mate. I guess I was wrong."

Rebecca choked back a sob as he eased himself into the passenger seat. He loved her. Those were words she would have given anything to hear just a few short hours ago. Words that would have made her fling herself into his arms with reckless abandon. But now those words only tore her heart to shreds. They made her realize what a complete fool she was.

Even though they were too far for her to hear, she knew Darlene was asking him what had happened. Justyn just shook his head, and then leaned back against the headrest with his eyes closed. Darlene glared at her in a way that was beyond chilling. Rebecca had the distinct feeling that it wasn't such a good idea to make a witch angry. What was worse was the horrible realization that she had just broken Justyn's heart, and most likely lost him forever. And whether he was her real life phantom or not, she wasn't sure she was ready to live without him.

Chapter Twenty-Seven

An entire week went by without one single word from Justyn outside of when he spoke to her as Erik. Even then, his eyes seemed to glaze over, and she felt like he wasn't really seeing her at all. She couldn't believe how much she missed him. She had even resorted to changing her routes between classes so she might catch a glimpse of him. But he didn't acknowledge her when she passed him in the hallway. She was invisible again—completely invisible.

Tom wasn't talking to her either, outside of the very casual, or the very necessary. Rebecca sighed as she watched him sitting quietly across the lunchroom. He had gone back to his old table with the basketball team, but he didn't join in with their conversation. He wasn't touching the pizza on his tray either, and she doubted that it had anything to do with whether or not it was actually edible. She had seen him scarf down worse. But everything had changed since Jay had died. It was like a part of Tom had gone with him. He looked so sad and lost without his friend at his side. And she had gone and made things even worse for him—just one more thing for her to feel guilty about. She was going to have to start a running list so she didn't lose track of all the reasons why she should hate herself.

"What are you moping about now?" Carmen asked.

Rebecca stirred around her chocolate pudding with her plastic spoon and sighed again, a little louder this time. "I'm moping because I've single handedly managed to alienate the only two guys who have ever given a crap about me in one fell swoop."

Debbie put a consoling hand on her shoulder. "You shouldn't be so hard on yourself. None of this is your fault."

Carmen snorted.

"I really can't stand it." Rebecca continued. "I just wish they would give me a chance to explain things. But neither one of them will even talk to me. I guess they must really hate me."

"What do you expect, Becca?" Carmen huffed. Rebecca was taken aback by the harshness in her tone. She had expected some sympathy from her friends. "You dangled yourself in front of them like a glorified fishing hook, and once you had them caught in your snare, you left them flopping around on the shore until they withered. Then you tossed them back in the water like so much garbage. Of *course* they hate you! To be honest, I'm a little disgusted myself."

Rebecca and Debbie were both equally amazed by Carmen's outburst, though it was a lot harder for Rebecca to hear. She felt her lower lip start to tremble, and had to fight back the childish urge to burst into tears like a little girl.

She didn't like it, but she had to admit that Carmen's metaphor was surprisingly accurate. Rebecca *had* dangled herself in front of both Tom and Justyn, using her voice as bait. She had enjoyed having the attentions of not just one, but two handsome guys. Before she had become an overnight diva, she had never had the attention of *anyone*. Once she had a small taste of what popularity had to offer, she couldn't get enough. She had secretly enjoyed watching the boys compete for her attention. And who *didn't* like the thought of two guys fighting over them? Feelings had been trampled because of her vanity. It was no wonder they couldn't stand the sight of her. She couldn't stand the sight of herself.

"That was a little harsh, Carmen," Debbie chastised. "Don't you think Becca's been through enough without you coming down on her, too?"

"Oh, sorry," Carmen said sarcastically. Her voice went up almost a whole octave. "I keep forgetting this is all about *poor* Becca. Who cares that Jay is *dead*. Who cares that Tom is devastated about losing his best friend *and* his girlfriend. Who cares that Justyn is most likely guilty of murder in the first degree. Let's forget about *all* that. Let's all just sit around and feel sorry for *poor* Becca because *she's* been through *so* much."

Carmen's face was beat red with fury, her dark brown eyes flashing dangerously. Rebecca flinched with every word that she spat in her direction. Each one was like a physical blow. It wasn't the first time Rebecca had seen her friend that furious. Carmen had a bad temper. It often got the better of her, and had ended in more than one suspension over the years. It was the first time that Rebecca had seen that temper turned on her.

"Carmen." Rebecca pleaded. "What did I do to make you so angry?"

"Nothing, Becca. Nothing—except you took away the only guy I ever really wanted."

Rebecca blanched. She had never expected to hear that. She had never thought that Carmen really *liked* Tom. Sure, they had both spent many a slumber party imagining him escorting them to the prom. Rebecca hadn't realized Carmen cared about him more deeply than the typical popular guy infatuation. As usual, she was too wrapped up in herself to see what was going on around her.

"If you were interested in Tom, you should have told me!" Rebecca exclaimed. "I would never have stood in your way!"

"It's not even *like* that," Carmen shouted. The cafeteria was pretty noisy, but a few people still turned around to stare at them. "I was *happy* for you at first. I wasn't jealous because I really believed a sweet girl like you would make Tom happier than a pushy big mouth like me. I thought you'd make a great couple. And what more could I want for my best friend than for her to have the perfect guy? But then that vampire freak comes along . . . ."

"He's *not* a freak." Rebecca interrupted. "You don't know anything about Justyn."

Who was Carmen to judge her? She flitted from one guy to another every week, and never worried about their feelings. And why did she constantly have to put Justyn down? Even if it was too late for it to make a difference, Rebecca thought she needed to make things up to him by defending him as much as possible, the way she should have all along.

"That's good, Becca." Carmen was about ready to explode. Maybe Rebecca should have just kept her mouth shut and let her vent. She could see the veins throbbing in her forehead. It wasn't a good sign. "Keep defending the serial killer. At this rate, you'll probably be the only two left to walk down the aisle at graduation."

"Don't you think you're being a *little* melodramatic?" Debbie asked her. "Come on, guys. We're friends. Sure, the past few weeks have been rough, but we can get through this if we stick together."

Poor Debbie. Always trying to keep the peace in a war zone. Always getting caught in the crossfire.

"You know what, Deb, if you want to stick with this two-faced backstabber, then that's fine," Carmen declared with a flip of her black hair. "But as for me, I've had it with her. This friendship is over."

With that, Carmen picked up her tray and tossed her uneaten lunch into the nearest trashcan. Rebecca watched her storm through the cafeteria doors with a heavy heart. Her senior year wasn't going at all the way she had planned. First, she lost her would-be boyfriend. Now her best friend was walking out on her, too. Had she really turned into a miserable, prissy diva, just like Carlotta? Had her stardom, however trivial, gone to her head? She must be doing something horribly wrong when everyone she cared about was turning their backs on her. Well, almost everyone.

"Don't worry about, Carmen." Debbie consoled. "You know what a hot head she can be. She'll calm down. She didn't really mean the things she said."

Rebecca gave her a half-hearted smile for the effort. "We both know Carmen doesn't say things she doesn't mean."

"You haven't done anything wrong, Becca."

"That's not true, Deb. I've done *everything* wrong." She sighed. "But I'm going to find some way to make it all right again."

Chapter Twenty-Eight

It was opening night.

The six weeks of rehearsals had seemed to go on forever while she waited for this night to arrive. Now that it was here, Rebecca wished that practices could have gone on indefinitely. She had gotten used to the auditorium being scattered with thirty or forty people at a time. She had thought a few more—a few *hundred* more—wouldn't really make that much difference.

She had been wrong.

Rebecca had made the mistake of peeking out from behind the curtain just as the orchestra was warming up. She had hoped to spot her parents in the crowd. She thought seeing their proud faces would calm her frazzled nerves. Instead of seeing her mother's round, smiling face or her father's enthusiastic thumbs up, she saw throngs of strangers filling row after row of seats. It suddenly seemed like the auditorium stretched out into infinity. The frowning faces that stared up at the stage seemed harsh and judgmental. How was she supposed to face that crowd? How was she going to make it through the night without having a heart attack?

Back in the girl's dressing room, Rebecca stared at her reflection in the mirror as she willed her pounding heart to slow to a regular pattern. She hardly recognized the face that stared back at her. Maybe it was because it wasn't really her face she was seeing at all. It was Christine's.

Her long, billowy gown was as beautiful as it was elegant. She was hardly worthy of something so spectacular. The iridescent skirt was sky blue with an over-skirt in a deeper shade of azure and a drawstring waist. It flailed out dramatically around her ankles. The matching bodice was complete with bell sleeves, a plunging neckline and a lace trim. It fit her curves snugly and was very flattering to her skin tone. The over-sized bustle under the skirt made it a little difficult to maneuver in tight corners but she was getting used to turning sideways when she had to walk through doors. A lace choker and a faux amethyst brooch completed the Victorian attire. Rebecca had never felt quite so feminine.

The costume was only the beginning of the trials of getting ready. She had sat through more than an hour of primping at her dressing table while three other girls worked on perfecting her hair and face. They yanked and poked, painted and brushed until they felt they had completed their masterpiece. They curled her long brown hair into perfect ringlets, and pulled it back on the sides with old-fashioned pearl combs. Her make-up was layered on so thickly, she was sure she would have to chisel it off when the show was over. Even with the excess of powder and blush, Rebecca still looked a little peaked. When she thought again about the crowd that was waiting for her on the other side of the curtain, she swore she saw herself begin to turn a little green.

"You look so beautiful, Becca!"

Rebecca did her best to force a grateful smile. "Thanks, Deb. So do you."

The simple black gown of Madame Giry was the dress of a Victorian widow. Even though it was much more matronly than Rebecca's dress, with a higher collar and a lot less puffiness, Debbie still looked exceptionally pretty. The straight skirt and button down blouse had a way of complementing Debbie's tall, stocky frame, especially with the long blonde wig that was pulled back into a braid.

"You should grow your hair long," Rebecca told her. "It suits you."

Debbie blushed a little. "Really?"

"Yeah definitely . . . it . . . ." She paused in mid-sentence. Rebecca moaned as her stomach did an acrobatic somersault worthy of the Olympics. She closed her eyes, and tried to will the waves of nausea away. The last thing she needed was to ruin her costume. "Ohhh, God . . . ."

"Becca, are you okay?" Debbie exclaimed. "You look like you're going to pass out."

"Just . . . just a little performance anxiety," Rebecca managed to stutter through a shaky breath. "Really, Deb, I have no idea how I'm going to make it through the show tonight. I seriously think I'm going to throw up the second I step out onto the stage."

"Come on, Becca, it's not as bad as all that."

Rebecca and Debbie both looked up in surprise at the new voice. It was a voice dripping with obvious sarcasm. Wendy had joined them, looking as perfect as any *Barbie* doll, even in the exaggeratedly elaborate pink gown of Carlotta. The cynical smile she wore could have been part of the costume, it fit so thoroughly with the nasty character she portrayed.

"Leave her alone, Wendy," Debbie barked.

She might as well have been a ghost. Wendy completely ignored her. "Just think of it, Becca. The curtain rises. The lights flicker on." She gestured with her arms for emphasis. "*You're* the star, Becca. A million faces will be looking up at the stage. A million eyes, and they will *all* be watching *you*."

"Knock it off, Wendy," Debbie said through clenched teeth. "Why do you always have to be such a bitch?"

Rebecca didn't say anything at all, but she felt her stomach lurch. Her face drained of what little color it had left and she had to hold onto the dressing table to keep her unsteady legs from going out from under her. Wendy knew exactly what she was doing, and she gleefully continued on with her torture tactics.

"Everyone one of those people will be waiting, Becca. Waiting for your voice to crack. Waiting for you to forget a line. Waiting for *you* to fail . . . ."

She could see it all playing out in her head, exactly the way Wendy described it. Everything would go fine until she made that one terrible mistake. Until she tripped over her long skirt or forgot what she had do to in a scene. At best, the audience would laugh—at *her*. Or worse, they would boo her off the stage and she would never be able to show her face in school, or anywhere else, ever again.

Rebecca couldn't take it anymore. Her stomach did one last painful flip, and she pressed her hand over her mouth and ran from the dressing room. She heard Wendy laughing heartily in the background at her abrupt departure, but it didn't matter anymore what Wendy was saying or doing. Rebecca's immediate concern was finding a bathroom. She realized almost instantly that she wasn't going to have enough time to make it all the way to the end of the hallway to the nearest ladies room. When she saw the trashcan in the corner, she made a mad dash for it, and quickly deposited the contents of her stomach.

She wasn't sure how long she stood there, pale and trembling, using the edges of the trashcan to try to keep herself from sliding to the ground. She wished that she could just die and be put out of her misery once and for all. Her stomach continued to heave long after it was completely emptied. She was feeling dizzy and was a little worried that she might pass out right there in the hallway, when suddenly she felt strong arms support her around her waist.

"It's all right, Becca." A gentle voice soothed her. A cool hand brushed across her forehead. "You're going to be fine."

She didn't need to open her eyes. She would have known that voice anywhere. She recognized the familiar touch of his fingers as they caressed her back. Just having him nearby was enough to make her feel better. Rebecca tried to hold back the sobs of gratitude that would have ruined whatever was left of her makeup as she threw herself in his arms.

"Oh, Justyn!"

He didn't push her away, but she could tell by his stiff posture that he wasn't nearly as enthusiastic about their reunion as she was. He gave her a quick hug before releasing her. She felt more than a little disappointed when he let her go.

"Are you sick?" It was a silly question considering he had just caught with her with her head hanging over a trashcan. But at least he cared enough to ask. That had to be a good sign.

"Just nerves," she admitted, and blushed when she realized the full extent of her humiliation. He had just watched her puke her guts up. How much worse could things get? "Boy, do I feel like an idiot."

He smiled just a little. "Don't be embarrassed. When I did my first play, I threw up every night for a week."

"Really?" Rebecca was surprised by the confession. "You always seem so cool and collected. I can't imagine you ever being nervous about anything."

"Looks can be deceiving."

That was true enough. No one knew it better than Justyn. At the moment, he looked no less than irresistible. The black cape, the ruffled blouse, the long formal tailcoat—they all made him look as though he might have stepped through a time warp. Without his normal facial piercings to give him away, there was no way to tell that he belonged to the twenty- first century.

The white mask that covered the left half of his face only added to his mysterious appeal. Rebecca wondered what he looked like underneath the mask. Only Miss King had seen a dress rehearsal of the make-up job Justyn insisted on doing himself. After he won her approval, he convinced her that it would have more shock value opening night if everyone, including the rest of the cast, were seeing his version of the phantom for the first time.

Justyn cleared his throat awkwardly. Rebecca hadn't realized she was gawking at him until that moment. She felt her cheeks start to burn. But still she couldn't tear her eyes away. He just looked too good. There was no way she *couldn't* stare at him.

"Well, if you're feeling better, I really should get going. I need to get ready for curtain call."

"Justyn, please, wait . . . ." Rebecca took hold of his arm and pulled him back before he could leave. "Can we talk?"

He wouldn't look her in the eye. "I don't think there's anything left to say."

"If you'd let me, I'd like to say I'm sorry," Rebecca said softly. "I'd like to ask for your forgiveness."

He nodded. "Apology accepted. But it doesn't change anything between us, Becca. You can't have a relationship without trust."

"But I *do* trust you, Justyn." Rebecca swore. "I think I always did. I just didn't know it."

He finally looked up at her, but it wasn't the look she expected. His eyes were glassy, glazed with terrible sadness. "But *I* don't trust *you* anymore, Becca," he whispered. "So, like I told you, there's nothing left to say. Except maybe goodbye."

Justyn disappeared behind the boy's dressing room with a whirl of his cape before she could even process what had happened. It was all over between them. She realized that she had ruined everything, and it was hard to care anymore about how her make-up looked as one tear snuck free and trickled down her cheek. It was hard to care about anything, including the play, when she felt like her heart was breaking into pieces.

Chapter Twenty-Nine

It was time. There was no way to procrastinate and no way to delay the inevitable. The opening scene had already begun. Tom and Carmen, both friends turned enemies, were out on the stage dressed as senior citizens. They were making bids on the phantom's old music box at an auction at the opera house, which leads them to reminiscence about the past, about the time when the phantom roamed. They would have to move like lightning to change back into their younger counterparts before they had to appear in the next scene.

The next scene—that would be her *first* scene!

Rebecca trembled; she trembled so hard it was probably registering on the Richter scale. Her hands were shaking as if she had Parkinson's disease. The phantom's theme song burst from the orchestra pit. She was sure the whole auditorium, even the people in the furthest rows, was going to be able to see how terrified she was. How was she going to survive? How was she going to make it through the next two hours?

She could hear the rumbles and squeaks as the stagehands changed the backdrop and props from an old deserted opera house to a new and elaborately decorated one. Then the curtains were pulled back and Wendy was on stage, strutting around in her jeweled gown with the chorus girls in line behind her, barking orders at everyone in true Carlotta style. There was no sign of any anxiety on her face. She didn't appear worried that she would make a blundering fool of herself. She was all confidence. Rebecca envied her.

She only had a few seconds left in the safety of the shadows, just a moment before her big debut performance. The only problem was that her legs were frozen in place. They were molded out of Jell-O, too unstable to carry her forward, even though she knew that she had to move.

"You're going to be fine."

Justyn. It was Justyn.

She was too terrified to be excited that he was there. Too scared to be impressed that he was actually speaking to her for the second time that night. Too numb with fear to let herself realize that it must mean he still cared that he was there at all, even if he was trying his best to hide it.

"That's easy for you to say," she muttered. Then she realized she couldn't breathe. "I . . . I can't do this. I can't . . . ."

"Yes, you can," he insisted.

"No, no I can't." She was bordering on complete hysteria.

"Becca, look at me . . . ."

He took hold of her shoulders, forcing her rebellious body to shift and face him. She couldn't help but stare into his eyes, so deep, so beautiful, so hypnotizing, even in the shadows of the phantom's mask. She wondered if he was using his witchcraft to put a spell on her. As she stood mesmerized by his eyes, she was undergoing a metamorphosis. Suddenly her heartbeat became more even, her legs felt a little steadier. She was no longer convulsing with tremors. She was still nervous, but she wasn't completely overwhelmed with terror.

Justyn nodded confidently. He could see he was getting through to her. She was calming down. "Good girl. See that. You *can* do this. You're going to be amazing." He lifted a gloved hand to stroke her cheek. "You always are."

Rebecca blushed. "I don't know about that."

"Trust me."

"I *do* trust you, Justyn." She hoped he heard the double meaning in her voice. "I'll always trust you."

His eyes softened. "If you get scared, just look for me. I'll never be far, even if I'm not in the scene. I'll always be watching you, just like the phantom watched Christine. Look for me and forget about the audience." He smiled. "I'll always be your biggest fan."

On the stage, Debbie was warning the managers about the dangers of ignoring the demands of the phantom. Rebecca knew *she* certainly couldn't ignore them. In that moment, if Justyn had ordered her to plunge off the George Washington Bridge, she could have taken the dive without a second thought. She couldn't ignore him, couldn't resist him, and couldn't deny him. Not anymore. She *loved* him.

She wanted to tell him that. Wanted to scream it at the top of her lungs. She wanted to declare her love. To fall down on her knees and beg him to forgive her ignorance and stupidity and just take her into his arms. But she couldn't squeeze the words past the lump of emotion in her throat.

"Justyn," she whispered.

"Hush." He put a finger to her lips to silence her. "We'll talk later. You're on now."

He was right. The managers were calling for Christine, the mild-mannered chorus girl, to sing for them. She was to take the place of Carlotta, whose diva-type tantrum had left them without a star for that night's performance. It wasn't out of character for her to be a little nervous, which was good because she certainly *was* nervous. With one last look at Justyn, whose wide smile of encouragement was half hidden behind his mask, Rebecca stepped out onto the stage.

The next two hours went by in a creative blur. She hardly realized that anyone was watching her at all; she allowed herself to get wrapped up in the storyline. Each song rang crystal clear; each line was delivered with perfect inflection. She worked well not only with Justyn, but even with Tom and Carmen. Their real life tensions were forgotten in the midst of bringing art to life on the stage. Anytime she felt a stab of fear or insecurity, she just looked for Justyn. As he promised, he was always close by. And his nods and smiles kept her on track. Before she even remembered to be terrified, they were at the closing scene, and Christine was stripping away the mask of the Phantom.

There were gasps all around them, both from the audience and the stage. Behind the scenes, and even issuing from her own lips were cries of startled surprise at the mangled mass of flesh beneath the mask. It was no exaggeration to say that Justyn was death walking. One lip was grossly enlarged, looking almost malignant. The skin on the left side of his face was puckered and red, a cross between a burn victim and someone who had put his face into the garbage disposal. The slight bruise he still had from his fall only added to the effect. He hardly looked human, but in the misery of his secret's discovery, managed to look more human than ever. Rebecca felt honest tears fill her eyes.

Things moved quickly as they neared the climax of the play. The Phantom had Raoul tied down with a noose around his neck. He was giving Christine the choice of watching her lover die or staying with him forever. In Rebecca's mind, there was no choice to make. She only wanted Justyn. Even with his face so horribly distorted by the make-up, she still felt nothing but desire for him. Nothing but longing as she crept slowly towards him. She moved carefully, with a little pretend apprehension. Christine was still afraid of Erik, still unsure of how far he would go to keep her with him.

Closer and closer she came, wading slowly through the mist created by the fog machine backstage. Closer and closer until she was standing directly in front of him, feeling her chest rise and fall with each heavy, passion-filled breath. Justyn was breathing heavy as well, feigning anger so well that Rebecca wasn't sure she *shouldn't* be afraid. But as he twisted the rope around Tom's neck a little tighter, making him gag, he winked at Rebecca, and she had to fight the urge to smile. She knew he was enjoying that part of the performance just a little too much.

Gently, she reached her hands up to touch his grotesque face. As she looked into Justyn's dark eyes, she realized that even if he really were deformed, she would still want him, still love him. He would still be beautiful to her on the inside. The audience had no way of knowing how very sincere the play of emotions that ran across her face truly was. Trust, devotion, love, longing—they all mingled in her heart and rang out clearly in her voice as she sang.

> *"Sad creature trapped in this darkness.*
> *A life filled with pain is all you ever knew.*

But know this, my tortured dark angel.
A part of me will always love you."

Then she kissed him. Pressed her lips against his as she was taken over by an unbelievable spark of passion. She hadn't intended it. Even though a small kiss, no more than a peck on the cheek, was part of the show—this was something much more. This kiss was deep and sensual, and it lingered for much longer than anyone expected, especially Justyn. It went on and on, and even the audience felt the effect of such pure, uninhibited emotion. Aside from the light fluid music issuing from the musicians, the entire auditorium had fallen into hushed silence.

When Rebecca finally let Justyn go, however reluctantly, she realized she was crying. Crying real tears that slid silently down her cheeks, leaving damp tracks in their wake. Not tears of sadness. Tears of happiness. Tears of inexpressible joy. A joy caused by the completeness that came with real, true love.

Justyn was crying too, crying and sputtering as he struggled to get back into character. Didn't he realize they were more in character now than ever? She could hear more than one loud sniffle among the crowd. She heard more than one hand rifling through handbags for a tissue. They had touched their audience more deeply than they had ever anticipated.

Back in the play, the phantom, overcome with mercy after being shown kindness for the first time in his life, released Raoul and ordered Christine to take him away, thus proving that he had a decent soul after all. Rebecca was tempted to rewrite the show at that point, and send Raoul off alone, but she controlled herself. Things were going too well to ruin them now. She allowed Tom to lead her away, and watched with fresh tears in her eyes as Justyn sang his final heart-breaking monologue.

Suddenly, it was all over. The play was over and she had survived. She had done more than survive. She had triumphed, just like Christine had triumphed in her first magical performance. Triumphed because of the watchful eyes of the phantom. Triumphed because of Justyn.

Rebecca was in a half daze until someone—she wasn't even sure who—came over and reminded her it was time to take their bows. The chorus girls went out first, followed by the more minor characters—the managers, Meg/Carmen, Madame Giry/Debbie. Then there was Wendy, whose applause was a little louder than her predecessors. Tom also received his share of shouts and whistles, mostly from the basketball players that filled two rows in the back of the auditorium.

Then it was Rebecca's turn. She lost a little bit of her former self-assurance. Again she felt a moment of nervous jitters. This was the moment of truth. If she had been terrible, the audience would still clap—after all, this was just a high school play and no one was going to be *that* cruel. She would be able to tell if the clapping was honestly enthusiastic or just sympathy applause. She took a deep breath and strode onto the stage with as much confidence as she could muster. She never expected the greeting she received.

The audience went wild. Absolutely insane. There were screams and whistles. Hoots and hollers. Many people were standing and shouting "Bravo", as if they were in a real opera house. The whole scene felt a little surreal, a little dreamlike. She waved at the crowd; everyone continued to cheer. She didn't think it was possible for the noise level to go any higher. Then Justyn came out and joined her at the front of the stage.

He took her hand and the two of them bowed in perfect unison. The few people still sitting could no longer hold their seats. The whole room seemed to shake with the thunder of the applause. Voices were growing hoarse from shouting. People, her parents among them, were shoving bouquet after bouquet of flowers into her outstretched arms. Even Darlene handed her a black rose after giving a dozen of them to her son. Rebecca was sure there was no way the applause could get any louder. She doubted that the natural high could get any more intense—until Justyn pulled her into his arms and kissed her. Miraculously, impossibly, the volume rose once again, doubling as the crowd went even wilder with appreciation.

Rebecca realized that this was it. *This* was fulfillment. She had found her calling. The stage was the place where she belonged. *This* was what she had always been meant to do. And Justyn was the one she was meant to do it with.

Justyn's arms were still wrapped tightly around her waist, his lips still pressed against her own, as the curtain slipped shut for the final time. She could still hear the lingering applause in the background, and she hoped that the moment would never end. She could have stood there, in Justyn's arms, with the sound of the audience as their own personal orchestra forever. She realized she was addicted. Completely addicted to the applause, to the sound of success. And she was even more helplessly addicted to *him*. Rebecca could never get enough of Justyn Patko.

Chapter Thirty

"You were awesome, Becca!"

"That was amazing!"

"Wow, great job!"

One after another—friends, family, cast members, classmates, and teachers—all came up to offer Rebecca their congratulations. The play was an undeniable victory. She had succeeded beyond her wildest dreams. It was an amazing feeling. A buzz that she thought she would never come down from. And all she wanted was to share those feelings of accomplishment with Justyn. She wanted to celebrate with him. After all, it was his triumph every bit as much as it was hers.

"Would you hurry up and get out of that dress? Everyone's waiting for us downstairs at the party."

Debbie tapped her foot impatiently as Rebecca set her garden of flowers down on the dressing table. She noted the excited flush of her cheeks in the mirror's reflection. It was such a refreshing change from the peaked thing she had seen looking back at her just a few short hours ago.

"Help me get out of this thing?" she asked Debbie.

It was impossible for her to reach all the snaps and buttons in the back of the elaborate white wedding gown she had worn for the final scene. It took Debbie a good five minutes. Finally, the puffy dress slipped to the ground, and Rebecca quickly stepped out of it. She was happy to be back in the casual jeans and sweater she had arrived in, even though they clashed with her excess of make-up and elegantly curled and pinned hair.

"Ready," she announced.

She grabbed her handbag and was just about to head downstairs with Debbie when she noticed a card sitting on her dressing table. It was in a dark red envelope, addressed to her in fancy silver letters. She picked it up and turned it over curiously. She wondered who it might be from, but she couldn't help feeling the tiniest bit of dread as she examined it. The handwriting wasn't the perfect calligraphy of her stalker, but it didn't look familiar either. Inside was a single sheet of paper, the same shade of blood red as the envelope, with just a few simple lines scrawled in the same fancy silver writing.

"Meet me behind the stage at midnight—the witching hour.

All My Love, O. G."

O. G. The opera ghost. It *had* to be Justyn. The note had his flair for the dramatic. And there was no hint of a threat, like there had been with the other notes, the ones from whoever was trying to scare her away from the play. She knew she would be there at midnight on the dot before she could even fold the note back into the envelope. In fact, she was extremely disappointed when she looked at her watch and realized it was only ten thirty. An hour and a half seemed like a lifetime when all she really wanted was some time alone with Justyn.

"What are you *doing*?" Debbie complained. "Come on! The party will be over before we get there."

"Okay, okay. I'm coming."

Rebecca left the note and her flowers behind. There would be plenty of time to retrieve them later, and plenty of time for her and Justyn to have their privacy. But for now, Debbie was right. She had to get down to the cafeteria and at least put in an appearance at the celebration. If she were lucky, Justyn would be down there anyway.

They had shuffled about halfway down the hallway when they bumped into Tom. He was still in costume, looking dashing in the fancy tailored suit of the French count. He gave her a wide smile when he saw her. It was so good to see that familiar, boyish grin. Rebecca couldn't help but smile back.

"Hey, guys," he exclaimed. "Great show, huh?"

"The best." Debbie agreed heartily.

"You were terrific, Tom," Rebecca told him. "It's easy to work beside you."

"Thanks. But you were the real star tonight, Bec." He gushed. "All I can say is . . . Wow! You were *unbelievable*. Really."

Rebecca blushed. "Thanks," she said. Then she paused for a minute, wanting to say so many things but not sure where to start. Finally, she decided to just keep things simple and honest. "Tom, listen, I want to apologize . . . ."

He shook his head, and cut her off in mid-sentence. "Nothing for you to apologize about. You didn't do anything wrong."

"That's very generous of you. But, Tom . . . ."

"No, really, Becca. You can't help who you care about. I wish it could have been me." He gave her a sad look of longing, and then shrugged his shoulders. "But it's not, and that's okay. I can deal with it. And I understand. I just hope Justyn knows how lucky he is."

She eyed him a little suspiciously. It all seemed a little too good, and too easy to be true. There had to be a catch. "And we're still friends?"

"Always." He reached out to give her an awkward hug. "Listen, I'll catch you guys later, okay? I need to get out of this monkey suit."

"I know the feeling. I'm glad that we live in the twenty-first century." Rebecca laughed. "We'll see you downstairs."

"See you later, Tom," Debbie echoed. Then she turned back to Rebecca as they made their second attempt to get down to the cafeteria. "See that, Becca. Didn't I tell you everything would work itself out? It looks like you're about to get everything you always wanted."

"It does seem that way," Rebecca said, a little tentatively.

She felt herself inadvertently shudder. Things were just a little *too* good to be true. Maybe this was the calm before the storm. Then she shook her head and silently chided herself for the pessimistic thoughts. She should sit back and enjoy the ride. Things were perfect. She just needed to accept it.

Well, things were *almost* perfect. As soon as she walked into the cafeteria, she locked eyes with Carmen. Her former best friend flicked her hair behind her shoulders, and gave Rebecca one long, dirty look. Then she turned on her heel to join the chatting chorus girls. Rebecca sighed. Things could never *really* be perfect when Carmen wasn't speaking to her.

"I'll go talk to her," Debbie offered. "Maybe now that you and Tom have patched things up, Carmen will want to make up, too."

"I sure hope so," Rebecca began.

She was interrupted by a string of admirers who had just noticed her arrival. Before she knew what was happening, she was swept into the crowd. She lost sight of Debbie in the mayhem that followed. Dozens of people accosted her, offering compliments and congratulations. Not the least of which came from Miss King.

"Rebecca!" She gushed, when she had her alone. "You stole the show tonight with that performance. And I'm not the only one who thinks so. There was a talent scout in the audience! He was here for Justyn, but . . . where is that boy anyway? I swear he is *completely* impossible."

Miss King scanned the room and Rebecca found herself following her line of vision. Justyn *was* absent from the party. Tom hadn't shown up yet either, and even Wendy was missing. It seemed like most of the main cast members were M.I.A. The only person she could pick out easily was Carmen, and that was because she was glaring at her with such obvious loathing that it made her hard to miss.

"You aren't going to believe this." Miss King continued. "He wants to . . . but I'll let him tell you himself."

Miss King was doing everything but jumping up and down for joy. But Rebecca was a little confused. A talent scout? From where? And why would he want to talk to her if he had come to see Justyn?

"Mr. Pessagno. Here she is! Here's our little starlet!"

Her director was already guiding her over to a middle-aged man who was surprisingly handsome for his years, so she didn't have time to ask any questions. He was wearing a very expensive designer suit, and had an air of almost regal importance. His gray eyes were filled with kindness, and his smile was sincere as he reached out a hand in greeting.

"Ah, the illustrious Miss Hope," he said. "It's an honor to meet you."

"Thank you . . . sir." She was so nervous; she had already forgotten his name.

"I was extremely impressed with your performance tonight," he told her. "Tell me, Rebecca, how long have you been taking singing lessons?"

Rebecca was surprised by the question. "Well I . . . I haven't taken any lessons, actually."

Now it was his turn to look surprised. To say he was flabbergasted would have been an understatement. Rebecca wondered if she had given him the wrong answer.

"A voice like that, and no lessons." He seemed like he was talking to himself more than anyone else. "Well, well, Miss King. It seems we have a savant on our hands. Such amazing, raw talent. With the right training, imagine the potential."

"She *is* amazing." Miss King agreed enthusiastically. Rebecca was sure the teacher was fighting the urge to clap her hands.

"Well, Miss Hope, I want you to know that the New York School of Performing Arts will be offering you a *full* scholarship. I honestly hope that I'll be seeing you next fall, you and your co-star, Mr. Patko."

Rebecca felt her mouth drop open. The whole world tilted on its axis. If Miss King hadn't chosen that exact moment to give her an excited hug, she might have fallen over. A full scholarship to the New York School of Performing Arts? That was more than she had ever allowed herself to hope for back when she had diligently practiced her violin day in and day out with no obvious improvements. She had never imagined her voice would take her where her fingers couldn't. She had never dreamed she was *that* good. She had doubted that she was good at all.

And even better, even more miraculous, was that Justyn would be there too. She wouldn't have to worry about what would happen to their blossoming relationship after graduation. They would be together. Maybe they would even have the chance to perform together again. She had just crossed the border from perfect happiness to complete euphoria.

"Rebecca, don't you want to say something to Mr. Pessagno?" Miss King urged, then she laughed a little. "I think she's in shock."

He smiled good-naturedly. "I understand. It's a lot to take in."

"I'm . . . sorry," Rebecca stuttered. "Thank you, Mr. Pessagno. Thank you so much for this amazing opportunity."

"You're very welcome," he said. "Now, I'm sure there are other fans who need to offer their congratulations. I don't want to monopolize your star, Miss King. But again, Rebecca, I truly look forward to seeing you next year and I hope I have the chance to work with you personally."

"Thank you," Rebecca whispered.

She was a little too shocked to say more, and before long she was overtaken by another tidal wave of supporters, this time including her teary-eyed mother, her grandparents, aunts, uncles and cousins. All of them were gushing with family pride. But Rebecca had trouble focusing on their heartfelt words of encouragement. She was too busy scanning the crowd for Justyn. Across the room, Miss King and Mr. Pessagno were apparently doing the same thing. Rebecca glanced at her watch and realized it was already a quarter to twelve. Justyn was probably waiting for her backstage. Rebecca excused herself from her family, deciding to seek him out before he missed his chance with the talent scout. *And* missed the chance for them to go to college together.

As she slipped through the cafeteria doors, she couldn't help but notice Carmen. She was still watching, still staring at her, and obviously furious. Rebecca stopped for a second. She thought about going over and trying to smooth things over with her friend, and even took a tentative step in her direction. But Carmen made such a disgusted face that it stopped her cold in her tracks. She wasn't ready to ruin the night with any nasty confrontations. Rebecca left things as they were with Carmen. She promised herself that she would have plenty of time to work things out later, and she went off in search of Justyn.

Chapter Thirty-One

It was with an eerie sense of déjà vu that Rebecca walked down the deserted corridor toward the auditorium. The clock was creeping towards midnight, and the school was deserted, except for whoever was still downstairs at the after party. The rest of the school was empty. It reminded Rebecca of the first time she met Justyn in the gym, except that it was a lot later and a lot darker. The only light was the subtle red glow of the exit signs. And it only got worse when she stepped into the auditorium.

It was very nearly pitch black in the large empty hall. Somewhere behind the stage, a dim light was flickering, giving her at least a beacon to guide her way. Most of the props had been pushed offstage at the end of the show, but Rebecca saw something hanging from the rafters. She heard the creaking as it swung slightly back and forth, like a tree limb being blown by a gentle breeze. She wondered what it could be, but it was too dark to make out any distinct shapes so far in the distance. She dismissed it. She concentrated, instead, on weaving down the empty aisles without getting too many bruises on her shins as she stumbled in the dark. Once she got backstage, she knew where the light switch was, and she could flip it on before she sustained any serious injuries.

Each step she took echoed in the total silence. Each footstep made a light thump against the hardwood floors. There was no other sound except for the slight breeze blowing through the empty hallway—until she heard a soft groan.

It was a low muffled sound, but very distinct. It was definitely the sound of someone in pain, definitely a guy. She started to move a little faster, no longer concerned with whether or not she tripped. Someone was hurt. Someone needed help. Maybe Justyn! Rebecca silently cursed herself for leaving her purse, along with her cell phone, back in the cafeteria with her mother. Now she didn't even have the option of calling for help if she needed to.

"Hello?" she called out. Her voice was so scared and small she could barely hear it. She did her best to pull herself together and made a more valiant effort. "Hello? Is anyone there? Justyn?"

Of course, there was no answer. There was only the creepy echo of her own terrified voice as it bounced back at her off the high ceilings and the continuous creaking coming from the stage.

As she got closer, and her eyes became more adjusted to the light, she thought she saw a pair of legs. There was a short moment of panic before she realized it was probably just the dummy that they used during the play, a stand in for Joseph Buquet, the stagehand who was murdered by the phantom. The crew had probably thought they would give a scare to the new janitor, who was by no means any more mentally stable than poor Mr. Russ had been. Apparently, being mentally challenged was a prerequisite for a high school janitor.

The silly thought made Rebecca giggle to herself. She realized that she was just being overly dramatic. She was getting scared in the dark just like a little girl, hearing things and seeing things that weren't really there. She hadn't heard any more groans. She had most likely imagined it the first time. No one was hurt. That was impossible. This was her perfect night, and her perfect man was waiting for her just beyond that curtain. There was nothing in the world for her to be worried about.

At least she hoped there wasn't. Her heart started to pound with an anxiety that she couldn't hold at bay. Why hadn't Justyn answered her when she called? Maybe he was running late. Or maybe he was too far back behind the curtains to hear her. Either way, she needed to see him, to make sure that he was all right. That was a better reason to rush backstage than the possibility of finding an invisible groaner.

Rebecca paused at the stage steps when she heard it again, louder this time. *Definitely* a moan of pain. No doubt about it this time. No wishing it away or making lame excuses. Someone *was* hurt. Someone needed help. And she was the one that was going to have to help them. But first she had to remember how to walk.

A slow, steady panic started to creep into her heart. It traveled like a slithering snake down her arms and into her legs, making them feel weak and useless, before finally settling as a tight knot in her stomach. Rebecca's mind was doing an instant replay of the last six weeks. The curtain falling at the first rehearsal, the notes, the calls, the flowers, Wendy falling into the mirror, Mr. Russ, Jay's accident. Some awful precognitive sense was telling her that all those events were leading up to *this* moment. This was going to be the climax of her own personal play. And for better or worse, it was going to end here. The villain would be revealed, but would the hero show up? Or would she, the heroine, wind up on the wrong end of a body bag? She wasn't naive enough to think that every story had to have a happy ending. But would hers?

She probably should have run away then. If her life were a B-rated horror movie, this would be the part where everyone in the audience would be screaming at the television set for the stupid girl to run the other way. But those people didn't understand the full power of morbid fascination, a thing Rebecca had become overly familiar with in recent weeks. They didn't understand the driving force of the need to *know*. To know *why*. To know *who*.

With more bravery than she knew she was capable of, Rebecca flipped on the overhead lights of the stage, flooding the small area with brightness. Her eyes needed time to adjust to the sudden change. She blinked a few times, and her vision focused. She was finally able to see the stage, and the scene that was set there. She was able to see everything clearly. A little *too* clearly

Rebecca started to scream.

She screamed and screamed and screamed until she had no voice left to scream anymore. No strength left to stand either. Her legs turned to Jell-O and gave way, and she slipped into a helpless, blubbering puddle on the floor. Her stomach heaved and she knew that if she hadn't already emptied it earlier, she certainly would have then.

She wanted to tear her eyes away, but she couldn't help herself. She couldn't stop gawking at the grotesque scene. She couldn't stop staring.

Couldn't force her eyes to close or her head to turn the other way. Couldn't stop herself from memorizing every single, terrible detail. The wide, unseeing eyes. The awful bloated tongue. It wasn't like on television, where it looked so clean. Not like the movies where a hanging body still looked vaguely human, as if the victim had just fallen asleep. This was nothing like that. This was so, *so* much worse.

If not for the blond hair and the designer jeans, Rebecca wouldn't have even recognized the person whose body hung limply from the stage rafters. There was no beauty left. No cocky grin. No malicious glint in the eyes. Rebecca would have given just about anything for one nasty, resentful comment to come out of those swollen lips at that moment. But there was no way that those lips were never going to open again. Just like there was no way that Rebecca was ever going to forget the horror of what she had seen.

Wendy hanging. Wendy dead. Wendy *murdered*.

Rebecca started screaming again.

Chapter Thirty-Two

Nobody came. Her screams didn't alert the Calvary, probably because there was no Calvary. No white knights riding in on their stallions, either. Not for her. Rebecca was on her own—unless you counted Wendy. But Wendy wasn't going to be offering any assistance any time soon.

She thought about trying to get her down. It somehow seemed horribly disrespectful to let her continue to hang there. Wendy would be angry if people saw her that way, looking less than *Barbie* doll perfect. She wouldn't like that at all. The fact that Wendy was well past liking or caring about anything didn't really register. Letting that register would mean accepting that Wendy was really gone, that she was alone with a corpse. And accepting *that* would probably shatter the thin layer of sanity that Rebecca was managing to hold intact.

It took a great deal of effort, but she managed to pull herself up from the floor. Almost as much effort as it took for her to get herself controlled enough to stop the desperate screams from pouring out indefinitely. She stood and examined the scene for a possible way to set Wendy free. As she did so, she meticulously wiped the dust from her pant legs, knowing it was ridiculous, that it was proof of her precarious grip on reality, but doing it just the same. She needed something, *anything*, however mundane to concentrate on so she didn't think too much about what was happening around her.

"Owwww."

There it was again, another low groan. It was followed by what could only be described as a muffled, barely audible plea for help. Someone was trying to talk over some kind of obstruction. There was no way it was Wendy. Her mouth was forever frozen in that terrible grimace. So it could only mean one thing. Rebecca wasn't alone. There was someone else, someone who was actually alive, in the auditorium with her.

Her breath came in short pants. Her knees threatened to buckle for the second time that night. She didn't know what she should do. Move forward and see who was in trouble, assuming someone *was* in trouble. Or run, as far and as fast as her wobbly legs would carry her. Common sense told her to get out of there before she wound up like Wendy. A nagging sense of guilt pushed her forward. If someone else was in trouble, she *had* to help them. Maybe it was a trap. Maybe it wasn't. But at least if she died, it would be with a clear conscience.

The sound was coming from just behind the curtain. It was only a few feet away, but it might as well have been across a bottomless pit. It was intimating to take those few, shaky steps. It didn't help that all she could hear was the constant creak of Wendy's body as it swung slowly back and forth. That awful sound was far worse than fingers on a chalkboard. It was making it hard for her to concentrate on taking that scary leap into the unknown.

Creaakkk. Creaakkk.

She wanted to cover her ears before the awful sound pushed her over the edge and into the black abyss of insanity, but she needed her ears to guide her. She had to save whoever it was who needed saving. She had to focus on that.

"Hello?" Her voice was hoarse from screaming. She hardly sounded like herself at all. "Who's there?"

Another muffled cry came in reply. Louder this time, with more infliction. It sounded almost like words, like a cry for help. And it was followed by a pounding that was very much like a foot banging against the hardwood floors in extreme agitation. It was insistent, determined. Whoever it was knew she was there, and they were calling to her in the only way they could.

Rebecca cautiously stepped behind the curtains. The lights were already on. It wasn't as bright as she would have liked, but she could see clearly enough. There was barely room to walk in the small room; it was so overcrowded with props. The platform that Justyn had fallen from was pushed into one corner. Miss King had decided to cut it out all together after the accident, so no one had bothered to repair it. She could see where the wood had splintered, and it made her shudder a little. She turned her head away from it and looked over at the piles of costumes, candelabras, fancy dressing tables, and the painted backgrounds from the sets that filled every corner. There were lots of props, even a few mannequins in full costume. But no living, breathing people were anywhere to be seen. Rebecca was still alone.

She almost sighed with relief. Maybe she had been imagining the moaning after all. Maybe there was no one there, no one in trouble, and she could go get help for Wendy and put the whole terrible day behind her. Of course, that would have been way too easy.

"Hummph! Humph!"

Rebecca jumped. The cry came from her immediate left. So close that she almost expected a hand to reach out and grab her shoulder. If they had, she would have likely died from fright on the spot, her heart exploding in her chest. But no one touched her. Instead, they just continued their muffled cries until Rebecca spun around, desperate to figure out where the sound was coming from. She didn't see anything but piles of discarded costumes. The room was empty.

She was just about to move a little further into the room when she noticed something out of place. The pile of clothes on the floor shifted ever so slightly. When it did, she saw a pair of white sneakers poking out from beneath one of Carlotta's pink shawls. Even as she saw it, the shoe started to pound on the floor. She noticed that the sneakers were attached to a pair of legs covered in faded blue jeans. With a shocked gasp, Rebecca ran to the corner, and started tossing away dresses, capes, and ballerina tutus. Underneath the mess, she at last found what she had been looking for.

"Tom!" she cried out. "Oh my, God, Tom! Tom, are you all right?"

It was a rhetorical question. There was no way he was going to answer her. Even if he wasn't dazed and only half conscious, with a stream of blood running from his forehead into his eyes, he was still gagged. A pair of nylon stockings were rolled into a ball and shoved into his mouth, making it impossible for him to do anything but mutter insensibly. When he tried to speak, it gagged him so badly, she was afraid he was going to choke to death on the spot. She quickly pulled it free, and waited impatiently for him to catch his breath.

"Tom, what happened? Who did this to you?"

Tom coughed, and gasped for what seemed like hours before he could speak. Even when he could, his words were broken and garbled. "Becca . . . we have to . . . we have to get out of here. Before he comes back. Jesus, Becca . . . he . . . he killed her." His eyes were wide with the same terrible memory that haunted Rebecca. "He *killed* Wendy."

"I know, I know." Rebecca sobbed. She wasn't even sure when she had started to cry. But now that she *had* started, she wasn't sure she would ever be able to stop.

"Get me out of here!" Tom struggled with the ties that bound him to the dressing room chair. "Before he comes back."

Rebecca's hands were already fumbling with the complicated knots. They stopped working completely when the implications of that simple word, "he", suddenly dawned on her. It seemed there was only one "he" that Tom could possibly be making a reference to. But still she needed to hear him say it. As much as she dreaded his answer, Rebecca had to know.

"Who did this to you, Tom?" she asked. She had no idea how she managed to keep her voice so calm and detached.

"He was wearing the mask, the whole phantom get-up. I didn't see his face," Tom told her. "But it *had* to be Justyn."

Justyn. It *had* to be Justyn.

To say that her heart broke would have been the understatement of the century. It shattered, no it *ruptured*. There was nothing left in her chest, but a gaping, bleeding, open wound that throbbed and ached like nothing she had ever experienced. How could anything hurt so much when there was no physical indication of any injury? How could she hurt so much that she thought even death might have been a blessing?

"Becca!" Tom shouted. "Hurry up!"

Rebecca snapped back to present, to Tom. It wasn't fair to let him go down with her. Her hands worked the knots like a robot. No longer her own hands at all. They were just mechanical appendages performing the task assigned to them. The rest of her body was numb. She had stopped crying, and she had fallen into a strange state that probably looked like calmness, but was really an agony so deep it had turned her into something of a zombie. But still, she was actually making some progress on Tom's ropes.

Rebecca and Tom were so involved with the intricate knots; they didn't even notice they weren't alone anymore. He was silent as any ghost. He made no sound as he slipped into the room. In true phantom style, he made his grand entrance, perched high above them on the wooden platform, clad in the blood red coattails from the ballroom scene. The costume was called *Red Death*, and how fitting it was. The outfit was sewn in blood red velvet and complete with a full-faced mask in the shape of the grinning grim reaper. It completely hid the true face of the phantom from their view.

> *"So now you come to my domain*
> *In this place you will find only pain.*
> *Your lover thinks he can save you*
> *But escape there will be none.*
> *Time to put aside childish games,*
> *The real nightmare has begun."*

Rebecca and Tom snapped their heads up at the sound of the grotesque song. The voice distorter garbled the words. Certainly, there was no hint of Justyn's angelic singing voice. Why the need for these games now? Why the drama? He was out in the open. It was all going to end now, one way for the other. There wouldn't be any witnesses when it was over, she was sure. There was no reason to pretend anymore.

"Justyn! Justyn, please . . . why are you doing this? Why do you need to hurt people? All this violence. For what? "

The reply was sad, almost whimsical, if it was possible to sound that way while speaking through a machine. Yet, Rebecca couldn't feel any sympathy. Not after the things he had done. The people he had hurt.

> *"To be a monster has always been my fate.*
> *There are no words to save you—it is too late.*
> *Blood on my hands is a curse I must bear.*
> *No hope for salvation. No love I can share."*

Even as he finished the last line, Rebecca saw the lights flicker on something silver in his hands. Even before he held it up and took aim, she knew with a horrible certainty exactly what it was. In an instant, Rebecca found herself staring straight into the barrel of a gun.

Rebecca didn't know much about guns. It wasn't very big, but she was sure it was big enough to do some serious damage. Even if she had thought of some type of escape plan, it would have been abandoned now that she had this new obstacle to face. Tom had somehow managed to free one arm, and was working on the second. But they couldn't run. Not with a pistol pointed at their backs, and a person they knew was crazy enough to fire it standing with their finger on the trigger.

"Justyn, you have to stop this!" Rebecca cried. She stepped in front of Tom, blocking him from the firing range. "Let Tom go. It's me you want. I promise I'll stay if you let him go."

"No, Becca . . . ."

Tom started to protest, but he was cut off by the eerie voice box, for the first time speaking in plain English and not using lines from the play. The cold, callous tone was enough to stop anyone in their tracks.

"You must care for your hero an awful lot if you're willing to risk your life to free him."

"I don't want anyone else to die because of me! Please, please Justyn . . . ."

"Owwwww."

Rebecca stopped short in the middle of the thought when she heard the moan. It definitely wasn't Tom this time. He was silent behind her, and somewhat paralyzed as he stared at the gun. The sound had come from the other side of the room, far on her right. She gasped, and looked around to find the source, while still desperately trying to hold her ground and protect Tom.

"Becca, Becca," the phantom tsked. "So quick to doubt the one you claim to love. Perhaps your love isn't an award worth fighting for, after all."

Even as he said it, Rebecca heard the moan again. Things weren't what they seemed. She realized that now. There was more to this story that she had ever thought. More players than any of them had known. Even before she saw the silver toed black boot protruding from the second pile of costumes, she realized what a fool she had been. Even before the costumes shuddered as someone struggled beneath them, Rebecca was flying across the room. She was on top of the costumes in an instant, tossing the clothes away in desperation.

And there was Justyn. Poor Justyn. In far worse condition than Tom was. His entire face was bruised and bloodied. It was hard to tell where the phantom makeup ended and the real wounds began. One eye was completely swollen shut, and there was a large gash across his forehead. He was tied, just like Tom, to one of the dressing room seats. He had been less than ten feet away the entire time, but he must have been unconscious. He was only starting to come to, and didn't seem to have any idea the kind of danger they were in.

"Justyn! Justyn, say something!"

"*Aghhh*, Bec . . . Becca? Ouch, my head . . . ."

Rebecca cried and kissed his bloody forehead, as gently as she could manage. "Oh, Justyn."

"How sweet. A lover's reunion."

Rebecca was so filled with relief to know that Justyn wasn't the killer, wasn't the real phantom, she almost forget that they weren't alone. The garbled voice brought her back to reality. The phantom had gotten closer. While she had worked to extract Justyn from the smothering costumes, the red-cloaked skeleton had inched his way down from the platform, moving as silently as a ghost. Now he was so close that she could feel his breath on the back of her neck as he spoke. But he was still partially hidden in the shadows so she couldn't make out who he was.

Rebecca turned to face him, furious, outraged. She used her body to shield Justyn. Tom was white-faced and silent, watching the scene. But the phantom had his back to Tom, so at least for the moment he was safe—safer still since the barrel of the gun was aimed squarely at Rebecca's chest. She didn't let it stop her. She held her ground firmly, and didn't flinch.

"Who are you?" she demanded. "Why are you doing this?"

"Don't you recognize me?" came the mechanical reply.

She should have been scared, terrified, when she was facing such a deadly opponent. But Rebecca was done playing games. Awesome fury had squashed all remnants of fear and squeamishness. It was ending. Right here, right now.

Rebecca reached out her arm, and in one quick movement, pulled away the skeleton mask.

Then she gasped as with a smirk of satisfaction, the phantom stepped from the shadows. Rebecca backed up a step, almost falling over when she recognized the familiar features—the short hair, the broad shoulders, the bulky frame large enough to fill out the masculine costume. The large strong arms, powerful enough to overpower two boys. Rebecca saw the face of the phantom. Saw *her* face. Not his. Not a man. The phantom was a woman, and one she would never have suspected. Rebecca couldn't fight back her tears or the awful feelings of betrayal as her tormenter was at last revealed.

"*I* am your dark angel."

It was Debbie. The phantom was Debbie.

Chapter Thirty-Three

"Debbie? Debbie . . . no! *Why?*"

Rebecca felt her anger slip away. It was so strange—this wild gamut of emotions, each one intense and uncontrollable in its turn. Now she found herself once again being overcome with despair. Emotionally, she was falling apart, despite her outward calmness. She knew that no matter what happened now, some permanent damage was being done to her psyche.

"Debbie, *no! Why?*" Debbie mocked her in a high-pitched, singsong voice. Somehow that scratchy sound was ten times worse, ten times more disturbing, than the voice distorter had been. "Why do you *think*, Becca? What was *always* the motive of the phantom?"

Rebecca couldn't answer, couldn't comprehend. None of it made any sense. The pieces hadn't fallen into place when the mask was stripped away, as she had thought they would. Instead, the whole puzzle had been knocked apart in one foul swoop, leaving her lost and more confused than ever. Debbie was her friend, one of her best friends. How could she hurt people, hurt *her*, in such horrible ways.

"What's the matter, Becca?" Debbie continued to taunt her. "Does the cat have your tongue? Would it help you to think if I took Tom out of the equation? Do you think that would simplify things?"

"No!"

The point of the gun was leveled at Tom, and Rebecca made a mad dash across the narrow room to throw herself back in front of him. Talk about roll reversals! Who was the hero and who was the damsel in distress, anyway? It seemed like she was the one doing all the protecting while both the guys were practically useless. Something that Debbie only seemed to find amusing.

"Seems like we can go on this way all night." Debbie mused. "With you playing at being a human shield. But I think it would be simpler, Becca, if you just stood right here in front of me." She gestured her forward. "You can't save them both, you know."

"Don't listen to her, Becca! Run!" Justyn shouted from his chair. "Don't worry about us!"

Debbie immediately went over and waved the gun in his face. "No comments from the peanut gallery, please," she instructed.

Justyn was unfazed. "Screw you, you crazy bitch."

Debbie laughed, almost good-naturedly, and took a step back as if she intended to walk away. But before Rebecca knew what was happening, she snapped back around, quick as lighting, and struck Justyn hard in the temple with the butt of the pistol. Rebecca gasped and covered her mouth with her hands when she heard him groan and saw his head wobble on his shoulders. It wobbled so much that he put every bobble-head doll in the world to shame.

Rebecca was ready to sprint back over to his side, but Tom restrained her. At first she was annoyed, thinking that he was *still* trying to keep her from Justyn, even after all they had been through. It took a second before she realized that he was only able to hold her back at all because his hands were free. Tom was free and Debbie had no idea.

"Do what she says until I figure something out."

He whispered just under his breath in her ear. Rebecca nodded, but she was skeptical. Would whatever plan Tom came up with include Justyn? She didn't think Tom would have a problem leaving his former rival behind if push came to shove. But Rebecca wouldn't be going anywhere unless they all left together.

"No whispering, please," Debbie told them, turning away from a half-conscious Justyn. "And Becca—I asked you nicely to come stand in front of me. If I have to ask again, I won't be quite so cordial."

Rebecca forced her shaky legs to carry her forward. She stood dead center between Tom and Justyn, hoping she would be able to shield whichever one came into more immediate danger. She tried her best to scope out the room for any chance of escape without giving it away, but Debbie interrupted her thoughts.

"Do you have an answer yet?" she asked.

Rebecca was confused. "An . . . an answer to what?"

Debbie rolled her eyes. "You asked me why . . . and I asked you the phantom's motive. Sooo, what's your answer?"

Rebecca thought hard. She didn't want to give the wrong answer. The only thing she could think of didn't seem logical. But Debbie was tapping her foot impatiently and swinging the gun around which didn't seem very safe. So she just blurted out the first word that popped into her head

"Lo . . . love," Rebecca stuttered.

"*Love*," Debbie echoed. "Yes, Becca. *Love*. It drives us all to do the most insane things. There's no rhyme or reason to it. Take for example the fact that you would fall in love with that Gothic freak . . . ."

"Who are you calling a freak, you psychotic whack job?"

"Justyn, SHUT UP!" Rebecca yelled.

She wished he wouldn't antagonize someone who was obviously mentally unstable. He looked like he wanted to say more, but Rebecca shot him such an angry look that it actually silenced him. Either that or he had passed out again, because his eyes closed. As worried as that made her, it was better than him running his mouth.

Debbie also looked annoyed about the outburst, but thankfully decided to ignore Justyn. "Do you have any idea, Becca, the pain of unrequited love? The kind of pain that Christine inflicted on Erik." She was silent for so long after that, Rebecca wondered if she was supposed to give an answer. The whole room hung in deadly silence until Debbie finally continued, her voice a little louder, a little angrier. "No, you *don't* know. You have no idea. You have men fawning over you all the time. You break hearts. You don't have yours broken."

"Debbie . . . I don't understand."

Rebecca was lost. Who did Debbie love? Justyn? That hardly seemed possible. She could barely stand the sight of him. Tom then? In all the years they had gone to school together, she had never seen Debbie look at Tom twice. Never once had she joined in at sleepovers when Carmen and Rebecca listed his many attributes. If she had, Rebecca would have never stood in her way. And there wasn't anyone else that ever came up, at least not that Rebecca could think of.

"Of course you don't understand, Becca," Debbie scoffed. "You never see what's right in front of your eyes."

"Then tell me, Deb. Please. Tell me what I did wrong so that I can fix it."

Keep her talking right? That was the key. That was what they always did in the movies. She only needed to keep her busy long enough to come up with a plan. She saw out of the corner of her eye that Tom was trying to inconspicuously reach into the pocket of his jeans. Maybe he had his cell phone with him. Maybe he was calling for help at that very moment. Rebecca hoped Debbie wouldn't notice. She tried her best to keep the attention focused on her.

"You *can't* fix it, Becca. It's too late. Too late for them. Too late for you. Too late for *us*."

"Us, Debbie? What do you mean by *us*?" She had to ask aloud, too shocked to believe it could mean what she thought it meant.

Debbie sighed in a combination of sadness and frustration. "Think about it, Becca. Who's always been there for you? Who supported you before the tryouts? Who stood up for you when Wendy was giving you a hard time? Who was the only one who stood by you through everything? *Everything.* Even when the guys and Carmen deserted you, who was *still* there?"

"You." Rebecca was playing along; doing her best to hide the disgust she felt now that she knew Debbie was a cold-blooded murderer. "You, of course, Deb. You're my best friend. You always have been."

Debbie laughed, a little bitterly. Rebecca swallowed hard. She was afraid she might have said the wrong thing—a mistake that could very well be her last under the current circumstances.

"Your *friend*. You know, I was okay with that for such a long time. But suddenly, you had these two buffoons fighting over you, treating you like a possession." She gestured at Tom and Justyn, each in turn, making Tom jump and Justyn, who had opened his eyes again, sneer. "They *disrespected* you. I couldn't put up with that. That's why they had to go."

"You're the one who needs to go," Justyn said with a roll of his eyes, a move that looked more than a little painful given the condition of his face. "Straight to the mental institution."

"Shut up, Justyn!" Rebecca and Debbie both shouted in perfect unison, albeit for different reasons.

"You see what I mean," Debbie continued. "They're animals, Becca. You deserve so much more! That's why I did all this. At first, I thought I would just scare you a little, and make you think it was one of them. I hoped that would make you stay away from them. That's why I sent the notes, and made the curtain fall. That retard, Mr. Russ, almost caught me more than once— first with the curtain, then with Wendy. He was always lurking around—so *annoying*. I thought that after what I did with Wendy, making her trip into the mirror, you would finally realize I meant business. But just like always, you didn't listen. That's when I realized that it wasn't going to be enough to just play games. I decided I had to kill the guys."

"Oh, Debbie . . . ." Rebecca couldn't help herself. She started crying again as the full magnitude of Debbie's illness hit her for the first time. She was sick. She was incredibly sick.

"I thought it was going to be easy," Debbie told her. "But I kept running into complications. The first time I went after Tom was at the Halloween dance. He had already left the bathroom when I went in to find him. Of course, I found Mr. Russ there instead. He confronted me about the accidents." She made quotation marks with the hand that wasn't touching the trigger of the gun. "He threatened to expose me. So what else could I do? I *had* to get rid of him. Luckily for me, the old guy didn't have much strength in him. He didn't even put up much of a fight."

"Debbie, you didn't . . . you *couldn't* . . . ." Rebecca already knew for a fact that she *had*. Actually hearing her admitting to her crimes out loud, and admitting it so matter-of-factly, made it seem so much worse and so much more real.

"My next plan seemed fool proof. I grew up in a house with a mechanic dad and four older brothers who followed in his footsteps. There's nothing I don't know about cars. It was easy to cut the brake lines. I was sure I would get Tom that time. But then he had to ruin everything by lending Jay his truck. Not that *that* moron didn't get exactly what was coming to him . . . ."

"*Aghhh!*"

That last comment was more than Tom could stand. He flung himself at Debbie, giving away their one advantage. He was still a little unsteady on his feet from his injuries, so Debbie easily sidestepped his desperate leap. When he tried to get to his feet he found the barrel of the gun less than a foot from his face, aimed directly between his eyes.

"Don't play games with me, surfer boy." Debbie warned. "I'm not in the mood."

"Just do it, Debbie." Tom was sobbing. He thrust himself closer to her, daring her. "You're gonna kill us all anyway, right? Why drag it out? *You're* the one who's playing games."

Debbie was thoughtful for a moment, and Rebecca found herself wishing the two men in her company would both keep their mouths shut for five minutes. Maybe then they would have a chance of surviving this nightmare.

"You're right, Tom," Debbie said. "I should just get it over with. But let's make it interesting, shall we? Let's give Becca a choice. Let's make our little game truly phantom worthy."

Rebecca didn't like the sound of that. "No, Debbie. Just let them both go. I'll stay with you. I promise."

"How noble." Debbie smirked. "Placing yourself out there like a sacrificial lamb. But no, you need to learn a lesson, Becca. And the only way you'll learn that lesson is by having to make a difficult choice."

"What . . . what kind of choice?"

"The choice between life and death, of course," Debbie explained. "So who will you choose, Becca? Tom or Justyn? Choose between them once and for all, and choose wisely, because one of them *will* die."

"No." Rebecca gasped.

"Screw her, Becca. Run!" Justyn tried to pull his arms free, desperate to come to her aid. Rebecca appreciated the sentiment, but it was pointless. He was too weak, and bound too tightly.

"He's right," Tom agreed. "Let her kill us. She's gonna do it either way. You just get out of here."

"Tick, tock. Tick, tock." Debbie tapped her foot impatiently. "Time is running out. Make your choice, Becca."

Her whole body trembled. She thought she had known what fear was before, when she was being terrorized, when she found Wendy's body hanging on the stage, when the gun was pointed at *her*. That was nothing. That was rated G in comparison to the way she felt now. She was afraid that someone was going to die right in front of her, and that she might as well be pulling the trigger herself. For Rebecca, that would be a fate worse than death.

"Debbie." Rebecca pleaded. "You can't expect me to pick who dies. You can't do this to me!"

"*I* can't do this to *you*?" Spittle flew from Debbie's lips as she screamed at her, eyes flashing, lips pursed in fury. Rebecca felt herself flinch. She took an inadvertent step backwards in the face of so much rage. "I *love* you, Becca! I've *always* loved you. And you don't even *care*. Now you need to know what it feels to lose someone *you* care about. You need to have *your* heart broken. So *choose*. Who do you love more?"

Of course, her first instinct was to scream out Justyn's name. She *couldn't* live without Justyn. She *loved* Justyn. But she also couldn't live with herself if she let Tom die because of her. She couldn't choose. She *wouldn't* choose. Instead, she started to sob again just as her shaky knees gave out beneath her. She slipped to the floor in a broken, useless heap.

"Oh, poor Becca." Debbie sympathized. "Poor, poor Becca."

"Shoot *me*!" Justyn offered. He puffed out his chest as much as was possible, considering he was pretty well strapped down. "Leave her alone and just shoot *me*! You know you want to, you sick, twisted, demented . . . *oufff.*"

Tom made one swift jump across the room and punched Justyn in the stomach just as it appeared that Debbie's eyes were actually going to bulge right out of her head. Even though Rebecca hated what it must have done to his still healing ribs, she was grateful for the intervention. Tom had just saved Justyn's life. Debbie had been ready to explode and Justyn had his finger on the detonator.

"Time's up," Debbie said through clenched teeth. "If you won't play, I guess I need to think of a new game. I know! This is perfect. You're going to love this, Becca! So, here we go . . . *eeny* . . . ." Debbie motioned the gun in Justyn's direction, very casually, like it was no more than a pointer or a ruler.

"Debbie, what are you doing?" Rebecca asked, forcing herself back to her feet.

"Meeny." She ignored Rebecca's question, and moved her hand so that the gun was now pointed at Tom.

"Deb, no, I'll choose! I'll choose." Rebecca begged. "Just give me a little longer to think. Please, just a few more minutes!"

Just until whomever Tom called on his cell phone finally arrives. Assuming he got through to someone at all . . . .

"Nope. Sorry, Becca. I like this game way too much to stop now." The point of the gun went back to Justyn. "Miney . . . ."

Rebecca knew what was coming—the last word, the last step in the game. Then the gun would go back to Tom, Debbie would fire, and Tom would be gone forever. Rebecca couldn't let that happen. She had to stop it; she had to save Tom. It didn't even matter if she killed herself in the process, just as long as Tom and Justyn were both safe. That was all that mattered.

Rebecca flung herself toward Tom. Using the full power of her body weight, she managed to knock him to the ground, landing hard on his chest and winding him momentarily. Rebecca thought she had bought herself at least a few seconds. But Debbie was smart. Debbie had tricked her. Before Rebecca and Tom could raise their heads to see what was happening—before Rebecca realized that the gun hadn't shifted at all but was stilled aimed at Justyn who could only sit in stunned, wide-eyed horror—Debbie laughed and pulled the trigger.

"Moe," she said.

No one even had time to scream as the bullet plunged into Justyn's chest.

Chapter Thirty-Four

Rebecca had never heard gunfire before. At least not up close and personal. She had no idea how loud it was. She couldn't help but notice the intense ringing that lingered in her ears long after the shot had died away. Even as she climbed off Tom and ran to Justyn's side, she could still hear the ringing. Along the way, she fully expected a second shot to take her down. She almost hoped it would. If anyone should have been hurt, it should have been her. Not Justyn.

At first, when she dropped down on her knees beside Justyn, she thought maybe Debbie had missed. She didn't see any blood, and he was still conscious, though he was paler than the palest shade of white. But too soon that fantasy was dashed. The blood hadn't been visible until after it had soaked through his black t-shirt and began to steadily drip into a puddle on the floor. Justyn watched it drip with the same kind of startled disbelief that Rebecca felt.

"She . . . she shot me," he muttered.

"You're going to be okay," Rebecca told him, and could only hope it was the truth. She also hoped he wasn't picking up on the hysterical edge in her voice. "You're going to be just fine."

"It . . .it . . . hurts."

He said it so matter-of-factly, Rebecca wasn't sure that it really *did* hurt. She even had the brief, crazy notion that he was just playing a trick on her; getting her back for all the times she had doubted him. She would have forgiven him if he were. Anything would have been better than the uncontrollable spasms that started to rack his body. The more she tried to hold him down, the more his body shook and trembled. She struggled to unbind his wrists, but his spasmodic movements were making it impossible for her to get a good grip on him.

Shock, she thought. *He must be going into shock.*

The fact that she was getting that information from reruns of *ER* didn't make her feel overly confident about her diagnosis. But shock was better than dying. Justyn *couldn't* be dying. That just wasn't a possibility that Rebecca was willing to consider.

She wished someone would help her. Anyone. In the background, she could hear Tom breathing heavily as he watched the drama unfold. Helpless to assist her, Rebecca realized, because Debbie was standing beside him with a huge smile on her face and the gun aimed at his chest. She was watching Rebecca's struggle with the true enjoyment of the deranged.

It was probably only a few seconds, even though it seemed like hours, before Justyn's body startled to relax. The violent shaking eased into an occasional shudder. He seemed relaxed, almost peaceful.

It scared Rebecca to death.

"Becca," he whispered.

His voice was so soft, so weak. He reached up his hand to try to touch her cheek, but he didn't even have the energy for that. Rebecca lifted his hand for him, touching the fingers to her lips. Her tears mingled with his blood. She was crying. Crying because her heart was breaking.

"Don't you dare say goodbye to me," she ordered.

"Becca . . . I . . . I . . . love . . . ." His eyes slipped closed before he could even finish the sentence.

"No!" Rebecca cried. "No, no, no, no, no! You can't do this to me, Justyn! You can't!"

"Oh, how sad."

Debbie's voice was probably the only thing that could have pulled Rebecca out of the deep chasm of grief she was starting to fall into. It was only her anger, her fury, her *rage* that gave her the strength to give Justyn one final kiss on the cheek before standing to face her former friend. The fact that she saw the slight rise and fall of his chest—knowing that he was still alive—empowered her even more. But she didn't have much time.

All feelings of guilt were gone. The slight pangs of sympathy she had felt for Debbie was also gone, replaced by the nagging need for revenge. Debbie had hurt Justyn. Debbie had to pay. But first, Rebecca was going to have to somehow gain control over the situation. She was going to have to get the gun.

She could see Tom out of the corner of her eye. Now that Debbie had turned her attention away from him and back to Rebecca, he was trying to send her some kind of secret signal. He was waving one finger, pointing it first at Debbie and then at himself. Rebecca wished they had an interpreter. They didn't have time for games anymore. *Justyn* didn't have time.

"Are you happy now, Debbie?" Rebecca demanded. "Another death on your conscience?"

"Happy? How can I be happy, Becca, when I don't have the one I love?"

There was a whole string of four-letter words Rebecca had never even thought about using before that suddenly seemed appropriate. It took a lot of self-control not to scream them at the top of her lungs—harder still to keep from flinging herself, claws barred, towards Debbie's unsuspecting face. But a plan was starting to formulate in her mind—one that wasn't quite as kamikaze. Tom just needed time, and a distraction. And Rebecca was just the one to give it to him.

"Did you even think of just telling me, Debbie?" Rebecca forced her voice to sound sympathetic. "If I had known . . . ."

"What if you had known, Becca?" Debbie interrupted. "What? You would have loved me back? You would have suddenly changed your sexual orientation?"

"You never gave me the chance. Maybe if you had, I would have felt something more . . . something more than just friendship."

The crazed look in Debbie's eyes softened to an almost whimsical twinkle. "And if I gave you the chance now . . . would you . . . *oufff!*"

Debbie was cut off in mid-sentence when the full bulk of Tom's weight crashed into her midsection, in pure football tackle style. The two of them crashed to the ground and scuffled around on the floor for less than a minute. But Debbie was quick to recover, and Tom was already hurt. She never lost her grip on the gun. She had the advantage. She swiftly kicked Tom in the groin, and before he could even double over, she hit him hard in the temple with the edge of the gun.

Rebecca wouldn't let herself cry out or run to his side as he slipped to the ground, unconscious. Tom was out. Justyn might not even be breathing anymore, for all she knew. Rebecca was on her own. She needed to keep her one small advantage. She had to let Debbie think she had a chance. If she lost that edge for even a minute, they were all going to be dead.

"Having four older brothers can have its advantages," Debbie said smugly as she pulled herself to her feet, completely unscathed. "So tell me, Becca. Were you a part of that little escapade? Did you know that your hero, Tom, was going to attack me like the territorial animal that he is?"

"No," Rebecca said. She was never very good at lying. She hoped it didn't show on her face. "No, of course not! I wouldn't let him hurt you, Deb. Never."

Rebecca was doing her best to hold it together. To not let the overwhelming desire to break down into hysterics take over. She had to stay calm. She had to stay on track. She was the only hope to save Justyn, who was coming closer and closer to bleeding to death with every second that passed. She needed to keep Debbie talking. She needed to stay in control. And she needed to figure out who was hiding in the shadows behind the curtains before Debbie noticed they were there.

A shadow was all she saw—a dim figure lurking in the darkness. Were they a friend or foe? She had no way to tell. Was it possible that Debbie had an accomplice? She didn't seem to need one. She was doing pretty well solo. She was strong enough that she could take on a teenage boy in hand-to-hand combat. But if it wasn't Debbie's phantom assistant, than who was it? She started to wonder if maybe the whole thing was an illusion brought on by severe stress and the very real desire for someone to come to her rescue. But Rebecca couldn't get that lucky. No one was coming to help her.

Then she saw a flash of black hair, and she knew. She knew who it was. Her would-be savior was Carmen!

Rebecca felt a little weak in the knees as relief washed over her. Carmen peered at them through the curtain, and put a finger to her lips. Rebecca did her best to keep her face blank, to try not to alert Debbie to the new arrival. For one glorious moment, she thought her prayers had been answered, but then reality set in. It was just Carmen—tiny, little Carmen. She was barely one hundred pounds. No match for Debbie when the boys couldn't take her, even if she *didn't* have a gun.

"Never?" Debbie was asking. "You'd *never* let Tom hurt me? Even if I killed your boyfriend?"

Rebecca forced herself to tear her eyes away from Carmen. She also had to remind herself that trying to gouge Debbie's eyes out at the moment would be considerably suicidal. Just the fact that she dared to mention Justyn at all made her furious all over again. But she couldn't give herself or Carmen away. She couldn't let Carmen get killed, too. Besides, she had to keep Debbie talking—keep her on track.

"My girlfriends will always come before some guy," Rebecca told her. She almost choked on the next words. "I . . . I love you, Deb. More than you know."

"Love me?" Debbie was skeptical. "As a friend, you mean?"

Carmen had vanished into the shadows. Rebecca wasn't sure what she would do. But she decided that she needed to distract Debbie as much as possible. That was their only chance. And there was only one way she could think of to do it—only one way that she could keep her attention away from whatever Carmen was planning and save all their lives.

It wasn't a pleasant thought, in fact in was downright revolting. Not because Debbie was a girl, but because she was a cold blooded murderer. But when she stole a glance in Justyn's direction and saw the puddle of blood beside his chair was spreading, she knew she had to do what she had to do. She had to bring to life to final scene of *Phantom* one last time.

"Maybe . . . maybe we could be . . . more than friends." Rebecca offered.

A brief glimmer of hope crossed Debbie's face before it hardened once again. "Liar. You can't mean that."

"No." Rebecca shook her head. "Let me show you. Let me prove it."

Debbie was skeptical. "How?"

Rebecca swallowed hard. She thought that under other circumstances, this might have been exciting—a forbidden thrill. But there was no excitement now, just a deep-rooted horror.

"Let me . . . let me kiss you. Let's see if I feel anything."

"You want to kiss me?"

What she really wanted to do was run screaming in the other direction, but she forced herself to give a different answer. "If you'd like me to . . . ."

Carmen had moved into the light. She was no longer behind the cover of the stage curtain. She was armed, but Rebecca had to wonder if it would possibly be enough. Debbie would really have to be preoccupied for Carmen to be able to sneak up on her. Which meant Rebecca would have to be *really* convincing. Her acting abilities would be seriously put to the test.

"I'll kill you if you try anything. I'll kill you if I even *think* you're trying to trick me."

Love or no love, Rebecca knew she meant it. "I'm not trying to trick you," she lied. "Let me show you."

She inched a little closer, taking slow, tentative steps. Debbie's hand was dangerously close to the trigger. One wrong move and she was dead. Debbie watched her with obvious longing as she moved forward. Gently, as lovingly as she could manage, she lifted a hand to stroke her former friend's cheek.

The mist of tears that filled her eyes might have seemed like touching emotion, but it was really only blind fear. Yet, she knew she had to be as tender as possible. It was a struggle to keep her voice steady, but she repeated the lines she had sung to Justyn in the finale of the play, hoping it would make her seem all the more sincere.

> "Sad creature trapped in the darkness.
> A life filled with pain is all you ever knew.
> But know this, my dark tortured angel.
> A part of me will always love you."

Even as the last note echoed off the high ceiling of the tiny room, Rebecca leaned over and kissed her. She pressed her lips against Debbie's with a desperation she hoped would be interpreted as passion. She didn't allow herself to shy away as her mouth was urged open, and Debbie's tongue began a tentative exploration. She forced her hands to lift so we could wrap her arms around Debbie's shoulders, pulling her closer, making her a more open target for Carmen.

Rebecca knew Debbie's eyes were closed in ecstasy because her eyes were wide open. There was no way that Debbie could have seen Carmen sneaking up behind them with a heavy, black candelabra in hand. She had no idea anything was happening at all until that cast iron candelabra came down hard on the top of her head. Then Rebecca and Debbie's kiss ended abruptly as, with a groan, Debbie slumped lifelessly to the ground.

Chapter Thirty-Five

Carmen was a statue. It was like someone poured quick drying cement over her head. She didn't move at all. Not even to breathe. The cast-iron candelabra was still raised high above her head, frozen in its place. Maybe because she was afraid Debbie was going to get back up. Or maybe because she was afraid that she wouldn't.

"Did I kill her?" Carmen asked in a strained, hushed whisper. "Oh God, tell me I didn't kill her."

"No . . . no, she's breathing."

Rebecca saw the slight rise and fall of Debbie's chest, so it wasn't a lie. But she also saw the blood gushing from the wound on her head where Carmen had hit her. She had to wonder how long that statement would hold true. Either way, she wasn't going to take any chances. She kicked the gun as far out of Debbie's reach as possible with the heel of her shoe before jumping to her feet and running over to help Justyn. Rebecca was smarter than the average B-horror movie heroine.

"Oh, God," Carmen repeated. Her voice rose in pitch several octaves. "They're dead. They're all dead, aren't they?"

Carmen was nearing hysteria. Rebecca had been there herself more than enough times in the last few weeks to recognize the signs. She might have found herself in the same condition if fear for Justyn hadn't overshadowed every other emotion. He was silent and still and the dripping blood was growing from a puddle to a pool with every second that passed. There wasn't any time to waste. Rebecca had to pull herself together. She had to take charge. There was no one else who was going to do it.

"Carmen, go check on Tom. Then get out his cell phone and call for help."

Carmen nodded and obeyed wordlessly, subservient for the first time in her life. She seemed relieved to have a purpose. The candle holder fell to the ground with a loud clank. But even over that noise, Rebecca heard sirens in the distance. She realized Tom must have gotten through to someone on his cell after all. At least, she hoped that was the case and it wasn't just wishful thinking.

Rebecca heard Tom murmur and moan as Carmen reached into his pocket to get the phone. She heard the three quick beeps, one long and two short, as she dialed the familiar emergency number. As soon as she got an answer, she began to explain their present situation to the operator, in hurried, heated sentences.

Rebecca was pretty busy herself; untying the complicated knots that bound Justyn's wrists to the chair. When she finally managed to succeed, she wondered if she had made the right decision. The full weight of his unconscious body fell heavily against her small frame. She was sure they would both go crashing to the ground. But before that happened, a pair of strong arms reached out and helped Rebecca ease Justyn gently to the ground.

"Is he alive?" Tom asked.

"Of course he's alive!" She didn't mean to snap at him, especially not when Tom was obviously not at his peak. His face was bruised and bloodied and almost as white as Justyn's. But it was such a terrible question. One Rebecca had been too afraid to ask herself, and one she certainly didn't want to hear. Instead, she focused on giving orders. "Help me stop the bleeding."

While she knew it was bad to move people who were seriously injured, it had to be far worse to just stand by and watch them bleed out. So Rebecca made an executive decision, and put Tom in charge of pressing a white ruffled dress shirt against the gushing wound on Justyn's shoulder.

His shoulder! Rebecca was more than a little relieved to see that it was only his shoulder that had been hit, not his chest as she had originally thought. There wasn't much chance that the bullet had hit his heart or his lungs or anything else vital. At least she didn't think so. She was also beyond grateful to the powers that be when she noticed his breathing got a little stronger. He even flinched when Tom's strong hands pressed down against his shoulder. Still, he had already lost so much blood. That couldn't be good. The fact that his face was so completely chalk white couldn't be good either.

"Justyn," she whispered. She tried to keep the tremble out of her voice as she touched his colorless cheek. She didn't want to give away how scared she was. "Justyn, can you hear me?"

"This is bad," Tom muttered. He was doing his best to keep the pressure on the wound, but the white shirt was already soaked through with bright red blood. "Really bad."

He was right. Rebecca certainly couldn't argue. But just the same, she wished he hadn't said it out loud.

"Yes . . . yes. We're behind the stage in the auditorium." Carmen was screaming into the cell phone, as if talking louder would somehow bring about faster results. "Yes, people are hurt, you moron! What have I been telling you? Well, tell them to hurry! Someone's bleeding to death here!"

Another statement Rebecca could have gone forever without hearing. She tried not to think about it. Tried not to look at the blood at all, and instead she concentrated on studying the rise and fall of Justyn's chest. Knowing he was still with her was the only thing that was keeping Rebecca sane.

Carmen went on barking directions into the phone while Rebecca and Tom stayed beside Justyn. Tom grabbed another shirt and did his best to stop the bleeding, even though he looked like he was ready to pass out himself. Rebecca stroked Justyn's hair, and squeezed his hand. She tried not to notice how cold his skin felt against her burning fingertips. In contrast to his black clothes, his pale face made him seem more vampirish than ever. Except for the fact that his beautiful, perfect, face was mangled. He might have really been the phantom at that moment. But it didn't matter. She would take him scarred for life if she had to, just as long as she had him for life.

"Justyn, don't you dare leave me. Enough with all this drama—open your eyes already! Just open your eyes and tell me you're all right." She sobbed as she laid her head gently against his chest. "Please, open your eyes, Justyn. Please! Do you hear me, you big jerk?"

She didn't really expect any response. She was surprised when she felt him shudder beneath her. She lifted her head just as he began to cough and gasp. It startled her at first, but then she felt a warm rush of relief as his eyes fluttered open.

"You . . . just can't make it through . . . a single . . . sentence . . . without insulting me."

Her eyes filled with fresh tears. "Justyn, oh Justyn . . . ." She was too overcome with raw emotion to even begin to express her gratitude in mere words. She didn't even care that he was still making fun of her.

"See that . . . ." He squeezed her hand back with more strength than she would have thought was possible. "This phantom wasn't such a bad guy after all. Didn't I tell you that all along?"

She actually laughed, even as the tears slipped down her cheeks. "And I told you that Christine wasn't really as helpless as she seemed."

"Of course not." He gave her a small grin that was more grimace than smile. "At least not this Christine. This Christine is my personal hero."

"Oh, Justyn . . . ."

"Lord . . . . Justyn," he corrected.

She rolled her eyes. "Lord Justyn . . . ." She relented, but then grew more serious. "I . . . I love you."

"I love you too, Becca." As weak as he was, he managed to use his one good arm to pull her down close enough to touch her lips. "Forever."

Tom and Carmen and even Debbie were forgotten in that one moment. That one moment that filled her heart with a complete and unbelievable happiness. Two soul mates were merging into one. She knew somehow that everything was going to be okay. Everything was going to be okay because Justyn was okay, and nothing else really mattered.

Just as she broke away from Justyn's embrace, the EMTs crashed onto the scene. Better late than never, Rebecca figured. Once they looked him over, they assured her that he was going to survive. And that was all Rebecca needed to hear. With a sigh of pure relief, she climbed into the ambulance to ride with Justyn to the hospital.

It was over. The nightmare was over.

Epilogue

Rebecca was just putting the finishing touches on her makeup when the blaring horn announced the arrival of her friends. She glanced once more at her reflection to make sure everything was just right. The deeply outlined eyes that stared back at her from the mirror hardly seemed to be her own at all. In fact, she might have been looking at a total stranger. Her choice of wardrobe for the evening was a far cry from her normal style. However, different didn't necessarily equal bad. It was a lesson that had been hard to learn, but in the end was extremely rewarding. And she had to admit that she was very impressed with the final results of her outfit. She just hoped Justyn would be. After all, she had done this for him.

"Rebecca! Rebecca, he's here!"

Her mother's shrill voice broke through the silence of her reverie. It was a voice filled with excitement, but tinged with the sadness of knowing her little girl was just about grown up. Rebecca had to wonder if her mother would still be excited when she saw her daughter's choice of attire.

She tore her eyes away from the mirror and looked towards her open bedroom door, feeling her heart start to race with familiar expectation. She always felt that way when she knew she was going to see Justyn. Her heart still thumped uncontrollably every time she saw him, even though months had passed. Every date left her with the same tingly sensation as their first. She hoped that feeling would never go away, not even when they were eighty.

Rebecca took one last, deep breath before stepping away from her dresser, and making her way down the hallway. As soon as she reached the foot of the stairs, she could see the small party who waited patiently in the foyer for her to make her grand entrance. Her parents were there, chatting pleasantly with the more eccentric Darlene as though they had all been friends for years. Thus proving that it was impossible for Justyn and his family to fail to win over *anyone* once they set their minds to it.

Then there was Justyn, so unbelievable handsome, so perfect in every possible way—at least in her eyes. He was standing off in the corner, shifting his weight nervously from one foot to the other, and looking up the stairwell in anticipation as he waited for her to appear. She was glad to see the magic of their relationship hadn't worn off for him anymore than it had for her.

He would have looked perfect to her in anything, but she never expected Justyn to be dressed the way he was. It was shocking. It was so unlike him. And it made her wonder if she had made a huge mistake. Justyn was wearing a completely modern, traditional black tux. From the red cummerbund to the black tie, it was as average and as commonplace as could be. No black eyeliner. No silver chains or metal tipped boots. No facial piercings, either. Who *was* this divinely handsome but normal boy, and what had he done with her Gothic boyfriend?

"Rebecca, stop lingering in the doorway!" Her father urged her forward as he lifted his video camera to the best possible angle. "The anticipation is killing us."

Now that she had been spotted, there was no putting it off any longer. Rebecca held her breath and started her slow catwalk down the stairs. As she turned the corner, she heard four people gasp in almost perfect unison, though she was pretty sure each gasp was for a different reason. Her dress swished at her feet with each step, and she hoped she wouldn't trip, especially since her father had the camcorder ready to capture every embarrassing moment.

"Isn't she beautiful?" Darlene gushed to her mother.

Mrs. Hope nodded, but Rebecca knew her mother well enough to know that of all the adjectives running through her head at that moment, beautiful probably wasn't one of them. Strange, bizarre, freaky, ethereal maybe, but beautiful—

"Beautiful doesn't begin to describe her." Justyn's voice was filled with such pure, honest emotion, it didn't even matter anymore what anyone else thought. "You did this for me?"

Rebecca shrugged her shoulders, and noted again just what Justyn was referring to as she glanced at her reflection in the living room mirror. The black make up, the black tight fitting gown with a long black train. Black spider web lace trailed the length of her arms and ended in a pointed tip at her wrists. Her face was pale as snow, making her dark eyes stand out in amazing contrast. The entire outfit seemed only fitting when she had chosen it. After all, Justyn was going against his very grain by attending the cliché senior prom at all. The least she could do was accompany him dressed as his Gothic queen.

"Unbelievable," he whispered as he slipped a corsage of blood red roses on her wrist.

"You really like it?"

He smiled at her insecurity. "There aren't words in any language that could express to you exactly how much I like it. Becca, my love, you are beyond stunning."

She felt herself blush at the sincere compliment and hoped it didn't ruin the effect.

"If you two love birds don't hurry up, you're going to miss your ride." Her father informed them.

Even as he said it, an almost musical honk emitted from the driveway. Rebecca peeked out the window and saw Carmen and Tom both hanging out the sunroof of the waiting limo, waving excitedly and gesturing them to come out and join them. They had gotten together not long after the play. It was true what they said about tragedy bringing people together.

"Your carriage awaits." Justyn offered her his arm, which she accepted gratefully. Not as much chance of her falling when he was at her side.

"Don't do anything I wouldn't do," Darlene called as they went out the door.

"*That* leaves us open for a broad spectrum of possibilities."

Justyn turned around to give his mother a conspirative wink, and Rebecca pulled him through the door before her father could ponder that comment long enough to have an angina attack. Tom threw open the door of the limo, and Justyn, in pure old-world fashion, took hold of her hand as she stepped inside. It was a good thing, too. For Rebecca, walking in high heels was a precarious endeavor.

"Wow, Becca. You do realize its *prom* and not Halloween, right?" Carmen asked as she gave Rebecca's dress a once-over. Her own light pink fitted gown looked spectacular, especially with the billowing black curls that cascaded down her back.

Tom grinned, as boyishly handsome as ever, especially in his tux. "Oh, leave her alone, Carmen. I think you look great, Bec. But of course, not as beautiful as you." He kissed Carmen's nose and the pout that was just beginning to form instantly vanished.

The four of them were a strange quartet. Yet, a quartet they had been for the last seven months, practically inseparable. That wasn't so odd for Carmen and Rebecca, who had been best friends since grade school. But a real comradeship had grown between Tom and Justyn as well. Rebecca wouldn't have believed it was possible if she hadn't experienced it firsthand. The surfer and the Goth, once bitter enemies, were now best friends and confidants.

Rebecca wondered what they were all going to do without each other the next year. With graduation looming threateningly, she realized they only had a few months left with their friends. Then Tom would be off to his ideal endless summer in California, and Carmen would be packing up for Rutgers University to study physiology. Rebecca and Justyn would both be attending the New York School of Performing Arts, thanks to the talent scout who had given them full scholarships. Darlene was already helping them look for a little studio apartment off campus. It was something Rebecca was dreading having to share with *her* parents.

"Why the serious face?" Justyn asked. "This is supposed to be a fun night."

"I was just thinking about how much I'm going to miss nights like this once we're all off in the real world."

"We'll keep in touch," Carmen said. "Thanksgiving comes pretty quick."

Rebecca didn't miss the quick sidelong glance she gave Tom. Her boyfriend was going to school on the other side of the country. At least Rebecca would get to be with Justyn. Of course, not being with Justyn wasn't really an option. She gave him a small smile, and gingerly touched the scar on his forehead. It wasn't nearly as awful as the hole in his shoulder, but it was still a lasting memento of the opening night of the play. It was barely noticeable to anyone who didn't know it was there, but for Rebecca it was a constant reminder of everything she almost lost. And everything she had to be grateful for.

It didn't take long for them to get to the restaurant where the prom was being held. They piled out of the limo and joined the other seniors in the elaborate ballroom. Red and white balloons and streamers, the school colors, decorated the hall. And every table setting offered a picture frame with the memorable words, "These are the days to remember." And that prom night was certainly a night Rebecca would never forget. Filled with fun, romance and even a few surprises—at least for Justyn.

Justyn didn't think much of it when Miss King, who was working as a chaperone, walked up onto the stage, and borrowed a microphone from the band. But the rest of the party at their table exchanged secretive smiles. Luckily, Justyn was too busy doing origami with his napkin to notice.

"Good evening, seniors. I hope you're all enjoying your night!" There were lots of hoots and hollers from the crowd on the dance floor. "That's wonderful! Well, we have one more little surprise for you—one more thing to make this a night to remember. The graduating seniors of the drama club would like to give one last farewell performance."

Lots of clapping erupted around them, and finally Justyn's head snapped up. On his face was a look of wide-eyed confusion. Rebecca had to cover her mouth to stifle a giddy giggle. Beside her, Carmen and Tom were smirking too. They were all pretty proud of themselves. It wasn't easy to take Justyn by surprise.

"What are you three stooges up to?"

"One last hooray," Tom told him.

Justyn narrowed his eyes. "And why wasn't I let in on this little secret?"

Miss King answered that question for them. "Without further ado, let me introduce Justyn, Tom, Carmen, and Becca. They'll be performing their own special rendition of *"Love Shack."*

Justyn's mouth fell open in dumb shock.

Rebecca smiled. "It's not *that* bad."

"You don't actually except *me* to sing that nineties retro nonsense, do you?"

"Blame it on me, Justyn," Carmen offered. "It's the only song with multiple parts that was anywhere in my voice range."

"Come on, dude, be a good sport," Tom said, and clapped Justyn on the back.

Justyn glared at him. "You're pushing it, *dude*."

"Do it for me."

Rebecca fluttered her eyelashes in what she hoped was a provocative way. They were so heavy with thick, black mascara, she couldn't really be sure. But when she saw Justyn's frown relax into that sweet smile she knew and loved, she realized that victory was hers.

"I can't believe I'm doing this."

"Come on, *Lord* Justyn—your fans await!"

Rebecca took his hand, and the two of them followed Carmen and Tom onto the stage. With the four-piece band as their back up, they sang—loud and clear and strong. The entire class joined in for the final chorus, and laughed at the silly, exaggerated expressions they wore as they got into character. Rebecca noted that Justyn didn't need the cheat sheet of lyrics she had pulled from her handbag. Apparently, he was a little more familiar with "that nineties retro nonsense" than he wanted to let on. It all went very smoothly. Rebecca wasn't even nervous about performing at all. The song actually ended way too soon, as did the rest of the night. Before long they were lost in the crowd on the dance floor as the last slow song of the night began to play.

"This is it," Rebecca whispered as Justyn pulled her close. "Sure there's a few more exams to take, but this is really the last big night of high school."

"Any regrets?"

"Only the weeks that I wasted that I should have spent with you." Rebecca smiled, but then grew a little more serious. "And of course Debbie."

"What Debbie did wasn't your fault."

How many times had she heard that? More than she could count. But it didn't really change anything. She still felt guilty, and at least partially responsible for everything Debbie had done. But she couldn't tell Justyn that. He would spend the rest of the night trying to change her mind.

Rebecca sighed. "At least she's getting the help she needs."

Justyn pulled her closer. "I wish you wouldn't torture yourself."

She should have known she couldn't hide her feelings from him. He practically read her mind most of the time. "I think it will be easier when we leave for New York. There are just too many reminders here. Of Debbie. Of Jay. Even of Wendy."

Justyn nodded. "I know how hard this has been for you. But Becca, I swear to you, if I can help it, no one will ever hurt you again."

Rebecca smiled. "Oh really, Lord Justyn. Are you going to be my hero? Are you going to ride in on your black horse and save me?"

She had only been kidding, but his eyes grew serious, and he actually stopped dancing as he raised a hand to stroke her cheek. "How about we save each other." He leaned down to kiss her. "Every day for the rest of our lives."

She had to swallow past a large lump in her throat before she could speak again. "Sounds good to me."

Rebecca sighed as he pulled her back into his arms. She rested her head on his shoulder, feeling the kind of bliss she didn't even realize existed before she had met him. Finally they had gotten it right. The final curtain had fallen. The show was over. And in the midst of art coming to life, Justyn and Rebecca had found true love.

Coming in 2013 from Author Laura DeLuca

Demon

Dark Musicals Trilogy, Book 2

Rebecca Hope was sitting high atop a deserted lifeguard bench, watching the waves roll in along the oceanfront, bringing with them an abundance of broken seashells and seaweed. Behind her, the sand stretched for miles. The distant screams from the roller coaster were the only sounds marring the peaceful beauty of the night. She watched as the sun dipped into the deep blue sea, turning the waters a murky gray. Looking out at the endless stretch of water made anything seem possible, but not even the spectacular beauty of the evening was enough to pull Rebecca from her sullenness.

"I can't believe the summer is already over." She sighed. "This is it. It's really our last night together. Tomorrow we're officially college students. "

Rebecca's boyfriend, Justyn Patko, gave her a supportive squeeze, but when she looked over at her best friend, Carmen Webber, her eyes welled with tears. They had been close since grade school. Rebecca wasn't sure how she was going to face life without her best friend by her side. They had never been apart for more than a few days.

Carmen waved her hand in dismissal, but Rebecca heard the catch in her voice. "Please don't talk about it. You know I don't like letting people see me cry." She squeezed the newly acquired teddy bear that her boyfriend, Tom Rittenhouse, had spent at least fifty dollars trying to win for her.

"Come on, guys." Tom gave Carmen a light jab in the arm. "It's not that bad. It'll be Thanksgiving before we know it. Then we'll have a big reunion. We'll all swap stories about college life and how hard we partied."

"Besides," Justyn added, "this is a beginning. Not an ending."

There was a commutative sigh as they considered that. It was the last day of summer vacation. It was bitter sweet, but they had decided to make the most of it. They drove the forty-five minutes to a little tourist town called Wildwood, a resort known for its free beaches and spectacular amusement parks. They spent the day sunbathing, exploring the boardwalk, and stopped for dinner at a little restaurant called Duffy's on the Lake. Finally, they headed back to the beach to watch the sun set on the nearly deserted shoreline.

"At least you two will be together," Carmen said with a wistful glance at Tom. "Tom and I are going to be on opposite ends of the country."

Rebecca couldn't argue. She knew how lucky she was. Tom was off to his endless summer in California while Carmen would be staying close to home and attending a state college in New Jersey. They were going to be a world apart.

Rebecca and Justyn had both been accepted to the New York School of Performing Arts. Their tuition was paid in full, thanks to the talent scout who had come in search of Justyn, but found a duo he refused to leave behind. They even arranged to rent a small apartment off campus, much to her parent's displeasure. Still, the fact that Rebecca was going to have her boyfriend by her side didn't mean she wasn't nervous about leaving her hometown and everything she knew. In fact, she was downright terrified.

Justyn seemed to read her thoughts, even though he addressed everyone. "Don't worry. After all we've been through his past year . . . college will be like one big vacation."

Rebecca saw Tom nod in the darkness. They were all contemplative for a moment, remembering the nightmare they had faced. During their high school drama club's production of *Phantom*, one of the students had stalked and terrorized them, even going so far as murdering two of their classmates, including Tom's best friend, Jay. Justyn had been close to death when the crazed killer was de-masked on opening night. Luckily, the gun shot only hit his shoulder.

Rebecca noticed Justyn grimace and try to readjust his arm on the cramped bench that was only meant for two. He was lucky he was an actor and not a pitcher because his shoulder would never to be the same. Rebecca still felt responsible. After all, it was *her* friend Debbie who had hurt all those innocent people, including Justyn—all because she had secretly yearned for a romantic relationship with Rebecca.

"Hey, babe," Tom said to Carmen, interrupting Rebecca's dark reverie. "How about one last stroll along the beach?"

Carmen nodded. The pretty Latina was trying so hard to maintain the tough girl façade, but Rebecca could see her eyes glistening as she climbed down the ladder that led to the sand. She watched them walk away hand-in-hand, but they hadn't gone far before Carmen finally fell apart. Tom wrapped his arms around her and stroked her long black hair. Rebecca, feeling like an eavesdropper on the intimate moment, averted her eyes to give them some privacy.

"You know, we really are lucky." Justyn whispered, and tilted her head to place a gentle kiss on her lips. "I've moved a dozen times in my life. I've left friends and family behind more than once, but I don't think I could bear to leave you."

Rebecca smiled, and studied his familiar face in the moonlight. His multiple facial piercings glistened against his pale skin and dark outlined eyes. His solid black ensemble should have made it hard to see him in the night.

When people saw Rebecca with the dramatic Goth, it took them by surprise. They made a strange pair. With her everyday jean shorts and curly brown hair, Rebecca was the poster girl for boring. Yet they made it work, and Rebecca couldn't imagine herself with anyone else. They were completely in tune with each other, and created a sort of magical harmony, not only with their voices but in all aspects of their relationship. She had even learned a few things from him. She touched the silver pentacle that dangled around her neck. She was still in the midst of her year and a day training; she had a few more months before she could call herself a full-fledged witch. Thanks to Justyn, she had discovered her spiritual path as well as her soul mate.

"I feel the same way," Rebecca told him, and leaned her head against his shoulder. "I couldn't imagine beginning this adventure without you by my side."

"Before we start this new chapter, there's something I wanted to give you." Justyn reached into the deep pockets of his black cargo pants and retrieved a little black box wrapped with silver ribbon.

"Really, Lord Justyn, you spoil me way too much," she said, addressing him playfully by his nickname.

He shrugged. "You are worth spoiling, my lady."

He kissed her fingers as he slipped the gift into her hand. She felt a warm blush rise to her cheeks and her heart fluttered. Rebecca loved the fact that even though their relationship had matured, Justyn still had the uncanny ability to make her swoon. With her heartbeat still accelerated, she examined the little box and shook it gently. Inside, she heard something rattle.

"But I didn't get you anything." She pouted.

"That's okay. This is for both of us."

She raised an eyebrow, a habit she had inherited from him. "Do you often give yourself gifts in velvet trimmed boxes?" she teased.

Justyn rolled his eyes. "Just open it and you'll see what I mean."

Rebecca unwound the silver ribbon that bound the box together. When she lifted the lid, she found two matching pendants, each laced to a long hemp chain. They were shaped sort of like seashells, with an endless spiral pattern that looped out from the center as the chambers grew larger. They were dark brown in color with a few hints of tan along the edges. The stones had been polished and smoothed on both sides, but when she lifted them, she could see that the two pieces fit together perfectly. She swore that the halves fought to snap together, like magnets in her hand. There was an energy pulsing and vibrating within the stones that even a novice witch like Rebecca could feel.

"They're beautiful." Rebecca whispered as she ran her hand along the intricate grooves.

"It's an ammonite." Justyn lifted one of the pendants, brushed her hair to the side, and hooked the clasp around her neck. His breath tickled her skin as his hands moved with graceful dexterity, giving her goose bumps despite the humid August night. "They're actually fossils that are millions of years old, named after Ammon, an ancient Egyptian deity. When they're divided in half, they're perfect mirrors of one another. Some cultures believe that if the two halves are given to lovers, it will bind them together forever. When made in necklaces, they're often called soul mate pendants."

"Wo . . . wow," Rebecca stuttered. As usual, the sentiment behind Justyn's gift was even more beautiful than the gift itself. It left her a little flustered. "That's amazing. How do you know all this stuff?"

"You don't spend eighteen years living with Darlene without learning a thing or two."

Rebecca laughed. Justyn's mother, Darlene, was definitely something special. EMT, exotic belly dancer, and Wiccan High Priestess were only a few of the titles she claimed. Rebecca knew she was a fountain of earth-based knowledge after years of studying the Craft. As Darlene's new apprentice, Rebecca was greedily dipping into that knowledge herself as often as possible.

"It's beautiful," Rebecca repeated, too overcome with emotion to think of anything more eloquent to say. "You certainly know how to make things interesting."

"Like I told you on our first date, I try not to be boring." He winked at her. "So . . . are you going to put mine on for me?"

"Oh yeah . . . sorry."

Rebecca giggled as she lifted the hemp chain. She wasn't nearly as graceful as Justyn was. She almost dropped the necklace in the sand three times before she finally managed to get the clasp locked. When she finally had it secured, he placed his hand over her heart where the ammonite lay. He did the same with her hands, lifting them to his chest. His dark eyes had lost all glimmer of humor. He met her gaze with a stare filled with genuine emotion. Beneath her fingers, she could feel the gentle, steady rhythm of his heart beating in perfect tune with her own.

> *"Our love will span both space and time*
> *In this life and the next you shall be mine.*
> *All eternity I will be by your side.*
> *For a love so strong cannot be denied.*
> *Spirit and flesh merged into one.*
> *So mote it be, for all days to come."*

When he was done with the recitation, he kissed her. Not just a gentle brush this time, but a deep passionate embrace that left her throat tight and her heart pounding with familiar yearning.

"I've never heard that poem before," she said, once she had caught her breath. "Who are you quoting?"

Even in the moonlight, she could see him blush. "I guess I was quoting myself. It was really more of an incantation than a poem, though. These necklaces are meant to be a symbol of our love, and it seemed a little spell work could only add to the power of the stones. There is power in words, Becca. Just like in there is power in nature."

"You mean, *you* wrote that?"

He nodded, but his eyes twinkled and the playfulness was back in his voice. "Well, actually, I just made it up as I was going along."

"Wow. Actor, singer, and now an improv poet slash chant writer. Is there anything you *can't* do, Lord Justyn?"

He smiled, and tilted her chin so he could look into her eyes. "I can't stop loving you."

This time when they kissed, they stayed wrapped in each other's arms. They embraced not only each other, but the silence that surrounded them. The cool ocean breeze stroked her skin in time with his hands. The moon's silver rays were reflected on the water, and the stars glittered like diamonds above them. It was a perfect night, and Rebecca wished it would never end. Before too long, a hand thumped against the wooden bench and Tom's cheerful face popped up from one corner.

"Hey, love birds. I hate to break up a tender moment, but Carmen and I really have to get going. I'm leaving for California at four a.m."

Rebecca sighed, but she knew Tom was right. They all had a big day ahead of them. They needed to get some rest. Justyn jumped down from the lookout, and ever the gentlemen, offered her his hand so she wouldn't fall on her face in the sand. Once she was securely on the ground, Rebecca noticed that Carmen's eyes were red-rimmed. She would never embarrass her friend by mentioning it, but seeing her that way finally broke Rebecca's thin grasp on her emotions. She threw her arms around Carmen and burst into tears.

"I'm going to miss you so much." She sobbed.

"You too, girl." Carmen couldn't hold back any longer either, and wept on her shoulder. "You better tell your parents to expect a big cell phone bill. And you two best not forget us when you're famous on Broadway. I want free front row tickets to every single performance."

Rebecca rolled her eyes and sniffed. "Like *that's* ever going to happen."

"With you two, it just might," Tom agreed. Justyn reached out to shake his hand, but Tom pulled him into a hug. "I'm glad we got to know each other, vampire," Tom teased. "You're not nearly as wacked as I first thought you were."

"You're not so bad either, *dude*," Justyn replied. "I might even miss having you around."

"'Til Thanksgiving?" Carmen asked.

"Until Thanksgiving." They all repeated. With one final exchange of hugs, the four high school friends parted ways to start their new adventures as college co-eds.

About the Author

Laura "Luna" DeLuca lives at the beautiful Jersey shore with her husband and four children. She loves writing in the young adult genre because it keeps her young at heart. In addition to writing fiction, Laura is also the sole author of a popular review blog called New Age Mama. She is an active member of her local pagan community, and has been studying Wicca for close to eight years. Visit her website at www.authorlauradeluca.blogspot.com for more information.

Laura DeLuca • 269

Made in the
USA
Middletown, DE